Christmas at Reedy Falls

PRAISE FOR ELIZABETH SUMNER WAFLER'S
A CLEFT IN THE WORLD

"In this suspenseful, exuberant story, nothing is predictable, but nothing is impossible."

—JACQUELYN MITCHARD, #1 *New York Times* best-selling author of *The Deep End of the Ocean*

"A heart-warming story of female empowerment and love, with—hurrah!—a middle-aged heroine to root for."

—ERICA BAUERMEISTER, *New York Times* best-selling author of *The Scent Keeper* and *The School of Essential Ingredients*

"An engaging, feel-good love story with plenty of plot twists."

—KIRKUS REVIEWS

"A heartwarming, hopeful story with glorious prose and inspiring characters."

—DARA LEVAN, author of *It Could Be Worse* and host of the *Every Soul Has a Story* podcast

Christmas at Reedy Falls

A ROMANCE

ELIZABETH SUMNER WAFLER

SHE WRITES PRESS

Published 2024
Printed in the United States of America

Print ISBN: 978-1-64742-806-8
E-ISBN: 978-1-64742-807-5
Library of Congress Control Number: 2024913278

For information, address:
She Writes Press
1569 Solano Ave #546
Berkeley, CA 94707

Interior design and typeset by Katherine Lloyd, The DESK

She Writes Press is a division of SparkPoint Studio, LLC.

To Porter

for all the weeks.
You are my earthly rock,
and I love you beyond measure.

CHAPTER ONE

Mamie

Charleston, South Carolina, 2022

It's difficult to parse a precarious situation when you're in the middle of one.

Despite my anxiety and inherent inability to parallel park, I manage to squeeze my Toyota Highlander into a space near the corner of Anson and Society without backing up onto the curb. It's the Tuesday before Christmas, and I'm picking up the man my roommate Abigay dubbed "Mr. Stunning Portfolio" here at nine o'clock. I rub my palms down my midi skirt, wishing my Smartwater was in the cupholder, and sigh, picturing the bottle on the kitchen counter, condensation now beading its sides. I need my smarts about me today.

The Christmas ringtone on my cell sends my heart to my throat. I snare the phone from the dash. Thankfully, it's not the man saying he's going to be late, but Abigay. A mixture of relief and annoyance washes through me.

"Are you already there?" Abigay asks.

"Ye-es. Why are you calling? What if he was here in the car?" I look wildly out the passenger side window to make sure Robert Fitzpatrick's not standing there peering in at me.

"Because you're the only person on earth who's perpetually ten minutes early for everything."

I sit up straighter and lift my chin. "I prefer to be punctual."

"Are you obsessing again?"

"A little."

"About?"

I look up again, but the guy's nowhere in sight. "About what he looks like."

"Enough, Mamie. It doesn't matter if he looks like Beauty's Beast. He's just your photojournalist. It's not like you're marrying the guy." I huff a laugh at the Beast reference. And as always, I'm comforted by the rising and falling quality of Abigay's Jamaican lilt. Even when she's reproaching me.

"You're right, you're right. I know you're right," I say to her, as has been our habit since watching *When Harry Met Sally.* "I just wish I knew what he's like and how well we'll partner on the project."

"No one could not partner well with you. Hey, they're calling our flight. Gotta buzz, Bee."

"Safe travels, Bee." Though we call each other Abs and Mames for short, Bee's a holdover from our first year at the Savannah College of Art and Design. The college mascot, the bee, was the perfect metaphor for how we saw ourselves: creative, industrious, and collaborative.

Now, Abigay and her fiancé Jake are headed to Vail for a swanky ski trip. But my getaway could be just as exhilarating. It's my first big assignment as a full-time feature writer for *Á La Mode Charleston,* a posh and on-trend magazine with a widespread readership. I get to write the inaugural article on the new dressed-for-Christmas Grand Bohemian Lodge in Greenville. Me! Abigay proclaimed it an epic opportunity, one that could meteorically boost my career. Staying at the hotel surrounded by its Native American vibes could alter not only the course of my career but also maybe my life.

It's now 9:04, and Robert Fitzpatrick's nowhere in sight. Why is he late? I check my lipstick in the visor mirror, straighten it, and take a cleansing breath. It's time for a self-pep talk. My managing editor, Farida, said the man who'd relocated from Boston to Charleston had a stunning portfolio and an eye for creating images that tell a story. "He'll make your words look great," she'd said. That didn't offend me. Grabby visuals are essential to a slick piece. They're what people notice first in a magazine spread. I just hope the project means as much to him as it does to me.

A white cat sitting against the red door of the Greek Revival home on the corner snags my eye. The guy didn't give me his address, but if he has a house in this neighborhood, he's obviously doing well. A hopeful first check mark for the photographer's experience goes into the pro column of my mental list.

At 9:10, I'm dusting the display screens on my dash with one of the wipes I use to clean my glasses. My mouth tastes of stale coffee. It must smell of it too. I rummage through my console for a container of mints. Its label promises three hours of fresh breath, which Waze predicts to be our drive time to the newly hip city of Greenville. A swag of Spanish moss caught between the street signs of Anson and Society sways with the breeze. What a pair those names make. Anson: my real last name and one of Charleston society's most historical. Because my mother is a snob and I refuse to become her, I took my middle name, Morrow, as my last when I landed the *Á La Mode* job. Knowing how alliteration makes my heart sing, Abigay gifted me a pretty notebook personalized with *Mamie Morrow* at the top.

I wait, almost fuming, for Mr. Stunning Portfolio. He's earned a second check mark on my list, this time in the con column, for his lateness and apparent lack of consideration. Strike one. A UPS truck zooms past, a beribboned wreath affixed to its grill. Christmas falls on Sunday this year. Though we should complete our work before Friday, the magazine offered to pay us to stay on through the holiday in the luxurious lodge. We had both accepted.

With things the way they are with my mother right now, I couldn't wait to put some highway between us. We're not on speaking terms. And I have no other family. I broke up with my last boyfriend, the baseball player, when he told me his five-year plan included marriage and two kids. Marriage is the last thing on my mind. Romance could make me take my eye off the ball. I'm "baggage free," though the back of my car—I tend to over-pack—says otherwise.

I'm a good writer.

Abigay and Farida have confidence in me.

I have confidence in me. Cue the Julie Andrews social media meme.

But why is he willing to spend days away from family and friends at Christmastime? He couldn't be married. Hopefully, his willingness to spend his time in Greenville speaks of his dedication to the assignment.

Still puzzling it out, I look up. And he is there. With his every long stride, my breath comes faster in my throat. What a guy! Sexy aviator sunglasses hide his eyes. But his squared-off shoulders showcase the perfect frame for his elegant and preppy clothes: oxford shirt, loosened silk tie, navy blazer, and hip leather brogues. The right side of my mouth twists into a grin at his footwear. In old Gaelic, "brogues" mean shoes that rough working men wore. And Mr. Stunning Portfolio presents as the antithesis of rough: a man of means. Looking over my car, he eases off his shades. Our eyes meet. My forehead is about four inches from the windshield, so I shrink back and give him a little it's-me wave. I trade my sunglasses for my regular ones, wishing I could give them a quick cleaning, and gather my long skirt in my fist. I bail out to meet him at the back of the car. Straightening myself to my five feet plus two, I incline my hand. "Hello. I'm Mamie Morrow."

His grip envelops mine. "Rob Fitzpatrick," he says, making such prolonged eye contact with me that for a moment the population of Charleston declines to two. His hand feels as if he had just set down a cup of cocoa. His eyes are warm too. Hazel flecked with brown. He takes his hand back and pockets it. I tear my eyes from his and become aware of kids stunting on the sidewalk and cars zipping along the street. "I'm sorry I'm late," he says. "I was on the phone . . . with my mom."

"Well." I pull at the neck of my now too-warm cropped green sweater. "We should still be okay on time." A pro-column check for his apology goes into my chart. But also a question mark. In light of my non-relationship with my mother, I'm curious about Rob and his "mom." But his tone had read like water on the pH scale. I fumble for the button that releases the hatch with a whoosh, then lean in to resituate one of my totes before standing back to give Rob access. He's knuckling at an eye as though a palmetto bug has invaded it. But he seems to blink it away before picking up his medium-sized bag and shoving it in next to my three. Meanwhile, I survey his profile and dark shiny hair. He unshoulders a few small bags and adds them so carefully to the mix that I know they must harbor his camera equipment. The something I'm finding familiar about him clicks. Sam Claflin. I'm dying to text Abigay. Rob Fitzpatrick resembles a cleaner-cut version of the actor who played Billy in the *Daisy Jones & the Six* series—little stick-out ears and all. Epic handsome. My voice rushes out an octave higher than normal. "I've heard so much about you. About your work, I mean." A blush comes on. "It's nice to meet you."

His voice is polite. "You as well. Farida thinks very highly of your writing. And oh," he says, pointing a pistol-like finger at me, "I really appreciate you driving. My car's . . . in the shop."

"You are welcome." I reach up to close the hatch again. My editor had spoken well of me to him too—woot! We get in the car. Feeling more accomplished, I climb up and into my seat while Rob sets a luscious leather satchel—definitely not vegan leather—on the passenger side floorboard before lowering himself onto the seat. But he grimaces as his knees scrape the dashboard. "Oh. Sorry about that. Scoot your seat back," I say. "Feel for your little thingy down there." *Little thingy?* My blush feels as bright as my hair. Rob gives me a pursed-lipped smile and shakes his head before reaching to adjust his seat.

A helpless giggle bounces inside my chest.

We buckle up.

I once heard someone say the most effective form of birth control is a Boston accent. But Rob Fitzpatrick's voice is nice. Deep and manly. How old is he? I'm intrigued by his trace scent of cedar or sandalwood. I bet it's his shaving cream. He probably uses one of those fancy shaving brushes.

Ahead, we're confronted with a road-closed sign. When Rob says, "Bang a uey," I realize I'm hearing Boston speak. A grin plumps my cheeks as I turn to look at him. "I assume that means to make a U-turn?" He returns the grin, and I note that one of his eyeteeth is canted. *Don't people of means in Boston get braces for their kids' teeth? My mother slapped the metal on mine when I turned ten.* But Rob's tooth works with his grin. The imperfection adds a certain charm. I can't put my finger on what his breath smells like. It's kind of woody but oddly . . . floral.

"Of course," he says, losing the *r*. "In Beantown, anyway."

"Is your family there?" He nods briefly, then looks out his window.

Okay, I guess we're not going to talk about that. I try and net a catchier bug. "So how did you come to choose Charleston?"

He looks straight ahead. "Charleston felt like a safe place to take a jump because of the slower pace. It's helped me slow down and be more intentional. And the creative community"—his face brightens with the word "creative"—"I've never been in a place where there are so many entrepreneurs. It's great for freelancers. Then there's the Southern history. The beauty." He flips a big palm indicating the scenery as we turn onto East Bay Street and head north. He's smart and thoughtful.

"Charleston's all that," I say, checking my side mirrors. "I'm curious about why people relocate. I've lived here all my life—except when I was in college. At SCAD. I feel his eyes on me again, flush, and babble on. "So I appreciate your perspective. I've been to Boston, but I don't think it's a place that I could . . . you know, thrive." I want to ask where he went to school, but at his silence, I change the subject.

"What do you think of southern accents?" The angle of the winter sun is blinding and hot coming through the window. I readjust my visor and bump the heat down. Rob slips out of his blazer. I spy the tag before he precisely arranges the jacket across his lap (Arrow New York). He gives me a shy smile, and I swear his eyes twinkle behind his shades.

"If angels came to earth, I bet they'd speak with southern accents."

My heart swells until it feels like it needs its own property line. Never have I ever heard a man say anything remotely that . . . charming, that clever. Or have I? A murky memory stirs and then flutters aside. I know next to nothing about this guy, but he sounds completely sincere.

"That's . . . sweet," I manage, my eyes on the road. He gives his left shoulder a small shrug, and it grazes mine. Obliquely, I watch him peer down at his hands, flex them, then tuck them beneath his expensive jacket. But not before I note their worn places. Small stains. White scar lines. I still, then suddenly recall what Helen Keller said about hands. That hands were more honest than faces, that hands were the true windows of the soul. Rob Fitzpatrick's hands are work-worn. I'd only felt their warmth before. Now his hands don't jive with my first impression of him. My sense of intrigue takes over. Who is this guy, really?

I have six more days to find out.

CHAPTER TWO

Rob

Mamie Morrow is nothing like I expected, yet everything I hoped.

I figured she'd be older than what her fresh-scrubbed face and casual style put forward. I pictured a stick figure in a suit and heels. Farida said Mamie was a go-getter. And she is that. Her energy could sand the finish off an armoire. From the little business we discussed the first hour, I'm confident she's a "hundo p" (her expression) into the project that could lead to bigger and better assignments for me in the South.

"Want some tunes?" she asks now.

"Sure."

She glances at me. "What do you like?"

I smile. "Probably not what you like."

She lifts her chin in a try-me gesture.

"Hey, we can listen to whatever you want," I say.

"Okay, but I like the old stuff. Crosby, Stills, Nash & Young, Fleetwood Mac, Joni Mitchell, Steely Dan . . ."

I grin and run a hand through my hair. She's caught me on the back foot. "So basically, Sirius XM's *The Bridge* playlist."

"Well, I guess *so.*" She smiles and lifts her chin, then slides her hands to a secure nine-and-three position on the leather steering wheel. "I'm an old soul. I mean, I appreciate Taylor

Swift's stuff and Norah Jones. And eighties pop." She looks at me before going on. "But it's the *early* rock that stirs me."

Something inside *me* stirs, turns over, and empties. I don't dare look at her. But two words tumble out. "Same here. With early rock." She nods at me and then gives me a look I can't read before moving to the fast lane to pass a van packed with family. The conversation lags.

"I've been told I'm an old soul too," I say. "My mother said that I came to life more thoughtful and understanding than my pack of brothers. That was the first thing that set me apart from them." Mamie does have an old-fashioned way about her. She's proper. The girl talks in a fancy font. Her name's not one you hear these days. But it suits her. I've studied old souls theory, but I've never discussed it with anyone. I sneak a look at Mamie, thinking I might bring it up with her this week. But before I know it, all I want to do is try and capture the radiant aura of her profile on film.

She accesses Sirius XM, and an Eagle's song thumps from the speakers. Mamie's running a one-sided debate about why we really should be listening to Christmas songs, but my mind's rebounded to when we shook hands behind the car. A current had bolted up my arm. I've never reacted to a woman's businesslike touch in that way. The connection was much more than physical, at least for me. And I didn't know what to do with it. Then she reached up to open the hatch, and her cropped sweater rode up. I wrenched my gaze away and pretended I had something in my eye, but not before I caught sight of a band of magnolia-petal skin. That time the current had zapped through me from head to toe. It's not this girl's competence I need to worry about, it's her appeal. Her spontaneity. She'd be too easy to fall in love with. I could screw up our work relationship and wreck the assignment that I badly need to be a success.

Rob

The miles pass and we agree to make a pit stop at the first decent-looking convenience store. That proves to be a challenge because Mamie nixes the first three. But back in her car again, hand sanitizer shared and the water bottles we bought installed in the cupholders, I sit back and watch the mile markers and the billboards advertising Jesus as the Reason for the Season, barbeque joints, and where to score guns and ammo for hunting season. It still amazes me that I'm now a geographical southerner. And especially how, after long months working in Charleston, Farida with Á La Mode plucked me from obscurity and awarded me this assignment based on my portfolio. I peek at Mamie, and a flicker of excitement moves through my chest about the week ahead. It could be fun working with a firecracker.

As "Reelin' In the Years" begins, she startles me from my thoughts. "How old are you, Rob?" She's just said my name for the first time. Her tongue seemed to curl before the R, making the single syllable richer than anyone ever has. My pulse takes an uptick.

"Thirty-one," I say, and then blurt out a reflexive "How old are you?" like my social filter's shot full of holes. She sits taller and gives me that chin lift again.

"I am twenty-six." *Not as young as I thought. The perfect age difference between a man and a woman, in my book.* I groan inwardly. But my good Catholic home training steps up. *Hail Mary, help me keep my head in the zone.* And now I'm thinking in baseball analogies, as if I haven't been trying to jettison that part of my life. I fumble through my jacket pocket for something to put in my mouth before something else I don't want to say comes out of it.

"Want a mint?" I ask her. She takes her eyes off the road long enough to regard the rectangle of purple I hold out, then furrows her brow.

"What kind are those?"

"Spencer's. I order them . . . from the UK." I sound like a total chowdahead: a Boston blockhead.

"Fan-cy."

Now I *feel* like the world's biggest, fanciest chowdahead. I tear away the end of the wrapper and shake loose a wrapped square. "Try one."

She wrinkles her fine-boned nose. "What do they taste like? Grape? I'm not a fan of grape."

"They're the violet-flavored ones."

She gives me a knowing look, one I can't decipher, then takes the mint.

She chews a moment as we listen to Boz Scaggs's rough falsetto. "They're good. Violet mints. Who knew?"

My chowdaheaddom slips to a safe level and I smile.

Mamie seems to study the dashboard and then exits from I-385 and into downtown Greenville. "Hey," she says around the mint, "we've made good time. We just have to turn onto Church Street, then make a right on Camperdown Way. What a fun street name to say. Camperdown Way, Camperdown Way. It sounds like a Dr. Seuss thing." I laugh with her before she eyes my briefcase on the floorboard. "Do you have a copy of the afternoon itinerary with you? Remind me what's when." I'm grateful she's steered the conversation to the project.

"Yah, hang on a sec."

"I take it 'yah' means yes in Boston."

I grin. "Yah. 'Yah huh' means of course. 'Yah nuh' means no way."

She looks at me like I'm an ape who just strolled out of the rainforest and ordered a Manhattan. "I'll try to rein it in. But I warn you: it's deeply ingrained."

But Mamie laughs. "Don't rein it in on my account. It'll be fun learning a new language." She taps her temple. "Good for the brain."

I laugh and pull out my cell to access the itinerary while we crawl through the midday traffic.

She glances over. "Oh, you have yours on your phone. I printed mine out. I'm old-school about keeping hard copies and using pretty paper planners and notebooks."

This girl. I read from my cell. "Okay, check-in is between noon and one o'clock. Lunch is at one thirty in the lodge restaurant called . . . Between the Trees. That's with Annelise, the manager's assistant, and the others. And at three o'clock, she's giving us a tour of the lodge."

"Check, check, and check," says Mamie.

"After that we're free. Do you want to meet in the lobby and come up with our game plan for the project?"

"Perf." She grins and bounces in her seat, her bun of hair bobbling. "This is going to be so fun!"

I laugh at her buzz. She's like a bumblebee. "I think we'll have fun with this."

"I'm psyched about the Native American art décor and collection."

"Is that a particular interest?" I ask. Her eyes are on the road, though her vision seems to leap miles ahead.

"I had an affinity for it. I mean, in art school. Only recently, though . . . let's say I've developed an appreciation for what it represents."

Nodding, I turn to look at her, and a memory comes to mind.

She goes on, "You know, the essence of Native peoples . . . from *genuine* perspectives. The way the artists bring the stories . . . and the wisdom to life."

While her words about this seem polished by much thought, I'm only just making my connection. She's quiet for a minute, and in the space, I find a place for my words. "Those are exactly the things I need to capture about the art. Before the pandemic, I went to the Boston Museum of Fine Arts, and there was this exhibition of Native American blankets. They really struck me, the colors and bold patterns. I remember reading that they were woven around the end of the Civil War. And I thought . . . how could all that beauty have come from people who were forcibly removed from their homelands? I felt an incredible respect for them and their art. It's like a testament to the human spirit. And the *creative soul*. As a creative, it shook me. I stayed there for over an hour absorbing the vibes. I hope to do that at the lodge." I slowly look at her.

Mamie regards me, her pretty face full of empathy and understanding. Returning her gaze to the road, she swallows, and I feel it in my own throat. "Spot-on. We can tap into those feelings and make our article transcend what the reader might expect to be a puff piece."

I peer at her profile. "Yes, that."

She places a soft fist over her heart and looks at me. "Hey, Fitzpatrick, we just might make a pretty good team."

I feel like I've been given a stamp of approval. One I didn't know I needed. I'm not just a photographer but a photojournalist. I smile. "Yah, we just might."

Another reason to focus on the work instead of Mamie Morrow's charms.

CHAPTER THREE

Mamie

Camperdown Way curls onto a wide brick promenade. From behind it rises the Grand Bohemian Lodge. My breath catches. Beside me, Rob lets go a low whistle. The online photos hadn't prepared me for the hotel's size or rustic *grandeur*, its many ells and arches, buttresses, and chimney tops. The nearby banks and parking buildings seem to melt away, leaving the GBL to stand alone in the crowning sun.

"It's"—Rob shakes his head—"way better than I expected." He twists in his seat and flashes a look at his small bags in the back of the car like he's dying to get his hands on a camera. I love it. His passion for the work bounces throughout the car.

I'm taking in the exotic sculpture flanking the huge front doors when a young man in a valet's vest directs me to pull ahead. I let the SUV roll along the brick drive that's studded uniformly with young trees and handsome iron lampposts. The maples are winter bare now, but the lampposts wear jaunty caps of wreath and ribbon. The job at hand has been the lead horse in my thoughts today, but suddenly, Christmas pulls ahead. My heart brims with the season's excitement, its expectancy. Then it occurs to me for the first time that I'll be celebrating with a stranger. But new experiences are good.

Said stranger's voice registers. "Did Annelise say we could valet the car?"

I rub my forehead. "Oh. Not sure. Maybe. Let's see." I put the car in park and roll down my window. A cool wind sweeps inside. A second valet steps up and greets us. "Hello," I say. "I'm Mamie Morrow on assignment with *Á La Mode Charleston,* the magazine." *On assignment.* I'm only slightly embarrassed by how heady it feels to say the words. The valet, whose name tag reads "Marco," beams and whips out a device from his jacket. He gives the screen a look and several thumb punches.

"Yes, Ms. Morrow and Mr. Fitzgerald. Welcome to the Grand Bohemian Lodge."

Rob whips off his aviators and leans into my side like a right tackle. His words crackle past me. "*Fitzpatrick.* My name is Rob Fitzpatrick."

"Sorry about that, sir," Marco says, and types something on his device. "Fitz*patrick.* Yes, Miss Annelise has you registered for complimentary parking." Though a whiff of Rob's annoyance still hangs in the air, he seems mollified. We get out, stretch our legs, and meet the valet around the back of the car. He's already busy loading our bags onto a pristine bellman's cart. It's so exciting to be among the first people to stay at the hotel for its inaugural Christmas holiday. I collect my purse and hand Marco my keys. Rob grabs a small bag, from which he extracts a smart-looking camera. It's colder here than in Charleston, and the chill sneaks right through my clothes. I'm glad I brought my winter coat. It's cloth and a fun, cheery red. Maybe I'll buy a scarf to wear with it while I'm here.

Mr. Fitz*patrick* and I enter the lodge and are met by a massive chandelier made of antlers—I'm guessing elk by their broadness. A rule of decorating is to draw the eye upward. Whoever designed the lodge knew a thing or two. Beyond the chandelier squats a huge four-sided fireplace made of river rock. On the hearth that faces the front door, a mother and a young child wearing a Santa hat sit stirring what must be cups of cocoa with hooky candy canes.

Oh, my word, bookcases full of old volumes rising to the ceiling. My gaze wants to be everywhere at once in the magnificently adorned lobby, but Marco, who has taken command of our cart, extends an arm to the left of the fireplace. "Registration's this way. They'll be right with you." He stands with one foot on the cart: a sentinel.

Rob's moving around the magnolia-garlanded fireplace snapping photos. A trio of well-heeled women in fur coats holding champagne flutes aloft sashay by. They catch sight of Rob and survey him as though he's on the dessert menu. *He's definitely fine.* Thankfully, before I take that notion any further, a dark-skinned young man with braids done up in a bun slips through a hidden doorway and into place behind the desk. Rob appears beside me, his face unreadable. The man introduces himself as Kwame and extends to us a professional welcome to the Grand Bohemian. He gets Rob's name right. I wonder if it's possible that Kwame received a transmission from Marco with the correct information in the approximately three and a half minutes since we arrived.

I hope that Annelise and the others have had Rob's name correctly noted all along. Because his earlier excitement and the connection we made have gone quiet. I can't fault him. I'd felt self-important—which is not like me but like my mother—when I dropped the magazine's name. Rob probably feels as if his name is already printed wrong on the pages of the article. To try and cheer him, I nudge the side of one of his long brogues—almost twice as long as my sneaker—and point out a God-tall glittering Christmas tree. I lean toward him and whisper, "Did Sasquatch sling that thing on his back and carry it all the way from Oregon?" When he grins and breathes a little laugh, I'm ridiculously glad. The photographer needed a recharge. For both our sakes. A high-octane afternoon brews.

Kwame hands us key cards to rooms on the third and fourth floors. Me on the third, Rob on the fourth. Thank goodness. If we'd had adjoining rooms, I might have been tempted to listen to him bump about, imagining what he sleeps in. Or if his chest is furry and dark like his hair.

I look furtively around as though I've said the words aloud and am relieved when Marco asks if we're ready. He shepherds us past a wall of glass cases full of elaborate Native American jewelry that he says is part of the permanent collection. I stop short when a silver piece, a sturdy bracelet, grabs me by the shoulders. Marco is going on about the permanent collection versus the collection that is for sale in the gallery, but he stops his bellman's patter and the luggage cart when he notices my preoccupation. "This is so much like one I've seen," I say, willing my hands away from pressing against the glass.

"There are a lot of them here," Marco says.

I relax my shoulders and step back from the glass.

"So many skilled craftsmen," says Rob.

"Will you get a shot of that bracelet, please?" I ask him. Not that I'll forget where it is. I smile at Rob when he complies. "I'm excited for the tour this afternoon." *The tour and later, time to myself, to wander the lodge.* To me, viewing art is a highly personal affair. With someone else, it's like they're reading a book over my shoulder, like they're taking part of my experience for their own, tincturing my experience with theirs.

The elevator walls are covered in small bone-colored hexagonal tiles. A coppery row forming a border near the ceiling isn't tile but what looks like pennies. Marco resumes his patter. "Those are facsimiles of Native American Buffalo coins," he says as though he minted them himself. "The real ones would be too valuable to glue in the elevators."

"Cool," Rob and I say in tandem, then share a grin. At my floor, Rob palms Marco a five-dollar bill and tells him he will make his own way to his room. He collects his few bags from in between all of mine, and then Marco and I move out with the cart.

Rob calls out to me, "See you downstairs at 1:25?" I straighten my purse strap. Five minutes would be enough time to hustle to the restaurant with about a minute to spare. Marco readjusts his grip on the cart. *I can do this. If Morrow and Fitzpatrick are to be a team on equal footing, I can't micromanage things.*

"Sure, 1:25," I chirp as the big doors slide closed.

Marco inserts my card into the lock of room 325. Expectation fills my chest. But the card is met with a red light. As he continues to try the card, I notice a small owl figure above my room number and trace it with my forefinger. *Why are you here, little one?* Marco opens the door and rolls the cart inside.

The first thing I notice in my suite is the starkness of the white walls and how they contrast with the eye-popping emerald green of the padded king-sized headboard. I hand Marco the ten I had tucked in my skirt pocket for that purpose this morning and thank him as he goes.

Across from the bed, two gray leather club chairs flank a marble-topped table, its base a sculptured tree trunk. A nice spot to work or to eat breakfast. Computer and phone charging stations have been thoughtfully and precisely placed. Smiling like a fool, I toe off my fashion sneakers, my favorite teal ones, and pad barefoot across the green-and-gray hatched carpeting to the bathroom. Squee! I'm a guest of the Grand Bohemian Lodge! The marbled bath is well-appointed and boasts a shower that could accommodate Santa and all nine of his reindeer.

I head back into the room and survey a counter lined with sleek kitchen gadgets, including an espresso machine. I feel like Iris Simpkins in *The Holiday* seeing Amanda Woods's home. Marco had called this a media room—like for the press, which I guess is me—woot!—with a Juliet balcony. I move to the window and throw open the sliding glass door. Thankfully, when I look down, no distracting Romeo wearing a velvet doublet calls to me, but the rush of a river does. The Reedy River! I stand, my hands on the railing, inhaling the blue-green smell. The falls splash merrily over boulders made smooth over time. Because the copse of trees along the side of the lodge are winter bare, I'm afforded the perfect view of Falls Park on the Reedy and downtown Greenville. Its mix of old and swanky-topped new buildings seems to vibrate with commerce. The pedestrian bridge, named the Liberty, links what they call the green at the side of the Grand Bohemian with the heart of the city. Even from my December perch, the grass is green and looks as smooth as a shaven cheek. The park beyond the bridge is dotted with color, people in parkas and scarves. Young children weave bright threads throughout.

I wonder if Rob is taking in the view from the floor above me and what of the vista he's likely photographing instead of resting for a few. I can't wait to wake up here tomorrow, maybe drag my duvet out here to the balcony and sip an espresso while reading the new novel I brought. My heart swells with gratitude for the days ahead and what they may bring.

Abruptly, I'm worn out from sensory stimulation: meeting Rob, riding side by side with him in the car for three hours, and our arrival at the GBL. At first I thought I might have overshared too much about myself with him, and way too soon. But when he opened up his feelings about the creative souls of Native American people, I felt we had made a real connection. And what we shared can't help but make the article better.

Mamie

I locate my phone where I left it on the bathroom vanity and set a thirty-minute timer. I climb onto the middle of the vast bed and starfish face down. I read somewhere that Indigenous peoples believed starfish symbolized regeneration, renewal, and self-sustainability. I should make this a daily practice. I begin with a deep seven-second-in, seven-second-out breathing pattern.

But the plethora of Native American elements that await me downstairs seize my thoughts and send them spiraling back to the real reason I'm here.

CHAPTER FOUR

Rob

It's tough for an English major from a city college to land a job in the field they love, but someone forgot to tell me. I've busted my hump working since high school. But I'm here. And on the brink of actually making a living from photography. I sit on the balcony of the sleekest room I've ever seen, my legs stretched out over the railing. Sighing with pleasure, I survey the heart of the city, decked out in the reds, greens, and golds of Christmas. My Canon R6 with a telephoto lens rests next to me on a side table.

I wonder what Mamie's doing downstairs. Probably precisely placing all her things or scribbling in one of her "pretty notebooks." I smile and shake my head. Despite her boho vibe, any chowdahead could tell she comes from money. She's polite and articulate but unpretentious. I like that.

Below, an elderly couple plods across the Liberty Bridge. They're holding hands. But from where I sit, it doesn't look like the grip is for support but because they're happy together. Laughing, they turn and look at each other. They are the most interesting subjects on the bridge. I'd wager they've been in love for a lifetime. I reach for my camera, but melancholy suddenly fills my gut and flushes away my inspiration. In the car, Mamie asked me about my family. Wishing I had something better to tell her, I kept silent, my mouth as parched as my past.

Remembering that feeling, I go back inside to snare a big bottle of complimentary Smartwater, then down half of it. The bedside clock reads 1:20. A text notification wakes up my cell. I pick it up: *Mamie*. What, when we traded phone contacts, made me not include her last name? Was it a harbinger that our partnership would transcend business? I like the intimacy of her first name on my screen. Abruptly, I'm back in high school study hall scribbling Olivia O'Keefe's name inside my three-ring binder. I hold the phone in my palm and read: *Are you ready, Fitzpatrick?*

I grin. No girl has ever called me that before.

The three dots pulse on the screen. She's waiting, probably bouncing on the toes of her little sneakers. I type: *Be there in . . . about ten.* I laugh out loud, picturing her outraged expression, and pocket my phone. I take a whiz and wash my face.

I reach for the elegant Satchel & Page briefcase my old friend Seamus gave me the day I left Boston.

I sling the wide strap over my shoulder and square it.

Mamie stands in the elevator niche at lobby level. I figured she'd be levitating, but she's utterly still before a huge portrait of a braided and feathered chief, or maybe it's chieftain. He's elegant, and where you'd expect fierceness, there's a gentleness about his eyes and a suggestion of a smile on his lips. I wish I knew what it is about the portrait that could make Mamie forget even for a millisecond about being on time for our lunch appointment. "Hi," I say.

She jumps about a foot and then looks at her watch. "*Robert* Fitzpatrick! It's only 1:24. You freaked me out! Not funny. I'm going to take a broom after you!"

Take a broom after me? I chuckle and shrug. "'Tis the season to be merry."

She covers an expanding grin with tapering fingers. Then she pockets her hand and takes a deep breath. "We can be merry later. Let's go."

"After you." The lobby's beautiful, but with Mamie in the lead, the scenery improves at every turn. She's taken down her hair—the color of the finest apricot jam—so that it flows over her shoulders. *Have mercy.* I trail the flowery scent that seems to emanate from her hair and watch her lean into her business persona. Her neck lifts and her walk loses its girlish bounce. Her strides are smooth. She looks to her left and right, offering people gentle smiles or nods. As we approach the art gallery, which seems to be the heart of the lobby, she slows until I've drawn up beside her. A signboard on an easel lets us know the Western landscapes of Harper Howard are on exhibition. "Look at this work," Mamie whispers as we weave through the space. I've only known her for a morning, but that's all I need to guess how torn she must be between stopping before the art and getting to the restaurant on time.

A stocky weathered-looking man in a feathered fedora booms a greeting from the restaurant entrance. "Welcome, travelers! Right this way," he says before removing his hat and introducing himself as Vaughn Reagan, the lodge manager. "Meet my team. Isla Collins, the finest, fine art curator south of the Mason-Dixon line. And Annelise Morrisey, my assistant extraordinaire." Mamie and I exchange handshakes all around. Isla's a tiny brunette in a black dress and pine-tall platform heels. A slip of a girl, my mom would call her. Annelise is a tall blonde with tortoise-shell-looking plastic glasses frames like Mamie, and she is dressed a lot like her, minus the sneakers.

"Look at the snowy owl," Mamie says to me, gesturing with wide-eyed reverence to a vivid blue-and-white acrylic.

"The stairs below the owl lead down to Spirit & Bower, our

special whiskey bar," Mr. Reagan says. "If you enjoy a fine glass, be sure and check out our cellar."

"Absolutely will," I say as Mamie echoes my comment with, "I love whiskey." *A woman drinking whiskey is seriously sexy. What's next from this girl?*

We move into the restaurant that's filled with the smells of garlic and butter. Looking up, I notice how the light fixtures resembling bundles of arrows perfectly highlight the wide-plank wood floors. They've spared no attempt at authenticity or expense on this place. "What does the name 'Between the Trees' signify?" Mamie asks.

"Nice, isn't it?" says Isla. "The name comes from a John Muir quote. 'Between every two pines is a doorway to a new world.' Some say the new world represents enchantment. Others say it refers to opportunities and perspectives."

"Oh, that's sublime," says Mamie. "The Grand Bohemian is certainly a new world for me." She flashes me a look and hurries to add, "For Rob and me, I mean. We're a team."

Isla smiles at us, a glint of curiosity in her eyes.

"Yah, we're eager to get started," I say, nodding at the group.

Isla welcomes a couple that Annelise says are prospective art clients and invites them to join us. We take seats at a long table. Vaughn is talking with Isla and the clients at one end. At my end, Annelise and Mamie talk about girl stuff. About how their hair looks decent this time of year without the humidity. Like I'm not even sitting there within earshot. When Annelise whispers to Mamie—just loud enough for me to hear—about the cooling boyshort undies advertised on Facebook and how they changed her life, I speak up. "Hey. This isn't stuff dudes need to know." I give them a dark look, shake my head, and pick up my menu. Annelise responds to something Isla's saying. But Mamie gives me a guilty look and mouths, *Sorry.* And just like that, her pretty lips are my sole focus. I watch her read her menu and purse her mouth in different ways. Her bottom lip is fuller than the top—

"Robert," Mr. Call-me-Vaughn Reagan says.

My head bolts back. I stare at the man and manage to get out, "Yes?"

"I understand you're from Boston."

I feel Mamie's eyes on my face. *Did Vaughn catch me studying her?* "Yah. Right. I grew up there. I relocated to Charleston eight months ago."

"You follow the Red Sox?"

I give him a sporting smile. "Sure."

"Good American League team. One of the best."

I nod at Mr. Reagan as the waitress asks for my order just before I have to discuss the Sox. Since Annelise had consulted the lodge's PR agency and they had laid out the specs and parameters for our work with *Á La Mode*, the rest of lunch is only sprinkled with business talk. Accompanied by the metallic clink of silverware at other tables, Vaughn mostly talks about the Greenville Grand Bohemian and how its theme differs from the others in the South and in the West.

Our food arrives promptly. I'm chewing a bite of a wicked good bison burger when I realize how I must look. Like King Henry the Eighth with a turkey leg in each hand. Looking around at the others, I wipe my mouth with my napkin. I have to hold back from bulldozing through the whole pile of hand-cut fries with sumac aioli. But it's the portion of Southern hospitality from the staff that's the most sating.

Mamie and Annelise chat like fast friends. It's 2:45. The time Mamie and I have to be together will slip by fast. But when I catch sight of the dessert, I swat away that concern. Before us is a bûche de Noël, or a Yule log, as they're called in South Boston. I have a big sweet tooth, especially for chocolate. One Christmas my mom splurged and got one for the brood of us from Old B's Bakery. My old man had thrown a fit at the price. But no one raises a brow at this inspiration that's over a foot long and presented on a copper tray.

Naturally, the icing is sculpted to resemble a knotted log, but what's special about the cake is the miniature model of the hotel made of chocolate pieces on top. It's situated between two incredibly realistic chocolate pine trees dusted with powdered sugar snow. "Wicked smart," I say, and Mamie laughs at the Boston speak. I smile. "My brother Smoky says that all the time."

Her green eyes now lily pads, Mamie pitches her voice low. "Your brother's name is Smoky? I mean"—she takes off her glasses and rubs at the lenses with her napkin—"not that there's anything wrong with that."

The burger churns in my stomach.

Just then, the chef appears and takes a bow. Mamie puts her glasses on and leads the clapping.

"Et voilà, Mamie, between the trees," Isla says of the lavish cake.

Mamie whispers to her, her voice barely audible, "I'm grateful for my elastic waistband."

My mind leaves my oldest brother and whooshes back to the magnolia skin I saw this morning.

The Yule log before us, we make an it's-too-perfect-to-eat show. But Mamie moans over a big slice, and Henry the Eighth scarfs down two. After coffee, Annelise consults her Apple Watch and asks if we'd like to take a half-hour break before getting on with the tour. *That gives me more time to meet with Mamie afterward.* "Sounds like a plan," I say, getting up from the table. "I should get my camera gear ready."

"Brilliant," Mamie says, laying her napkin to the left of her plate and rising. "I need to gather my note-taking things. See you directly," she says to Annelise and me before scurrying back through the lobby.

I'm thanking Vaughn again for the delicious lunch when he reaches into the breast pocket of his coat and takes out what looks like gift certificates. Four of them. "I'd like you to experience dinner at Between the Trees." I'd gotten an eyeful of the prices on the dinner menu. The magazine's footing the bill for our accommodations but only provided a stipend for meals. Has Vaughn Reagan, like Johnny Carson's Carnac the Magnificent, sussed out the truth of my upstart status and beleaguered budget? I shake my head and take a step back. I tell him I can't accept them.

But he smiles warmly. "I'm sure you'll want to get out and enjoy some of Greenville's great dinner spots. Don't miss the city Christmas tree on Main Street at night. I recommend Sassafras Southern Bistro and Jianna for their wonderful food and service. The chef at Jianna makes the pasta himself. And if you venture out of the immediate area, Ji-Roz offers the best Greek in town." He winks. "Tell Angelo I sent you." He inclines the vouchers. "But please use these to dine here whenever you like. You don't want to miss our Christmas Eve feast." He tweaks his red-and-green bow tie and then gestures to a man at the host stand. "Make your reservations with Josh. He'll take care of you."

The only thing worse than Vaughn knowing my financial status would be for him to think I'm an ungracious man, even if I am a Boston Southie. I take the certificates, slip them into my pocket, and then offer him my hand and my thanks for his largesse.

Should I tell Mamie the truth? Or lead her to believe I'm flush?

As I walk away, Vaughn calls after me, "Your article could help put the Grand Bohemian on the map in the South. We're excited about that."

The gauntlet's been dropped.

Floored by the burden of proof I owe to Vaughn and the hotel owner, I turn and give him a high wave.

CHAPTER FIVE

Mamie

A t the door of my room, I smile and tap the owl, then insert
my card into the lock. Two tries later, I'm in. I'll let the
front desk know about the faulty card when I'm back downstairs.

The huge lunch has made me drowsy. It's the perfect opportunity for another starfish meditation before the tour. Stretching
out, I take off my glasses and scrub my face into the sumptuous
duvet. I think I might sleep, but the real reason I'm here seizes
my mind again: the box.

It was my mother who, though unwittingly, helped me
realize why I was drawn to Native American art. The once
ungentrified Colleen Atwater had "married well" and become
an Anson. Apparently, it didn't take long for my father to realize her true character because he only stuck around until my
third birthday. I remember little about him. Really only three
things: his wavy red hair, his smell of cigars and bergamot, and
his booming voice as I hid in the phone closet under the stairs.
He must have been awfully eager to be rid of Colleen because
he left her not only the house on Tradd but a whack-load of
money. As far as I know, we never saw him again.

But I wondered if my father had loved me.

I remember being held by strong, corded arms. But try as I
might to make the memory arms fit below the plump face and

shoulders of the man whose portrait gathered dust in the attic, I could never reconcile them. Colleen didn't talk about my father or any other family, for that matter. The topic was a street with no outlet. It was as though only the two of us had ever existed. And on our cold, cold planet, her mission was to make my life the one she had never had. While she played bridge and lunched with the other mothers at Virginia's on King Street she learned how to cultivate what they insisted were the right qualities in me. She sent me to the finest girls' school. In college, I would be courted by the best sororities and make my Charleston debut.

But the rudder of her Project Mamie boat fell off when I chose the College of Art and Design. The joke was on her: there were no sororities at SCAD. But there was Abigay, Native American art, and the seed of a career in journalism. Since then, by Colleen's account, the trajectory of my life has been a succession of disappointments.

It was Abigay who helped me understand that there was something innately wrong with my mother. She said Colleen was missing the part of her heart that could make her love me for who I am. She said I was someone special in the world. I loved Abigay and college and thrived creatively, despite my mother and the ghost of my father.

One afternoon two months ago, my mother called and asked me to come to Tradd Street. That's how she refers to the graceful Georgian mansion where I'd grown up South of Broad: *Tradd Street.* "A package came for you," she said in her habitual five-words-or-fewer fashion. I racked my brain for something I might have ordered that could have shown up at her house instead of my place.

"Well, what does it say, Mother? Is it, like, an Amazon box?"

"It is from another origin."

Nonplussed, I told her I'd come, and then ended the conversation. I called out to Abigay, who was propped up on the sofa with her sketch pad, binge-watching *Virgin River* on TV. I told her where I was headed.

"Tell Colleen I said hi." Abigay, an up-and-coming fashion designer and the divine offspring of a Jamaican flight attendant and Caucasian American professor, and I roomed together through grad school. When my mother met my roommate for the first time, she complimented her on her *pretty golden tan.* Abigail took it in her typical unruffled stride, but I squirmed with humiliation. Then the Fletchers arrived. My mother took one look at Abigay's effusive and lovely mom's ebony skin, and her skin paled. She and I had a hushed row in the parking lot, and I suggested she not visit again until she could find a modicum of grace. After grad school, Abigay and I moved to Charleston, where we found a modest two-bedroom apartment. Mother never did pop in, proving that, for all her airs, grace eluded her.

"I'll smother her with kisses."

"Ha. Hurry back and tell me what's in the box, Bee."

Ten minutes later, I drove beneath moss-laden oaks and through open wrought iron gates into my mother's cobblestone drive. Carolina wrens chirped, restless in the trees. I hoped Gladiola was working because my mother's housekeeper is the only pleasant part of the household. Though I suspected she found little reason to be glad on Tradd, she was always happy to see me.

I knocked on the screen door. But it was my mother's slight shadowy figure that approached. We exchanged greetings as she unlatched the screen. The sheepish look on her face should have been a tip-off that something big was about to go down. I entered the foyer, smelling cinnamon and the lavender polish Gladiola uses on the antiques.

"Is that Amber Autumn tea I smell?"

"Yes," she said, standing in place as if she had grown roots.

"Well, may I have a cup?"

She sent a darting glance to the living room, where I spotted a cardboard box atop the English three-door chest.

"I'll bring the tea."

While she hurried into the kitchen, I entered the living room and approached the chest. The "to" label on the box was immaculate and penned in a beautiful firm hand that read, *Miss Mamie Anson*. But the "from" label was unreadable. It looked as though it had been scrubbed at. I lifted the box, weighing it in my hands. It felt light for something that seemed so full of portent.

My mother came back in with a tray, her steps mincing, though the rattling of cups and saucers and spoons made me fear a crash.

I put the box down. "Here, let me take that." I took the tray and set it down on the English tea table in front of her favorite chair. "What is going on here, Mother?"

I think that was the moment she figured out the jig was up on the titanic-sized bit of information she was keeping from me. She plopped down on her chair, and a light cloud of dust lifted around her. *Had she let Gladiola go?* "Guess you better open it."

I picked up the package again and took a seat on a chair across the table from her. On my lap, the box felt as though it writhed with the troubles of the world. "Who sent this?"

Colleen's head was down, her jaw tight. Then she looked up without meeting my eyes. "I don't know."

"You don't know," I said flatly.

"It's your grandfather's personal effects."

"My *grandfather*? What grandfather?"

"My father, Tate Atwater."

"*Your* father. Your *father*? I'm twenty-six years old, and you've never told me about him?" My thoughts tangled and spun. "He's dead?"

Tears ran down her cheeks through channels I hadn't noticed the last time I'd seen her. "Mm," she said, nodding her head. Then her apparent sorrow unleashed what is for her a verbal tsunami: "Evidently, Tate wanted you to have his things when he passed. Someone else sent them."

My thoughts were on a prowl, riffling through our past. "Who?" I ran my fingers over the return address label. "I can't read this."

"Must have been a friend."

"Well, why to me? Did Tate Atwater know me? Know *of* me?"

Now that she had the upper hand again—the knowledge, the power—my mother collected herself, sat up, and poured cups of tea. She stirred hers until I thought I'd scream. She took a sip and locked my gaze with hers in such a way that I surmised her tears had been of the crocodile variety. "When you were three, your father and I went through a bitter divorce. The situation was . . . unsuitable for a young child. Neither your father nor I had family to send you to while we . . . worked things out. Except for my father in New Mexico."

"New Mexico!"

"Yes." She closed her eyes. "He was a Navajo Indian. Lived in the Navajo Nation."

My mind became a flaming torch of righteous indignation.

She sat there with her eyes closed like a kid who thinks you can't see them if they can't see you. I got up and paced the Persian rug, my hands in my hair. "You sent me to stay with my *Native American grandfather. On a reservation.* By myself. When I was three."

"The airline provided an escort."

I halted in my tracks and gaped at my mother. "How long was I there?" I closed my eyes and tried to force a memory.

"You were there eight weeks."

Eight weeks. I collected the box and sat down again. I looked at the return address label, then glared at my mother and punctuated my next words with finger stabs to the box. "Did you scrub off this label?"

"I didn't want you stirring up anything with those people."

"Those people?" I looked at her black hair. *"Mother dear,* you are one-half Native American. And that makes me one-quarter! How could you keep this from me? This is my life, my *identity* we're talking about! My *heritage!"* My skin sizzled with panic. "What else have you kept from me?"

"Nothing else, really. I gave you the box when I could have hidden it away. I never saw any point in you knowing about Tate. But maybe I was wrong."

A sob swelled in my throat. "He could have loved me!"

"He did love you, Mamie. He was crazy about you."

This was the linchpin moment I would come back to rub like a rosary. The only other question that mattered pecked at my brain. "How do you know?"

"We spoke on the phone that summer. After. All he could talk about was you. He asked me to let you spend summers in the Nation. But I didn't want you growing up in that world." I fell heavily back into my chair and slumped. *How fun that would have been for a kid.* I wrapped my arms around my torso and rocked back and forth, realizing how very little I knew about my family. And how my mother had made me feel that I shouldn't ask.

"What about your mother?"

"Irish Catholic. Catherine Mary Morrow. Died giving birth to me."

Oh, my Lord. My grandmother and my middle name. She never told me. "On the reservation?"

"Yes, but I wasn't reared there."

"Where, then?"

"In Santa Fe . . . with a . . . foster family. Tate climbed in a bottle after my mother died. But eventually, he got sober. And came to visit me often. He was a good father, in his way." She sniffed. "But Tate's world wasn't for me. When I was eighteen, I boarded a bus for the East Coast."

I felt like the brain-imploding emoji on a keyboard and struggled to string words together. "You didn't think . . . that you being a *foster* child . . . and half Native American was . . . relevant information? That I might have been mildly interested in knowing about this whole other . . . universe of yours?"

My mother pursed her lips and gave a slight shrug.

Outrage pulsing through me, I looked at the ceiling toward the attic where my school things lay moldering in an old toy box. *Had I been tasked with making a family tree in second grade? What a farce that project would have been.* I caught sight of my face in a trumeau mirror. It was ugly, blotched and contorted. I took a breath and faced her again. "You said there was nothing else, really, that you were keeping from me. How much *nothing else, really*, is there?"

"How much more do you want to know?"

"You know what?" I pushed my hands out as though holding her at bay. "I don't want a single other thing from you. This is the most bizarre . . . script flip . . . I could have ever imagined." I got to my feet and picked up the box containing the personal effects of the grandfather who had loved me. I strode to the door. My hand on the screen frame, I turned back. Colleen's head was bowed. "Mother?" She refused to look at me. But at that moment I didn't care if I ever saw her face again. "You did me . . . a great injustice. I am going home. Do not call."

Though my hands were clumsy with their shaking, I managed to start my Toyota. On the passenger seat, the box held its secrets.

The tears came then.

I howled with loss all the way to my apartment.

Someone once said that grief makes a permanent home in your heart. But in the two months since I learned about my grandfather, there seems to be a bit more wiggle room every day. The day I received the box, I opened it sitting on my bedroom floor with Abigay. Written in beautiful cursive on an envelope tucked inside was *For Mamie*. On the back, a note by a different hand read, *Per your grandfather's instructions, I send these with my best wishes. TB.*

"Wonder who TB is," Abigay said. "A friend, maybe? Or could it be family?"

"Maybe. Oh, Abs, what if Tate remarried and had another family? What if I have half-siblings out there somewhere?"

With the hope of learning more, I opened the envelope and slid out a sheet of notepaper.

Dear Mamie,

  The summer you spent here was the happiest time of my life. Your bright chatter, curiosity, and sweet nature filled my days with laughter. You turned ordinary things like making the morning biscuits into moments of delightful discovery. I know you have grown into a wonderful young woman who sheds light on others and makes the world a better place. Not being a part of your growing up is the roughest path I ever traveled. But I am at peace now. See enclosed a photo from your time in the Nation.

  Your loving Grandtate

Grandtate. Was I the one who named him that, or did he suggest it? I read the letter twice before sharing it with Abigay and felt the chambers of my heart loosen and sigh. I ransacked the box for the photo without success.

Mamie

They say that daughters who grow up without a father may have issues. I googled it in high school one day after another dismaying "Donuts with Dad" event. There's even a name for it: fatherless daughter syndrome. Girls with that awful label can struggle with a sense of self and self-esteem. Even intimacy and trust. A classmate whose dad had died and I were the only students in our grade who grew up without knowing a father's love. At least her big jokey uncle stepped up each year to fill the role. I wonder what it would have been like to have had my grandfather there to support me. At least I now know that the strong arms I recall holding me when I was little were his. I feel like I have a healthy sense of who I am. Abigay's probably had a lot to do with that. I'm nothing like my cold and duplicitous mother.

But I have to wonder if there's an underlying reason why I'm so career focused and in no hurry to get married. I don't think I have intimacy issues. Maybe trust ones because I was abandoned by my father? But maybe Tate's love was so powerful that it's stored up in my soul. And someday I'll be able to trust a guy enough to commit to him the way Abigay has with Jake.

I smile and start a text to her: *How's the snow bunny? All great here. Lodge is rustically gorgeous. Mr. Stunning Portfolio is epic handsome. Merry Christmas.* But before adding a heart and hitting send, I delete the "is epic handsome" and replace it with "seems like he'll be great to work with." If Farida hadn't tasked me with the Grand Bohemian assignment, I would have begged her for it. I'm here to get in touch with my heritage. This hotel buzzes with Native American vibes, and our tour starts in twelve minutes.

I step out from the elevator downstairs holding the notebook Abigay gave me and am surprised to see my photographer in the lobby. He's slung about with the small bags I recognize from the car and talking with Annelise. She holds a notebook of her own, and a pencil is tucked behind an ear. I greet her and tell her I'm a pencil girl too before lifting my brows at Rob. "Who's the early bird now?"

He holds up a sleek camera. "Got some wicked good worms."

I grin. "Well done."

Annelise suggests we start with the ballroom. The space is opulent, the walls papered in gold-and-white animal prints. But Rob stands riveted before an entry wall of arrowhead collections in beautifully framed shadow boxes. "Wow" pops out of me.

Annelise says, "The arrowheads are part of Mr. De Renne's private collection. Most of the art in the hotel is." *The guy must be a mega-millionaire.* I open my notebook and scribble a few notes. Rob positions shots.

"What are the arrowheads made of?" I ask.

"Mostly stone," Annelise says, and consults her notebook. "Sorry. Flint, jasper, and obsidian."

"Interesting." My mind returns to the box and to the small leather pouch of arrowheads my grandfather left me. I wonder for the first time if they're valuable. But selling one would be like selling a toe.

I swallow around the lump in my throat as Rob says to Annelise, "So those are igneous rocks. Imagine being pierced through with one of these bad boys." He clutches his chest and pretends to stumble backward.

I grimace. *The way my mother pierced my chest.* "Right?"

Annelise smacks her forehead. "There's a Christmas ball Saturday night. I don't think I told you."

A ball! I picture the elaborate antler chandeliers all lit up and a band playing Christmas jazz. I bet Rob would ask me to dance. He'd take my hand . . . our chests would draw close . . .

Annelise gives me a sidelong look. Certain my face is a pomegranate, I peer down at a random notebook page. "Did you bring anything dressy?"

"I didn't. I mean, nothing formal."

"You know what? We have three days," Annelise says to me. "There's a consignment shop with glam stuff downtown. We could go shopping."

I imagine the boutiques festooned for the holidays, serving Christmas cookies and punch to customers, everyone feeling festive. "That sounds so fun."

Rob seems to survey his outfit. Annelise says to him, "You're probably fine in a jacket if you didn't bring a suit." She must have read his solemn expression. "But there are no rules. It's all good." She leads the way back to the lobby. Behind me, Rob's violet-y exhale brushes my neck. Chill bumps gather there. I give my head a mental shake and march after Annelise. *This is business and self-discovery, not romance, Mamie. Rinse and repeat.* Annelise turns. "Let's go out on the bar balcony and look at the egg before we hit the gallery."

"The egg," Rob says. "Okay, I'll bite."

I smile at his pun. Tourists come through the balcony door, oohing and aahing at the lobby. *Everyone loves the hotel. Just wait until our article hits the stands.*

On the porch hulks a large open oval structure made of mosaic stone. "Voilà! The egg," says Annelise. "A heating element underneath keeps it warm all the time."

I reach out and touch it. "How neat is that?"

"Sit in it," she insists. "People take selfies here all the time. Couples especially love sitting in the egg at night."

She tips me a wink. *What the heck? I have to set her straight.*

Rob sits right down, his hair grazing the top of the egg's opening. He runs a hand over his hair and settles himself on the stones, his long thighs sticking way out. "Man, it *is* warm."

Does he expect me to sit with him? Like we're a couple?

I freeze, deliberating on the implications of sitting or not sitting when Annelise pulls her cell out of her skirt pocket.

"C'mon, Mamie, I'll take the picture." But Rob extends his Canon to her and suggests she use it.

Deciding that not taking a seat would brand me a poor sport, I do. Rob and I were relatively close in the car, but now in the egg, we are arm against arm, thigh against thigh. The temperature of the stone seems to spike with every second. His sandalwood scent wreathes my head.

"Say, 'Merry Christmas!'" Annelise sings out.

I smile for the camera, but my thoughts steal my brain. It feels way too good sitting close to him. My phone pings in my skirt pocket. If it's a text from Abigay, I owe her a big thanks for the escape hatch. I stride to the balcony railing, dig out my phone, and bend over the screen. I glance back. Annelise is laughing as she tries to help Rob extract his lengthy limbs from the egg. He looks so funny. And cute. Definitely cute.

The text is from Abigay: *Oh, Bee, it's so fun imagining you flitting about the Grand Bohemian with an intriguing photographer. Sneak me a pic of him! All fun here with my love in a winter won-derland. XO.* Glad to hear from Abigay and that all is well with her and Jake, I'm ready to move on from this unseemly scene. I straighten my spine, shake my hair out, and collect my note-book. "Ready? I'm dying to see the art."

"The library is just through here," says Annelise. "You might want to hang out there to meet or write or whatever."

We move to the doorway where inviting furniture covered in elegant, textured, and earth-toned fabrics is cozily arranged. I can't help but step inside.

"Now *this* is a library," I say, my eyes lifting to high shelves of books. "Are the books real?"

"Not only are they real, but most are first editions. Mr. De Renne's collection."

"Oh, my word. That's amazing. No wonder you shelve them high." Rob's gone all clicky with his camera.

"Get this arrangement," I murmur to him, indicating a square vase of natural greens, white and dark purple blossoms, and pheasant feathers. He does. I long to take off my shoes and pad around on the brown-and-white carpet that resembles the spotted coat of a fawn.

"Mamie, you'll appreciate this," Annelise says. "It's our corn maiden doll representation, hand carved. Isn't she sweet?" The stout figure placed between hardcover books and other Native American accessories wears a green husklike collar and a skirt of tricolor Indian corn.

Birdlike wings unfurl in my stomach. "She is," I manage, my eyes glued to the maiden. I think of the corn maiden doll my grandfather crafted for me not out of wood but of beads, hundreds of them in shades of blue. I wonder if he had named her Bluebell or if I did.

Rob appears at my side and takes several snaps of the corn maiden. I recover my voice. "Will you send those to me, please?"

"Yah huh," he says, "I started an album to send to you."

With a little smile, I remind myself that "yah huh" means of course. "Cool. Thanks."

Isla clips past the doorway, and Annelise calls out to her. "Are you ready for our media team?" *Media team. I like that. Infinitely better than partners or, heaven forbid, a couple.*

"Hey! Your timing is perfection. My feet need a minute."

In the open gallery space, I pause over a glass-topped case of Native American jewelry and have to tear myself away when Isla offers us seats in Lucite chairs. Cedar seems to be the choice of fresh greenery here. I love the way the local florist draped it over portrait frames so that it spills over their edges, especially my favorite, the splendid chief's portrait by the elevators. A painting over the curator's desk captures my eye, and I do a double take. It's an Indigenous woman, a braid falling over one shoulder. Her sinewy arms knead bread in a wooden bowl. My own arms prickle with a sudden chill. Rob's asking Isla about the photography of Bob King, an uber-talented local.

I get to my feet. "Excuse me for a second?" I rush to find a moment of hush. When I spot a ladies' room, I barrel my way in. I have the room to myself. Standing head down before the long vanity, I put my hands on the granite and close my eyes. An old wooden bowl had been one of the items in my grandfather's box. The day I opened it, I ran my fingers over its scuffs and fissures, hoping to remember something, but came up with nothing. Now a vision comes. Hands as gnarled as an apple tree incorporate wet ingredients into a wooden bowl of flour. I'm wearing a blue dress and red round-toed Keds. *There's only one way to make biscuits,* a smooth tenor rings in my head. *See how the shortening and buttermilk take only the flour they need for the batter and leave the rest in the bowl? It's magic.* Enchanted, I smile up at the man, but before I reach his face, the memory seems to whoosh down the sink drain. I regard my face in the mirror as a single tear leaves my right eye. But it's a happy tear. Abigay gently reminded me that I might never remember much of my time in the Navajo Nation. But *here in this place,* I'm beginning to, just as I'd hoped. I lick the tear from my lip as if to possess it and return to the gallery.

CHAPTER SIX

Rob

Mamie comes back to the gallery, humming a Christmas tune. I can almost feel the vibration in my sternum. The smile that commandeers my face at the sight of her is that of a total chowdahead, an infatuated one. I fake cough into my shoulder to cover it.

Mamie puts her hands together and then uses them to prop her chin. "Isla," she says, still standing, "I've been wondering about the owls in the lodge. Why owls? What do they represent, wisdom?"

Isla looks up from the iPad she's using to show me photos of the hotel when it was under construction. "Oh, glad you asked. I love the owls." She sits back and crosses her legs. "Indigenous peoples believed owl energy could connect them with inner wisdom. It could give one the ability to see through deception to the truth."

"Nice," Mamie utters at the same time that I say, "Cool."

"It is cool. Owl energy," Isla says.

"Sounds like a name for a late-night bar," I put in.

Isla laughs. "It does! Oh," she says to Mamie, "and the way the lodge nestles into the surrounding trees is reminiscent of owls nestling into the trees at night. You may hear one or two."

Mamie's expression is thoughtful. She bends over her

notebook again. I hope she's recording Isla's words; they seemed to carry insight.

"What's next?" Mamie asks, brightening and sticking her pencil behind an ear.

Isla stands. "I'd love to show you the jewelry. The pieces in this case are for sale. Most of these were worn by men," she says, looking at me.

"Hmm." Isla glances out the windows at a bunch of teenage boys pretending to joust with each other in front of the lodge. The gangs in Boston cross my mind. Then I think of my hood and lift my eyes to the heavens, imagining myself there, sporting a big honking beaded tribal necklace. Pop would howl his ridicule at a man wearing something like that. A woman, sure, especially if it meant putting more cleavage out there. A man, no. My brothers wear gold chains and show off their chest hair. I wouldn't be caught dead wearing jewelry, period. Except for a wedding ring. I guess that's another thing that separates me from them. Though I'm no Ivy Leaguer, I like the traditional New England classic style where preppy is a sort of coastline casual. In Charleston, it's even more so. In Greenville too, by the looks of three guys striding through the lobby. Since I've been in the South, I've felt like I belong here.

Mamie seems fixated on another bracelet. "The turquoise is so beautiful," she murmurs. Her hands, which have been resting on the rim of the case, have gone shaky. Puzzled, I look at her face, but she's intent, her head tilting as her eyes follow the designs on the bracelet. She clasps her hands behind her as Isla tells us how authentic turquoise is named. "This milky turquoise is called Sleeping Beauty because it was unearthed from the mine of the same name."

"Where?" Mamie asks, her green eyes as alert as a doe's.

"New Mexico, pre-1960s. The mines were closed shortly after."

"What tribe?" Mamie persists.

"Navajo," Isla pronounces.

Mamie breathes out.

A ray of afternoon sun steals through the window and lights the small smile that plays across her pink mouth. What is she thinking? Does she *want* the bracelet? The price mounted on the velvet next to it reads $1,800. Mamie seems too sensible to wear anything that expensive or fancy. "Interesting stuff," I admit as I get several shots of the piece.

"Thanks, Fitzpatrick," she murmurs, her eyes never leaving the case.

Two to one, she'll want to use a photo of the bracelet in the article. Maybe that's what's on her mind. "How are the stones' authenticity proven?" I ask Isla.

"The Navajos signed their work with a stamp or etching of some kind on the inside, a mark that's individual to the craftsman."

Christmas comes early in Mamie's eyes. "Could you take it out so we can see the marking?"

Isla surveys the kids now entering the hotel through the gallery door. She gives us a meaningful wait-a-second look. When the kids move on through and toward the lobby, the curator slips behind her desk and takes a set of keys from a drawer. She locks the outside door. "We don't have a lot of unaccompanied minors coming through, but we can never be too careful." She clips back to the case.

"Of course," Mamie says, eyeing the keys. Her chest rises and falls, rises and falls.

Isla opens the case and takes the bracelet out for Mamie's inspection. Mamie bends close.

"You're welcome to pick it up," Isla says.

"Really? Thank you." Mamie picks it up as gingerly as one would the Magna Carta. "So this marking here"—she points to the inside of the cuff—"identifies the artist?"

Isla nods. "Yep."

Mamie holds the bracelet closer to me, but I've already moved in with my camera. We're finding a rhythm, and we haven't even met to strategize our schedule yet. Maybe we're playing the assignment intuitively, which is pretty amazing.

With both hands, Mamie gives the bracelet back to Isla. Isla uses a white cloth to wipe it down and then replaces the piece in the case. Mamie buffs the glass with her sleeve while Isla returns the keys to the drawer, pulls out her purse, and sets it in her computer chair. Hoping Mamie's ready to get down to business as we planned, I ask her where she wants to meet. "Oh. I don't know. Didn't you want to see the bourbon bar? And I wanted to get a look at the spa. Can't we meet *tomorrow?*"

Isla gives her watch a peek that Mamie doesn't seem to notice. I speak up. "Isla, can we see those things tomorrow?" Mamie gives me a ticked-off twist of her mouth. *What?*

"Of course. You guys are totally free-range. But if you need more info for your story, be sure and let us know. Either Annelise or I are here every day. Well, except for Christmas Eve and Christmas Day this week." She grins with wide eyes as though she can't wait for the time off and tilts her head at a fir dripping with ornaments and feathers next to a high-backed oval-shaped purple velvet banquette situated just beyond the gallery. "I'm woefully behind on my home decorating."

"I totally understand," Mamie says, not looking at me.

"They just set up a hot chocolate bar in the lobby, if you're interested," says Isla. She collects a blazer from the back of her chair and her purse. "Enjoy."

"Thanks, Isla," I say. "We appreciate your time."

"We do, so much," Mamie chimes in. "See you tomorrow."

"Of course. Everyone's happy you both are here. Have a great first night."

We watch the curator leave through the lobby, a woman

on a mission. Mamie lowers her head and looks at me over her glasses like a strict teacher. "So we'll meet now. Where?"

I don't know why she's turned into a porcupine, but we need to clear the air.

"How about the library? Annelise suggested it."

"Okay, but I'd like to get a hot chocolate first. I mean, if that's okay."

The sarcasm doesn't suit her. I hope it's short-lived and not a character trait that's just showing up. "Yah huh," I say, mildly narrow eyed.

Her face flushes. "Would you like one too?"

"No, thanks. I'm good."

"Okay, then. See you in the library," she says, turning. I pick up my bags and then make a pit stop. Above the signs for both the men's and ladies' rooms are small owl emblems like the one above my room number. That must be what got Mamie wondering about owls. I wash my face and gargle with the mouthwash and little cups the hotel provided. I think of my mom and wish she could see how nice this place is.

People are roaming around in the library, but they leave when I walk in and set my camera stuff in one of two adjacent chairs. While I wait for Mamie, I take a few photos. Bronze sculptures of Native American men on horseback and a couple of masterfully finished pieces of furniture that I know are antiques. I'm taking a seat when Mamie comes in with her hot chocolate. It's precariously piled in a paper cup with whipped cream, tiny marshmallows, chocolate shavings, and peppermint crumbles.

"That looks good." I search her eyes to assess her mood. "Wish I hadn't had two slices of that dang Yule log."

She gives me her natural smile for the first time in hours. The gritty lens over the afternoon swipes clean. She takes a sip of her cocoa. "Yum. Listen, I apologize for getting salty. I usually have a low patch from overstimulation on the *second* day of a trip. But I get over it. And I'm kind of a control freak . . ."

A weight slips off my shoulders. *The real Mamie's back. At least I hope it's the real Mamie.* "Aw, you're okay, kid. I know a lot's riding on this for you. It is for me too. But let's try to have some fun. Remember, 'tis the season to be merry."

She holds her hot chocolate cup aloft and smiles. "Cheers to that."

"Cheers. By the way, are you an only child?"

She stares at me for a long moment. "Ye-es." Then she grins. "*And* an eager beaver overachiever. How could you tell?" We share a laugh. "What about you? There's Smoky. Do you have other siblings?"

"Five brothers."

"Five! Ding dang, that's a lot of Fitzpatricks! A lot of *testosterone.*"

Especially if Pop's around. "Yah, sometimes *too* much."

Mamie seems to read my face or maybe my voice and gives me a sympathetic look.

"Let's talk schedule," she says. "You were spot-on about meeting this afternoon instead of waiting 'til tomorrow. Now we can start work in the morning."

I smile. "I'd like to begin with the exterior. Get a sunrise shot of the lodge."

She nods her head thoughtfully. "Starting outside's like beginning with the big picture, then moving to the details—to the gestalt of the place. I like that."

Gestalt theory. Mamie's whip-smart, unlike some of the girls I've dated. Not that this is in any way a date. "Well, that was easy."

Mamie opens her notebook, pulls the pencil from behind her ear, and holds it aloft. "How about I write out the schedule and then type it up tonight? I can email it to you." She gives me a saucy look. "And then *you* can look at it on your *phone.*"

I watch her write something, her hair falling over her cheek, and realize I'm treading infatuation-infested waters. I throw myself a mental work-life preserver before I swim out any farther. "That works." I cross one leg over the other at the knee.

"I like your socks," she says, pointing at my ankles with her pencil. "They're colorful."

The preserver slips from my grasp. Mamie's gotten personal, noticing my clothes. But now I'm glad I blasted my budget to buy them. My old friend and mentor, Seamus, taught me about masculine charisma. *Looking refined makes a man feel confident and therefore more successful.* I want Mamie to see me that way. I nod a disconcerting thanks to her, then punch up my weather app. "Okay," I say after the glitchy app finally displays the daily sunrise forecast. "A few clouds in the morning—that's good. More color in the sky, so I need to be set up before . . . seven fifteen."

"Perf. I'm bringing the coffee."

"You *are?*" I grin. "Okay, then. But I like mine black and strong enough to dissolve a spoon."

Mamie hoots a laugh.

"Is there a Dunks down here?"

She turns her head to give me a side-eye. "Excuse me? A dunks?"

"Dunkin' Donuts. 'Dunks' in Boston."

"Ahh. Well, not downtown. But I promise to find you a good cup."

We iron out a working separately and working together schedule that pleases us both.

Annelise sticks her head in the door. "Hey, y'all, I'm headed home. It's five o'clock," she adds in a singsong voice. "The bar's open."

I stand up and stretch my back that's still stiff from contorting myself in the egg. "Thanks. Have a good night." *Maybe*

Mamie and I can get a drink and then have dinner later. But I don't want her to think she has to spend all her time with me. I watch her as she stands and tells Annelise to have a lovely night. *Lovely. That's Mamie.*

"Will you have a drink with me?" I ask when we're alone.

"I will," she says. She collects her still half-full paper cup and stuffs her napkin into it. "I've had enough sweet stuff for one day."

We gather our things and head out into the bustling lobby ringing with the lilt and sass of southern accents. From overhead, Earth, Wind & Fire's version of "Jingle Bell Rock" begins. Two spots are left at the polished black and azure-veined bar. We take them. Mamie bends her head down to look beneath the surface, and her hair sends a bouquet to my nose as it brushes my thigh. *Mind on business, Fitzpatrick.* "Yay, there are hooks under here," she says. "A good bar always has purse or bag hooks." She hangs up her computer bag and purse and asks me if my things will fit on the hook beneath my space. They do. That settled, we order drinks from a bartender named Tucker; Mamie orders a Weller, rocks. *A girl who drinks whiskey . . .* I order the same and we settle back onto leather spotted calf-hair stools. After Mamie's low patch, I realize I feel more comfortable around her because it proved that she was human. She's not perfect. And neither am I.

Maybe we'll be perfectly imperfect partners.

My heart chimes in. *Maybe more*, it says.

CHAPTER SEVEN

Mamie

I nurse a whiskey at the Grand Bohemian Lodge lobby bar with the *epic-handsome Rob Fitzpatrick* whom I've only known since eleven minutes after nine this morning. A surreal day if ever, oh ever, there was one. The Native American elements I experienced on the tour made me feel closer to my grandfather. Maybe as close as I'll get. I only wish I'd had more time with the silver bracelet. But I'm grateful that Rob captured the artisan's stamp on film.

Tucker, the bartender, chats Rob up about Greenville's ice hockey team with the unlikely name of the Swamp Rabbits. "The puck drops at seven thirty tonight," Tucker says, giving me a winsome wiggle of his brows.

I touch my breastbone. "Me? Thanks. But I'm not a fan."

He cuts his eyes at Rob. "Guess it's not exactly a romantic thing to do." Rob huffs a little laugh and adjusts the knot in his tie.

A blush climbs my neck. "Oh no, we . . . we're working on a magazine feature. May I have a glass of water, please?"

"You bet." Tucker moves away and takes someone else's drink order before pouring my water. Rob peers into his whiskey as though some special wisdom dwells at the bottom. *What's he thinking?* I stir my whiskey with a fancy arrow-shaped swizzle stick, then glance up at the expanse of windows behind the bar. It's nearing full dark outside, and the window becomes a mirror. In it, I find Rob and me. Twice today we've been mistakenly thought of as a couple. Do we look like one? Small and neat, tall and rangy. Our *body language* doesn't suggest intimacy. Is it something in the way we look at each other? Something in our eyes? Though I've been preoccupied, one thing's bankable: I like him. A lot. He's a good guy.

The mirror Rob turns to look at me. I still, and watch his image move. I can feel his eyes on my hair, my chin, my chest. Someone would have to take away my girl card if I didn't recognize that Fitzpatrick is into me. We haven't talked much about our personal lives, but I think that if he had a girlfriend, my radar for that would have pinged all over the place. I haven't seen him texting and grinning at his phone screen the way someone in love does. The way Abigay does with Jake.

I take another sip of my drink. It's a good thing I feel I'm too young to get married or I might find myself in Abigay's Chuck Taylor sneakers, too far gone on *Rob* and writing a mediocre piece. His sleeve brushes mine and sends a note of sandalwood to my nose. Then again, since we're spending Christmas on Sunday here, we have until Monday, the day we drive home. What's wrong with a little Christmas flirting just for tonight? I've totally got this.

My elbow on the bar, I rest my chin on my palm and turn to him. When he looks at me, I slowly smile and give my eyes a couple of slow bats. Does he mind my glasses? The light in *his* eyes and the way he curls the right side of his mouth up says he doesn't mind a thing.

My chest is warm from the whiskey. Tucker returns with two glasses of water, one for each of us. "If you're ever here durin' baseball season," he says, "you should *catch—bada bing—*a Drive's game. My *girlfriend* loves goin'." I hide my grin at the bartender's goofy matchmaking efforts behind the rim of my water glass. Rob's shoulders are shaking with suppressed laughter.

"Another round?" Tucker asks.

"Why not?" Rob and I say in tandem, and then grin some more. Tucker moves off.

The drink has loosened my tongue. "I do like baseball. I dated a player last spring. He was with the Charleston River-Dogs. A pitcher." Rob seems to hang on my every word. "My roommate Abigay says I fell out of like with Blake and into like with baseball. I follow the Braves."

"Hmm. Your roommate . . . Abig*ay*, short for Abigail?"

"Nope. Her mother's Jamaican. It's a family name. What about Smoky? What's that short for?"

He picks up his glass and sips the last of his whiskey. "You wouldn't believe it if I told you."

"Really?"

"Really."

I seem to have come a little close to the bone and wonder about his brothers again. Maybe his family is as messed up as mine.

He changes the subject. "So do you and Abigay share an apartment? Or a house?"

"A two-bedroom apartment in a four-square house. It's comfy." I don't want to reveal any more about my family while we're having fun. I wipe the condensation from my water glass and then reach for a fresh napkin from Tucker's stash. "What about you? Do you have a . . . home in Charleston where I picked you up?"

He takes a long pull from his drink and then sets it down. Sitting straight, he locks his eyes with mine. "I live in a garage apartment behind a great old Georgian. I'm also sort of my landlady's handyman."

Someone bumps me from behind and I turn. Rob and I have been too deep in conversation to notice that people are queued up two-deep behind us and jockeying for position. "Want to move to a table? Somewhere where we can talk . . . maybe get an appetizer," I ask him.

"Absolutely." He manages to catch Tucker's eye and make the universal sign for "check." I'm reaching for my wallet when Rob takes care of our tab. He earns another check in my pro column for being a gracious man. We collect our highball glasses and bags and score a prime spot on the banquette near the gallery. The bracelet's been the top card in the deck of my mind, but now the garage apartment and the handyman's work shuffle to the front.

I'm wondering which thread to pick up in our conversation when a waitress appears and introduces herself as Whitney. She lays fresh cocktail napkins on the oval cocktail table in front of us. The room is growing warm and loud. Rob shrugs his blazer from his broad shoulders. I practically have to yell our appetizer order of a Bohemian Hunt Board with local cheeses and cured meats to be heard.

"Quite a few office parties going on tonight," Whitney says, tilting her head toward the area around the great stone fireplace now teeming with revelers in festive dress. I count four slinky red dresses, one with a jaw-dropping décolletage, and look ruefully down at my boho cropped sweater and skirt. "What else may I bring you?" the server asks.

"I should switch to wine," I say, and Rob nods. We ask for two glasses, a pinot grigio for me, and a pinot noir for him. Whitney moves off, leaving me to surreptitiously inspect his broad shoulders and swell of chest muscles the way I hadn't been able to in the car. My pulse picks up and so does my babble. "I know you're supposed to pair your wine with food, but I only drink white. I want to like red, but I just don't. It's a temperature thing."

Rob doesn't respond to my remarks. He's busy flexing and surveying his hands. When he looks up, he leans a little closer. His eyes implore me like he's about to say something that urgently needs saying. "My photos have sold well in three Charleston galleries. And one in Savannah. But I'm just getting established with the photojournalist thing. This is my first assignment."

Why did he tell me that? Has he picked up on some deep-seated prejudice in me? His disquietude works its way under my skin, making it feel too tight. "Well, me too," I insist, "as a features editor." I search my purse for an eyeglass wipe but come up empty. I down the last sip of my whiskey. *Farida. She suggested and therefore vetted Rob for the assignment. She went on and on about his portfolio. The photos she mentioned must be those that are selling in galleries. Farida's an outstanding businesswoman. She doesn't make staffing mistakes. Abigay would fuss at me for obsessing again. Do I feel I'm more competent just because my name's on the Á La Mode masthead? Where's my humility? I'm acting like my mother. Oh no, I can't be. I am not my mother.*

Rob's big shoulders rise toward the not-so-crisp crease now in his collar. Whitney swoops in with our wine just in time to give me a minute. Rob mumbles his thanks to the server. I take a sip of my wine, still feeling his anxious eyes on my face. I recover my grace. "C'mon, Fitzpatrick. Everyone has to start somewhere. I'd love to see your portfolio."

A cloud seems to move from in front of his face. His shoulders visibly relax. And mine follow suit. His lips break into a mile-wide smile. "Thanks," he says. "I'd love to show it to you. Get your feedback." He takes up his glass. "We forgot to toast before."

I grin. "We did. You make it." I collect my stem.

"I know a lotta funny ones, but tonight . . . how 'bout to partnership?"

I smile and clink my glass with his. "To partnership."

We sit back and enjoy our wine, listening to Christmas jazz.

A three-star-Michelin-chef-worthy charcuterie board arrives. We dig in, hopscotching the board through hard cheeses, prosciutto and chorizo, nuts, artisan crackers, olives, and pickled winter veggies. We talk about cooking. (I'm not a cook, but Rob is.) We talk about travel. (Rob hasn't been to many places, but I've visited Europe twice.)

Whitney comes by and I take the check. "My treat, Fitzpatrick."

He smiles. "Thanks. I'll get it next time."

"I'm not keeping score. It's Christmas!" Abruptly, a need to see the photos Rob took today turns me inside out. "Since you have your camera with you, will you show me the first photos?"

He reaches for his camera as though I'm about to snatch it up. "They aren't organized yet."

I flap my hand. "I don't care about *that*."

"But I do. And I haven't edited them. I planned to do that tonight."

"I promise I don't care if they're perfect."

He sighs. "I promise to show them to you soon. It's a personal thing."

My brain buzzes with doubt. *Is he hiding something from me?* "You're the photojournalist."

The happy hour crowd is thinning. People are likely headed toward Between the Trees or downtown for dinner. Rob asks, "Would you like to get some dinner?"

Abruptly, I'm ready for a shower and my luxurious bed. And if my roommate/therapist is available, a much-needed phone chat. "The charcuterie was pretty filling. And I'm feeling road fuggy. I think I'll just order room service."

He gives me a thumbs-up, but his smile is short. "Sounds like a plan. Guess I'll do the same."

I gather my things. "Have a good night, Fitzpatrick."

He nods once. "Good night, Morrow."

I make my way through the lobby, musing over our toast. We raised a glass to partnership, but maybe we should have toasted to trust. I hurry to the elevators in hopes of spending a minute alone with my favorite piece of art: the formal painting of the chief. Standing before it, I wrap my arms around myself. "Good night, Grandtate," I whisper.

As the elevator ascends to the third floor, I lean against the back wall, pondering the painting downstairs. Warm, fuzzy waves move through me each time I see it. Because I have no photo of my grandfather, my mind is making the man in the portrait into his image. I'd like to think that, after Grandtate got sober, he had the painting chief's regal bearing, gentle eyes, and irrepressible-looking smile.

I reach my room, give the little owl a perfunctory tap, and insert the key card. A red light. My tired shoulders slump. I say to the hallway, "Mother of pearl! Why didn't I remember to get a card?" I stump back to the elevator and toward the front desk. The lobby has mostly cleared. Only a few couples are gathered by the great fireplace. Through the main doors of the hotel strolls Robert Fitzpatrick. Where has *he* been? How awkward is this when we've already said our goodnights? I can't let him see me.

I leap behind one of the massive Christmas trees and peek through its branches like some sleazy detective. I wish Rob would move on to the elevators, but at the registration desk, a pretty clerk I haven't seen before greets him by name. Rob walks to the desk. I wait, taking long breaths of the pungent-as-a-candle white pine in which I've stuck my face. The clerk leans toward him, rests her elbows on the surface, and grins at my photographer. Only minutes ago, *I* was flirting with him.

Until suspicion plucked a hair out of my head and made me worry why he wouldn't show me the photos. The woman giggles and flips her hair at something Rob's saying. He glances in my direction and I bolt back, jostling the tree. My heart pounding, I grab a branch to still it. My thoughts dip and dart. Rob was supposed to be *my* Christmas fling. And now he's standing there like Johnny Depp's Don Juan DeMarco.

A couple of plastic bags swing from one big hand. One of them reads, *Pablo's Tacos*. What happened to room service? He was gone for such a short time; the food must have come from a truck. The other bag bears the name of a pharmacy, and when he stops swinging it, I make out a small white-and-navy bottle that looks like Woolite. *What's he washing by hand?* Toying with a bouquet of pheasant feathers on the tree, I watch him saunter to the elevator. I count to ten and head to the desk for the new card. Kwame's there now, and I'm glad I don't have to talk to the hair-flipping femme fatale.

I reach the door of my room again. This time the key works. I enter, kick off my sneakers, and flop into a chair with my phone. *What time is it in Colorado? Six.* I have to talk to Abigay. Maybe I can catch her getting ready for dinner. I snare my phone and click on her name. She answers after one ring.

"Mames," she says with an exclamation point in her voice. "I was just thinking of you and hoping you'd call."

I grin. "Hey, Abs! Are you having the best time ever?"

"I am! We are. But I'm big-time sore from skiing."

"I bet. A good soak in the hot tub will take care of that."

She laughs. "No doubt. After dinner, though. We're going to a fancy steak place. We can walk there from the chalet. It's so romantic being where there's snow at Christmas. Having dinner with the fine MSP? Catch me up."

I hate laying a downer on her, but we've always been truthful with each other. "No, I'm sitting in my room. I messed up, Abs."

"*What?* How? What did you do?"

"I just . . . Well, things were going great. We had drinks and I started flirting with him."

"Yay! That's my girl."

"And he was *totally* into me," I said, remembering with a frisson of pleasure.

"No doubt."

"But then I started doubting him again and asked to see the photos he's taken, and he wouldn't show them to me. Said they weren't *edited* yet."

"Listen up, Mamie . . ." *Uh-oh. I'm in trouble when she calls me by my name instead of Bee.* "You're going to have to make a decision right now. You either trust Rob or you don't."

"I know."

"And you know what? If he *feels* your mistrust, it could affect his job performance."

"You're right. You're right. I know you're right."

"The guy deserves the benefit of the doubt. And if he's as sweet as you've said in your texts . . . Well, what if he is the one?"

"The one?"

"Your forever guy."

"Hey, that's not what this is."

"C'mon, this is a meet-cute if I've ever seen one."

I tuck my feet beneath me and smile, letting the sensory lollapalooza of a car ride and how Rob and I had connected so quickly wash over me again.

After a moment, I say to the person who knows me best, "I promise to think about it."

CHAPTER EIGHT

Rob

In a red coat, white turtleneck, and a dark green overall-looking garment, Mamie's like a bright winter bird hopping along the far end of the curved bridge. My tripod's set up facing the hotel, and I expected her to come through its big-wreathed front doors, but instead, she's heading toward me from downtown. Feeling the wind pick up, I raise the collar of my jacket and then collect my Canon with the midrange telephoto lens. I take a few shots of her. It looks like she's singing. My mom says people who sing out loud have happy hearts. Like Seamus O'Malley with his show tunes and bass voice. What I'd give to be the one who fills Mamie's heart with song. The morning wind off the Reedy River brings her words to me. From a silly '60s tune about loving life and feeling groovy.

She reaches the end of the bridge. Looks up. Sees me. Her green eyes are bright and clear in the brand-new light. *Groovy.* She calls out, "Fitzpatrick!" Hearing Mamie Morrow say the words "I love you," even just *singing them* in the vicinity of the name she calls me, lassos my heart. If only. Her small hands are swaddled by fingerless gloves. Her pink-with-cold fingers hold a large cardboard caddy loaded with two huge cups and a rolled-up bag.

"Good morning." I survey her haul and squint. "How did you get out so early?"

"I made an espresso and pounded it, then struck a trot."

I close the gap between us. "Struck a trot?" I point a pistol finger at her before relieving her of one of the cups. "*That's* one wicked good southernism." I notice the camel-colored leather boots she's wearing today, then glance at my feet. I'm wearing the same shoes I wore yesterday. The only fine pair I own.

She grins. "Well, you know. I try. I was playing the alley cat out foraging before the dawn." She sets down the caddy. "This isn't Dunks but a spot that had a line already, so it must be good." I blow through the hole in my cup lid and then take a long pull. The brew is surprisingly great. She picks up the bag that reads, *Top Me Up*, unrolls it, and holds it out to me. "Smell."

The scent of freshly baked pastry and cinnamon fills my nose. "Oh man."

"Right?"

"Yah. Smells like my mom's cinnamon buns."

Mamie pulls her cup from the caddy and takes a sip, her eyes on me. "Think she's making them now? For Christmas, I mean?"

I grin. "Bet she is . . . this *huge*, like, restaurant-sized pan full." Mamie looks like she wants to say more but instead opens the bag so I can take a pastry. She hands me a napkin, and we lapse into a cinnamon-roll silence. Lights are beginning to bloom inside windows. Clouds are moving in beyond the lodge. It's my moment. I brush the crumbs from my coffee-cup-warmed fingers and turn to the tripod.

"Beautiful!" Mamie cries as the clouds turn vivid orange and hot pink against a backdrop of eastern sky.

I take a series of shots, watching the angles of the lodge's dark gray roof create the perfect contrast with the changing scene. When I think I have what I want, I turn to Mamie. "Want to see?"

"Uh, yah huh," she says, pronouncing of course the way I do but in her soft drawl, and I laugh out loud. I move away from the camera and direct her to step up and peer into the view-finder. She stands on tiptoes. She adjusts her focus. I click back through the last few shots for her. "Oh wow," slips from her lips.

Such tender-looking lips. No lipstick today. *What would it be like to kiss her?* I've never kissed a girl as petite as Mamie. One so much shorter than me. *Would she have to stand on tiptoes every time?* I'm working it out in my head when Mamie finally lowers herself to her heels again. She looks from the camera to me in a way that makes me fear I've spoken out loud. My heart jerks in my chest.

"Oh, Fitzy," she says, almost breathlessly. "This is incredible work." *Fitzy?* "These are so inspiring. They make me . . . *feel* the words I want to use for the caption. But how do you choose exactly the right photo?"

As her praise fills my chest with renewed confidence, I exhale every bit of doubt about my work. The temperature must be dropping because I see my breath. Either that or Mamie Morrow's stoking a furnace in me. I struggle to talk shop. "So . . . I took about thirty shots. That's typical. I'll upload them to my laptop and use editing software. I can spend an hour or two editing a shot I find promising."

"No more dark rooms."

"That's right. Digital technology has superseded the old ways. But I learned the art of photography by shooting with film. Film forces you to slow down and be more judicious because negatives can't be deleted." Mamie's eyes light with a knowing smile. I pause. "What?"

"Well . . . I just remembered what you said in the car that day. When you said Charleston had made you slow down and be more intentional. Intentional, judicious." She holds out both palms and mimics weighing the words. "There's a relationship." *Hmm.* "I feel like they show you're growing as a creative."

I like that. I'm humbled. "Thank you, Mamie."

"I mean it. I'm happy for you. You rock. You do."

I laugh and smile into her eyes.

"I'm marveling here. I had no idea it was that much work. An hour or two on *one* image. It's like the revision process of writing."

"Yah. We have that in common. Two creatives." I shrug like I've tossed off a casual remark. But when she looks at me, I try and gauge her reaction. Her lips twitch with what looks like emotion, and abruptly, she's on her tiptoes again, this time to wrap her arms around my neck. My heart trip-hammering, I lean into her hug and lightly squeeze her to me. The electric current that zaps me is much stronger than the bolt I felt when we shook hands the first day. I want to hold her and smell her flowery hair until sometime in the next millennium, but she pulls away after a moment and gives my right shoulder a friendly little pat.

"Two creatives out to conquer the world," she declares. "One story at a time. I'm glad Farida paired us."

"Yah. Me too, kid," I say, reaching out to touch her nose. "Your nose is cold. Want to head inside?"

She holds up a wait-a-sec finger, takes out her phone and brings it to life, then assumes her business persona. "So according to the schedule, we're supposed to go our separate ways now—you editing and me writing—until lunchtime." *No. Not now.* But she regards the sky and drops her phone back in her pocket. "You know what? I'd rather take a walk. What say you? Want to play hooky, Fitzpatrick?"

My smile's all over the place, and I run my hand over my mouth. "Sure. I'll just run my camera stuff up to my room."

Mamie trades her glasses for sunglasses from deep inside her coat pocket. I like that she doesn't fuss with a big purse full of stuff.

I'm hoisting my tripod when a teenage girl and boy stop in front of us. The girl says, "Are you a real photographer?"

I grin and shake my head.

Mamie jumps in, "He sure is."

"Do you take portraits?"

"Sorry, I don't have the pedigree for that."

Mamie smiles and says to the kids, "How 'bout I take your picture with your phone so you'll have it? Over on the bridge overlooking the falls." The couple thanks her and heads for the bridge. "I'll do it while you take your things up," Mamie says to me.

"Cool." I turn from her and plod inside through the gallery door. Isla is with a customer but waves to me. The lodge is toasty. Families mingle around all four sides of the big fireplace. A guy with a baby girl in his arms bounces her. She has a green bow in her hair. Green. I can't help but think of it as Mamie's color. The guy kisses the baby on her cheek. I think being a dad one day would be cool.

With the right woman by my side.

Mamie waits for me at the bridge. She's taking pictures of the falls with her phone. As I approach, she calls out, "Smile, Fitzpatrick!" She snaps a picture of me, looks at it, and grins.

"Man, it's even colder now," I say, jamming my hands in my pockets.

"Let's get moving. We'll warm up." We tread the bridge and end up in the park. "Oh, it's *sweet*," Mamie says.

"It is nice," I say, nodding around at the scene. Twinkle lights and swags of greenery outline the canopied terrace of a French bistro to the right. A tall fir strung with garlands of popcorn, cranberries, and what looks like Cheerios rises from the center of a circular green-gone-brown grassy area that is surrounded by a low brick wall just right for sitting down to rest or enjoy the park.

"Look at the little sign," Mamie says. "*For the birds.* I value that."

Seated on the brick wall is an old guy with long hair playing a guitar. The case at his feet flutters with dollar bills. He's singing a not-bad version of "Hark! The Herald Angels Sing" through his bushy beard.

As we wander the park, Mamie points out the coffee place she found this morning. "Let's get another cup!" We head into Top Me Up, and I order two more big coffees while Mamie goes to the ladies' room.

"This one's on me," I say, handing her a cup when she comes out. "I'm not keeping score. It's Christmas!"

She laughs, obviously remembering how she'd said the same words to me yesterday, and then toasts me with her steaming beverage.

We've known each other for two days, and we already have an inside joke. I like that. I like it a lot.

We mount a tall and deep-stepped flight of concrete steps to get to street level and arrive on Greenville's thriving Main Street. Every lamppost wears greenery and red bows. Across the way, I see the sign for Jianna, one of the restaurants Vaughn recommended to me. People are gathered there, bundled on its balcony, laughing and drinking Bloodies—as my brother Roger calls them—with huge celery stalks in the glasses. I sip my coffee, grateful for its warmth. We head up the street, Mamie chattering about how festive everything is.

Several blocks down, a line of carolers in authentic-looking Dickensian costumes have gathered at an enormous Christmas tree before a stately-looking building. "O-oh, *tidings of comfort and joy, comfort and joy, o-oh, tidings of comfort and joy,*" they sing, ending their song to applause from shoppers.

Mamie joins in the cheering with a "Woot!" She clutches my elbow. "Aren't they good?"

"They are. Impressive." But what I like best is Mamie's touch.

She regards my upturned blazer collar. "I want to get a scarf. It's definitely colder here than I expected. And let's get you one too."

I shiver, and as if on cue, a new chill snakes around my neck. "I concur."

She smiles and sings again. "O-oh, *tidings of comfort and joy.* Look, they might have them here," she says, stopping in front of a shop. "Do you want to go in with me?"

I look through the door of what is clearly a ladies' boutique. "I'll wait here, if that's okay."

"Okay, be right back." She trots inside, and it's as if the sun has been extinguished. But she pops up behind the glass in the door and gives me first a thumbs-up, and then a show of all five fingers. *Five minutes*, she mouths.

Hanging with Mamie, my cheek muscles are going to have to get used to being stretched into grins. I'm glad I bought some tooth-whitening strips at the drugstore. I check my phone and deal with an email.

Mamie steps back out in four minutes, wearing a bright-green-and-white scarf. I like that she knows what she wants without equivocation. She styles and profiles the scarf for me.

"Nice." *Why didn't I bring my Canon?* Mamie has me swerving off my game.

She sets her coffee down on a dusty window ledge and digs into a handled bag. "I found one for you. Went ahead and grabbed it."

"Aw, you shouldn't have done that."

She shrugs a shoulder and pulls out a navy-and-red houndstooth-style scarf. "They were two for one."

"Well, thanks. I like it." I take the end of it, but she holds onto the other end as though we're playing tug-of-war.

"Wait, the tag—"

I can't hold in a chowdahead grin as she holds the scarf to her mouth and chews through a strip of plastic. She pokes the tag in her pocket, then rises on tiptoe again, leans in, and loops the scarf around my neck. Our faces are inches away. Her eyes are on the scarf, but I'm dumbstruck watching her mouth work as she ties the wool cloth in a complicated knot. My heart warms along with my neck.

I'm a heartbeat away from kissing her when she lowers her heels and steps back. "Voilà," she says. "Have a look." She takes my arm and turns me to the window. Instead of admiring the scarf, I survey the pair of us in the glass.

We complement each other.

Mamie makes me look better.

She makes me feel better.

Maybe she's the girl to make me a better man.

I turn to her with a smile. "Looking good."

"Right. Lead on, Fitzpatrick."

CHAPTER NINE

Mamie

Rob and I continue our walk along Main Street, letting the day take us where it wants. We wander down this side street or that, poke through this shop or that. Rob looks ah-maz-ing, even more handsome in the new scarf. We carry matching shopping bags from an upscale stationery and gift store, where we found great presents and had them wrapped, Rob to mail to his mom and his friend in Boston, and I for Abigay. I made a mental note to ask him about Seamus, but the idea of Smoky gnaws at me more.

Every hour we spend together, I feel as though we're more in sync. I've come to anticipate and enjoy his Boston speak: the quirky way he says "yah" for yes, "yah huh" for of course, and "yah nuh" for no. The violet scent of his breath. The many iterations of his grin that I'm coming to recognize. In his big gangly way, he's adorable.

I want to know more about him.

But the way he looks at me, as though I'm the perfect version of myself, makes me feel shy, which is not like me at all. I glance over at him, and he meets my eyes in a way that finally gives me the temerity to ask about his family. "You never told me about Smoky."

He huffs a laugh.

"No. Really, I'd like to hear about your brothers."

Then I feel bad about the anxiety that plucks at his features. "I don't mean to pry. I just . . . As an only child, I mean, I think it's pretty phenomenal having five sibs."

"No, it's okay," he says kindly. But a note of resolution enters his voice. "Smoky's not short for anything. I didn't mention my old man and brothers when you were talking about baseball the other night . . ."

We stop at the crosswalk. Cars and trucks jockey to change lanes and make the light. The white pedestrian symbol flashes, and as we cross the street, Rob takes my arm. I like that he seems to feel protective of me. But on the other side, he lets go and puts his hands in his pockets. I bet they are cold. I wish he had a pair of gloves. He seems to survey the people around us, and I sense he's about to spill his guts.

"I didn't grow up surrounded by light the way you did in Charleston but in a dark part of South Boston, a sooty train trek to Fenway Park." He looks at me. "Pop named my brothers after Red Sox players."

"No way," pops out of me.

Rob shakes his head. "I'm serious. No one could make this up." *Oh, my word.* He lifts a hand and flips up the thumb. "Smoky, my oldest brother, his name is Smoky Joe Wood Fitzpatrick." *Oh no.* Rob adds fingers to the cocked thumb as he counts. I cringe in anticipation. "Cy Young Fitzpatrick. Cy." *That's not bad.* "Roger Clemens Fitzpatrick. Roger." *Roger's good.* "Lefty Grove Fitzpatrick. Lefty." *Lefty. Okay, his father is an eccentric. A lot of creatives are eccentric.* Rob completes the hand by adding the pinky. I wince inside, preparing for the worst, and get it. "Mookie Betts Fitzpatrick. Mookie."

Mookie? My mind's blown. I blurt out the million-dollar question. "And you are?"

He lowers his hand. I wait, dread squatting in my belly. "Robert Edward Fitzpatrick. Rob."

I breathe a silent sigh of relief. "That's a beautiful name!"

Rob doesn't respond to my compliment but rubs his hands together and continues. "The Sox were in a slump the year I was born. Pop let Mom name me." *He let her name him? Eccentricity is one thing, but overbearing and controlling is another.* My heart stings for Rob and his mom.

We turn a corner and tacitly stop walking under a red awning. Rob turns to me again. "I'm the son of a coarse man, Mamie, who owns a pub in a shabby old Irish Catholic neighborhood."

He's searching my eyes as though my reaction means everything to him. Why would it mean so much? Is he falling in love with me? Despite whatever attraction we're feeling, we're first and foremost work partners. And friends now, I think. I take him by his forearms and give them a little shake. "Thank God we're not our parents, Rob. You are anything but crude. You're a class act."

He pulls his arms back and then pinches the bridge of his nose as though a bangeroo of a headache's set in and screws his eyes shut. He opens them but stares beyond my shoulder as though if he looks at me he can't go on. "Pop's not an unkind man. I mean, he was never cruel to me. I don't want you to think that. He's just self-centered. The regulars like him. Their butts have kept the fake leather booths smooth and the business afloat. But we all had to help out. He had me filling salt and pepper shakers and ketchup bottles after school when I was nine. Maybe that helped make me a responsible kid? But on baseball season Saturdays, my old man—his bookie consulted and his bets placed—had all of us guys ensconced in the cheap seats. I enjoyed it as much as the others until high school, when I realized my brothers were becoming like my father. Only Smoke . . ." He stops and looks at me as though he has just emerged from a cave. "Mamie, oh man, I'm sorry." He puts his hands together and gives me a little bow. "I'm a jerk, laying a downer like this on you."

My heart lightens. I give him my most radiant comfort-and-joy smile. "No worries, kid." My Boston speak brings a small smile to his face again. "We're getting to know each other. That's a good thing. Right?"

He reaches out to touch the tip of my nose again. "I'd say so."

"Believe me, Fitzpatrick, if you knew about *my mother* and our family secrets, you'd outrun the fastest man alive for the next bus out of here."

I meant to make him laugh with the simile, but instead, he frowns down at me with what seems a quickly tossed mix of surprise and empathy. "Really," he says flatly. "I'm *sorry*, Mamie. I figured you had the perfect life."

"I think I'm realizing that no one has a perfect life. And I'm Irish Catholic too," I add stupidly, as if it helps. Rob nods but then is quiet again, rocking back and forth on his heels.

I hope he doesn't feel he overshared with me. I think about my parents, my mother, and what her prejudices and schemes did to me. I can't help but wonder how Rob's family dynamic affected him. Why does learning more about him and his upbringing suddenly feel like everything to me?

Is it because my *flirting* with Rob has become *falling* for Rob?

We move on. I'm caught up in a vortex of my thoughts. I suspect Rob is too, though we exchange an occasional smile. In front of a funky French café with a decorated bicycle tethered outside, we pause to allow a big group to pass us by. Another thought drops from my brain to my tongue. "Do you believe creativity is genetic or cultivated?"

He gives me his what-suddenly-made-you-think-of-that grin but then answers, "I think it can be both."

We move on. "Is your mother a creative person?"

He nods slowly as though the idea is only just resonating with him. "You know what? She *is*. She can draw like nobody's business. I remember watching TV at night with the family, lulled by the familiar scritch scratch of her pencil, and then feeling her eyes on my face. I'd cover it with my arm, like *Aw, Ma, not me*. She'd just smile and whisper, '*Hush*,' and '*Be still*.' A wall of the kitchen, the most light-filled room of the house, is still covered, as far as I know, with these incredible likenesses of her boys. At all ages. It's like her little private gallery. The sketches weren't framed, just carefully tacked up with pushpins. But it was pretty cool. We guys gave each other the business when a new sketch would go up, but secretly, we liked them. I think it must be hard to give six kids individual attention. But the drawings made me feel special. The way she *saw me* put on paper made me feel loved."

"That's *so super sweet*. I'd love to see the ones of you." Rob either blushes or develops a sudden case of windburn. I poke him with an elbow. "So you inherited your creativity from her."

He looks down at me as if I've single-handedly invented a catalyst for a bold new way of thinking. "Guess I did. Never really thought about it."

"Well. Here's a Mamie Morrow proclamation: That's where you got it." He grins his whatever-you-say grin.

He picks up what sounds like a loose thread from what he's already told me. "When we were growing up, she had the seven of us to feed and clothe, plus five loads of laundry to do a day. I guess the sketches were her creative outlet. But after we left the nest—all my brothers got married young—she took watercolor classes with some ladies in the neighborhood at a Hobby Lobby. Turns out she has a knack for painting too."

"That's so cool. Good for her." Wistful longing steals through me. *If only I'd had a mom like that*. I stop short of the next corner, where an empty bench rests outside a sports store. We tacitly take a seat. "Show me a photo of your family? On your phone?" I think about the work photos he hasn't shown me yet, but I trust him. Rob will show me when he's ready.

He takes his phone out and thumbs it alive but hesitates a moment. "Okay." He locates his camera roll and scrolls through shots. "Here's one my aunt Bridey took a few Thanksgivings ago. My uncle Gus is next to Pop." He hands me his iPhone and I take it, the metal still warm from his pocket. My heart's headed for my throat at what I'm about to see. I scan the picture of the brood crowded around a dinner table. The super handsome, scruffy-haired Fitzpatrick who *has* to be Rob snags my eyes.

"Your hair was long!"

He lets go of a breath he must have been holding in the form of a huffy chuckle. "Yeah, it was. That was before I started interviewing."

"It's sexy long." He looks more like Billy in *Daisy Jones & the Six*. *Note to self: Tell Abigay.*

He offers me a challenging gaze. "You don't like it now?"

"No. I mean, yes! I love it short." I pinch and stretch the screen every which way to take in the whole group. "I just like it long too." I survey Rob's brothers and dad, who sort of remind me of the men in *My Big Fat Greek Wedding*: beefcake, cocky— not polished like Rob. I only skim over his pop, whom most of the boys resemble. But there's something about the guy sitting next to him. I look at Rob. "Is this Smoky?"

His mouth opens slightly before he speaks. "It is. What are you, a clairvoyant?"

I puff a laugh through my lips. "Women's intuition. He's the only one who has your pretty, kind eyes. And I believe he's your favorite brother."

He stares at me as though blown away. "Woman, you see a lot."

I've glimpsed the woman at the end of the table but have

deliberately avoided studying her, saving her for last. Finally, I focus on her, stretching out the image. "Your mom." Rob looks so much like her. The big hazel eyes, the same shade of dark hair, the same smile. I notice that, though she's at the Thanksgiving dinner table, she's still wearing what looks like a vintage apron with cherries on it over her clothes. I hope she's not poised to jump up and fetch things for the men during the meal.

I've never seen my mother in an apron in my life. For a moment, I allow myself to conjure her face, her shrewd eyes, her pinched mouth. I'm glad Rob didn't ask to see a photo of her. Two women from very different worlds. Rob's mom looks happy with her lot, while my wealthy and privileged mother looks defeated by life. I suddenly feel bad that I haven't spoken to her in so long and disappointed with myself for not buying her a Christmas present. Maybe it's not too late.

Rob chuckles. "Mom doesn't like that picture because she forgot to take off her apron."

I realize that I don't know her name. I softly ask him for it.

"Treasa. T-r-e-a-s-a. It means 'strength' in Gaelic."

"She's beautiful, Rob . . . and so are you."

He stares at me as I hand him back his phone, which he fumbles but the bench slats catch. He looks like a man with everything on his mind but with no way of expressing it. I scoot back against the bench, and he follows suit. Then I lay my head on his big shoulder. After a moment, he shifts his head close to mine. We rest awhile.

I'm grateful he can't see the tears that coast my cheeks.

A horse-drawn carriage moves down the street. I swipe at my face. The clip-clop, clip-clop helps drown out a loud protest from my over-caffeinated and abruptly empty-feeling tummy. A surprisingly sleek white horse rears its head and lifts its feet high. "Nice," Rob murmurs as we move apart. Tucked into the carriage in a blanket resembling Rob's scarf is a young couple with a crowing baby. They look utterly happy and carefree. All things downtown Greenville seem fresh and new and young. The bundled driver, his eyes so brilliantly blue that I can see them from where I sit, wears a top hat. He doffs it to us as he passes. The work Rob and I have to do—that somehow handed the reins to what's happening between us—takes them up again.

We stand and stretch ourselves. I'm scanning the cityscape without success for the gray roof lines of the lodge—where our computers and Rob's cameras wait—when a commotion behind us diverts our attention. "Where are we headed?" Rob asks. I'm visualizing the Waze map from Tuesday morning's trip. *Wait, was that only yesterday?* Like the white horse, I give my head a mental toss.

"If we want to head back to the lodge, I believe we turn on Church Street, the next block, I think."

"Lead on, Morrow."

I grin. "That's the spirit." In a parking lot close to the hotel, we stumble upon a small food truck city. Gaily colored lights and Christmas tunes from tinny speakers call to a laughing and jostling crowd. The loud people appear to be tourists. Others in suits and business attire queue up and study their phones as they inch along. If locals flock here, it must be the place to be. The dizzying smells of cilantro and cooking onions meet my nose.

"Hey, Fitzy, how about buying me a taco?"

CHAPTER TEN

Rob

When we arrived back at the hotel from our walk, Mamie said she wanted to freshen up and get her computer bag. "Meet back here in twenty?" she asked. I practically tripped over myself agreeing without questioning her about the schedule that mandated separate work times. I came here with all my eggs in one basket, to concentrate on a shoot that could help pave the way for more publication work in the South. But my growing feelings for Mamie are arm-twisting me into risking it all. It's like the judgment-making part of my brain shuts down whenever she's in eyeshot. I'm afraid I can't be certain if what I feel for her is real because the lobe that controls fear breaks down as often as my twenty-year-old Nissan.

My car. The reason I was relieved when Mamie offered to drive us here. I took public transportation in Boston and didn't need a car. In Charleston, my landlady, Mrs. Aiken, just happened to have the old Nissan in the garage below my apartment. Her son had taken away her keys, and she said she was still mad as a hive of hornets about that. She wanted to give it to me, but I paid her for it by refinishing a few pieces of her furniture.

While Mamie and I waited in the lobby for the elevator to our rooms, I almost asked her about the Native American chief portrait on the wall, and why it drew her in so intently. But I sense that it's a personal thing. Only time will tell if she opens up to me about it. But that's the thing; we only have six days together before Christmas Day on Sunday.

In the serviced, well-appointed bathroom of my room, whose door I probably would never have darkened without Seamus's mentorship, I brush my teeth. The white strips I used last night have my teeth looking good, despite my crooked front one. I caught Mamie noticing it the second day. I closed my mouth and ran my tongue over my top teeth the way you do if somebody tells you that you have spinach between them. I felt self-conscious and couldn't help but wonder if she thought my teeth were unattractive. I wash my face thinking about how I had told her I thought she lived the perfect life. She *looks* utterly perfect to me. Those green eyes, that pert nose, that flowery-smelling hair, and her lovely pink mouth. I shout out loud when I realize I've dribbled toothpaste down my shirt. I grab a towel, wet it, and dab unsuccessfully at the stain before glancing at the bottle of Woolite I bought at the drugstore. I'll wash my shirt and socks tonight, hang them from the floor lamp in the corner, and iron the shirt tomorrow. It's the nice new white one that I want to wear to the ball Saturday night when I hope to hold a dream of a girl close to me.

I rip the shirt off and then pitch it into the corner. Thinking of Mamie, I take a packet from the other box I bought at the drugstore and slip it into my pants pocket. In the bedroom, I rummage through my suitcase for a clean T-shirt, put it on, then poke my arms through the dark green collared sweater I bought for the trip and pull it over my toothpaste-dribbling, lovestruck epic chowdahead.

Seamus taught me that clothes make the man and encouraged me to put my best foot forward. Before the trip, I invested in three outfits' worth of nice clothes in hopes I'd look successful. I survey my look in the full-length wall mirror. The first two days, I wore the Arrow blazer with a shirt and tie—the blue shirt the first day and the white one today. I'm alternating two pairs of trendy argyle socks. Now I look casual—but still business-like—in the green sweater and a pair of camel-colored pants. Mamie must wear casual boho-style clothes all the time, but she still looks refined. In her case, it's the woman who makes the clothes, not the other way around.

I turn to pick up my packed satchel and then shoulder it.

Could a girl like Mamie fall, like, really fall, for a guy like me?

I make it downstairs with a good five minutes to spare. Mamie's already in the lobby with her computer bag, warming herself by the fireplace. I grin and shake my head at the queen of get there early.

She eyes the length of me. "Fitzpatrick! You look nice."

With a sheepish glance down at my sweater, I realize it's only a shade or two different from her green overall things and also the sweater she wore the first day. I hope she doesn't think I wore it so we'd match or some dweebish thing like that. "Thanks."

"Green's my favorite color."

"Yah nuh. Really?"

She catches me off guard by giving my upper arm a little punch, her green eyes merry. "That's one for the sarcasm," she says, all saucy. I hold my arm and pretend to grimace, then laugh with her. She's put on red lipstick, her hair up in a business bun. Attached to one of the overall-like straps that fasten with pretty buttons is one of those old-fashioned Christmas pins like my mom wears on her Mass coat. Mamie's is a gold bell with red and green flowers around it.

"Nice pin, Morrow," I say, then wave my hand up and down her outfit. "What do you call that thing you're wearing anyway?"

"It's a jumpsuit! Super comfy. Abigay and I love them. And they have pockets," she says, putting down her bag and modeling them by pulling her phone from her right hip pocket and a lipstick tube from her left. But she frowns and puts the tube back, then pulls out a card instead. "Here. It's my biz card."

I take it and check it out. On a pink background, the swirly logo for Á La Mode Charleston is in the top left corner, and *Mamie Morrow* with *Features Editor* underneath is emblazoned in lime green across the center.

"Is this mine to keep?"

"Sure. May I have yours?"

"Actually, I don't have one yet."

"Well, you need one right this minute," she urges, "to make connections."

"I know. I'm just not sure what to put on it at this point."

She tilts her head at me as though perplexed. "I'll help you work on that, if you want."

"Yah huh," I say. *Of course I want that.* Though I'm creative, I could use some design pointers. And a dream of a teacher is right in front of me in a jumpsuit, little ankle boots on her feet. Hopefully, my vulnerable brain won't make her into a Mrs. Fraser, my pretty ninth-grade English teacher who, when she sat on the edge of her desk and swung a high heel, turned every boy in the class into a slack-jawed cretin. Man, that behavior would never fly these days.

I feel like we've reached a new level of intimacy by talking about working on something together that doesn't have to do with the assignment. One that makes my spot by the giant hearth the best place on earth. "Can I convince you to get a hot chocolate with me this afternoon?" she asks, wiggling her eyebrows at the snazzy little bar set up near reception.

I smile. "Why not?"

As we stand in line for the cocoa, we decide to work not in

the library but at a table in Between the Trees, where there are plenty of empty spots this time of day. With warm cups of decadence in hand, we make our way there and find a corner table for four where we can spread out our things. A nearby brass-plated outlet lets us charge our laptops. I manage to concentrate on editing the photos I took, including the sunrise shots from this morning, although over my screen I can't help but notice when Mamie tucks strands of escaped hair behind her tiny ears or toys with one of her pearl studs. Or when she sips from her cup, leaving red kiss prints on the rim. Lucky cup. Or when she surprisingly taps her computer keys louder than any human. Normally, I'd be supremely ticked at anyone else for that, but this is Mamie, and everything she does either makes me laugh, causes my heart to beat faster, or warms me to the core.

Neither of us speaks until Mamie stretches her neck and back and proclaims that we've been at work for two hours and six minutes. I pull out my mints and offer one to her. She nods with big eyes. We take turns watching each other's things—the way people do at an airport gate but really shouldn't—while taking bathroom breaks. When I come back to the table, Mamie gives me a side-eye I can't decipher, but then she's quickly heads-down again. Minutes later, she moves her phone to her lap and types something into it, seems to study her screen, then jumps back onto her laptop with the look of someone who's just grappled with a tough decision. *Tap! Tap! Tap!* Like shell pops.

Knowing she's going to want to see my photos after our work session, I dig back into my task. Before I know it, I've edited seven photos, and the clock on my laptop says it's 5:24. Despite my Mamie distractions, I've made great progress. Being with her makes me more productive. It's like she has a force field that wrenches more creativity from me. It's exciting being with a woman with that kind of energy. I save all my work and then ask her how much longer she wants to stay.

"Oh. Wow," she says. "We almost missed happy hour."

I laugh. "There are still thirty-five minutes left. Want to head to the bar?"

She looks at her phone, then drops it into her pocket and studies me. She looks from my hair to my eyes, my nose, and my mouth, which wobbles in response. Then she lowers her chin and peeps up at me in a way that stirs me more than any of her other gestures. "Why don't we go straight to the banquette?" she asks softly. "See if it's available. It's quieter there."

"A plan if I ever heard one." We collect our things and I rise on trembling knees. We take the path through the gallery. Isla appears to have left for the day, and I hope she's getting quality time with her family. Yesterday she and her assistant put up a new collection of paintings.

"Let's look at the new art for a minute," Mamie says.

"Well, sure. I'm easy."

We check out the realistic landscape work of a South Carolina artist. Unlike the usual big-sky Western works, the subjects of the new paintings are locales in our state, many of them of the marshy low country, which draws us both in because of Charleston. "Here's one of Greenville," I say, and point to the historic pedestal clock in the painting, the same clock that's across the street from where the massive Christmas tree stands this time of year. "I like that one."

"I do too. The colors are yum."

I grin and fight the urge to tousle her hair. She's so dang cute. We move on to the gallery, and Mamie takes a minute to look at the bracelet again. But when she sees me noticing, she adjusts the computer bag on her shoulder, straightens her spine, and strides on. "There's another painting in the permanent collection that I wanted to see again."

I follow her around a corner. She stops before a painting of a river scene. A Native American wearing braids and contemporary clothes sits at one end of a canoe, paddling and smiling at a small red-haired child holding onto its sides at the other end. *A red-haired child.* Mamie reaches out as if to touch the figure of the child, but then withdraws her hand and pockets it. The painting is so realistic I can almost hear slow-moving water lapping at the hull of the canoe.

Mamie looks up at me. Something in her eyes seems to ask, *Do you see?* She pauses, and then as though waking from a delightful dream, she smiles. "I'm ready if you are." *What did she see?*

Moving in her wake, I stroll into the lobby. Two other couples are seated on the banquette, but one of them moves down to make room for us. I smile. *Southerners.*

"I hope Whitney is here tonight," Mamie says as she situates her bag. "I like her." She raises her hands to her hair and slowly removes the tortoiseshell clip that holds her strawberry-jam-colored hair. She gazes into my attentive eyes and runs her hands through her waves before clasping her hands daintily in her lap. "Oh, there she is," she says.

"Who?"

She grins. "Whitney." *Whitney?* She digs into a pocket, pulls out her lipstick, and then proceeds to apply a coat of fresh red. Gobsmacked, I watch her every motion.

Whitney's appearance startles me. "Hi, you two," she says, smiling and looking from Mamie's face to mine. She lays red cocktail napkins on the table in front of us. "What may I bring you tonight?"

Mamie unclasps her hands. She lays one of them on my arm. I feel like I've just ingested the massive glowing orb from atop the nearby Christmas tree. "Want to have just a drink or two, then walk into town for dinner?" she asks, and gives my arm a little squeeze. *Anything you want. Whatever will make you look at me the way you are looking right now.*

Rob

I force words from my brain to my lips. "Ah. Yah. The Hunt Board last night was wicked good but a little heavy for an appetizer." We place a wine and two glasses of water order with Whitney, and with a last enraptured smile, our server moves on.

Mamie takes back her hand, and I'm afraid she's going to start talking shop, but she asks me a question that feels like one of those icebreaker things people play at parties. "What's the most embarrassing thing that ever happened to you?"

I smile. "Hmm." I'm trying to think of a single incident. "Okay, it's not a one-time thing, but I was teased about my ears when I was a kid." As soon as I say the word "*ears,*" Mamie's eyes move back and forth from my right ear to my left. "It gets worse. Pop took all us guys to the barbershop and had our hair buzzed."

She smiles gently. "I think your ears are cute."

At her sweet words, another childhood memory stirs. From the *Rudolph the Red-Nosed Reindeer* cartoon. When the girl reindeer, Clara or something, tells him he's cute. My face turns that red. Does that mean that she's falling for me, despite or maybe even because of my imperfections? *Man, I hope it's because of.* Oh, to have Mamie Morrow whisper something into my ear one day. I clear my throat, then tweak one of my ears. "All the better to hear you with," I say. Mamie squeezes her eyes shut and giggles as our server shows up with our wine and water. I pick up my wineglass.

Mamie says, "Wait! We have to toast."

I laugh. "Okay, okay. Here's to Christmas."

She brings her glass close to mine, and her expression turns solemn. "To a Merry Christmas. And to trust."

Why to trust again? I give my head a mental shake and abruptly remember the side-eye Mamie gave me this afternoon in the restaurant. The way she took her phone out after that and stabbed at the keys made me wonder if I'd done something wrong. Whatever it was, I want and need her trust.

With brio, I clink her glass with mine and say, "To a Merry Christmas and to trust." Mamie nods, and her lips form her prettiest smile. We take our first sips and enjoy the wine for a few minutes, watching the merrymakers in the lobby to the sound of that Wham song "Last Christmas."

"So if we're telling truths here, what was *your* most embarrassing moment?" I ask.

Mamie purses her lips and toys with the stem of her glass, then answers, "Okay. First, you need to know that I have the worst singing voice in the state of South Carolina."

"I find that hard to believe."

"No, really. I do. I love music, but I don't have the pipes." She sips her wine and then gives me a small grin. "So once when I was thirteen, I think, I was in the album section of a Barnes & Noble after school. They had these big honking headphones you could put on to listen to a . . . oh, you know," she says, spinning a hand in the air toward herself as though wanting me to help her think of the words.

"A sample track."

"Yeah, yeah, exactly. I was listening to a Gin Blossoms song, getting into it, and started singing along, my eyes closed."

I bite the inside of my cheek to hold in a laugh because, though I can see where this is going, I want to hear Mamie tell it. I could listen to her southern voice—with more notes than a harp—reading a tax return.

She picks up her water glass and takes a big sip. "What I didn't know was that the headphones were connected to the overhead speakers for some reason. When I finished the song, opened my eyes, and took off the headphones, people all over the store were laughing and clapping. I was so mortified; I ran out of there like a scalded haint all the way home."

I throw back my head and let out a guffaw. "A scalded *what*? A haint? Is that like a ghost?"

Mamie whaps me in the chest with a fancy little throw pillow, and I grab it. "Yes, it was a term for a haunt or ghost in the low country. Didn't you read *To Kill a Mockingbird?*

"Yah huh. I did."

"Scout uses *haint* in the book. Anyway, the Gullah people in the low country painted their porch ceilings *haint blue*." She makes a high sweeping gesture with a fine hand to indicate the ceiling above us. "Haints wouldn't enter the house because the blue looks like water, which haints aren't able to cross. Haven't you noticed how most of the porch ceilings in Charleston are painted that light blue-green color?"

I run my hand through my hair. "Yah, my landlady's is that color. I just thought it was a pretty color. This is fascinating." I grin. "So a *scalded* haint, though. What does that mean?"

Mamie laughs. "Like a scalded dog—you know, like accidentally scalded from skulking around an outdoor fish cooker. Another southernism for you. They're guaranteed not to come back."

"You're going to make a real southerner out of me yet."

Mamie looks into my eyes. "I hope so."

Whitney comes by and suggests another round. Mamie and I say, "Yes, please," at the same time, and then smile at each other and nod as if to say, *I dig being with you.*

And then, just like that, a fantasy I've had for two days becomes a reality. Mamie walks her fingers toward me on the banquette in a playful way and then covers the back of my hand with her small palm. I look down at it but don't dare move an arm muscle. It's her move. I keep talking, hoping she won't pull back her hand. "So who are the Gullah?"

"You don't know about the Gullah? They're a precious people. You probably haven't lived in Charleston long enough to know about the barrier islands where they live. The Gullah are African Americans whose ancestors were once enslaved, but they're all about honoring family values. They cultivate a super-rich culture—crafts that fetch these huge sums, seafood cuisine traditions—"

Whitney arrives with the wine. She eyes Mamie's hand on mine and smiles at us again. Mamie must notice because she blushes, takes her hand back, and thanks our server. She drains her first glass. *Is she worried the staff will think we're unprofessional if we become more than partners while working on the project?* I hold the throw pillow to my midsection because it feels like I've just been punched, disappointed beyond all reason.

"Oh," Mamie says brightly, "you know the Charleston market. I mean, have you been there?"

"Uh, yah." *Excellent timing there, Whitney.* "I've driven past, but I've never been inside."

"Well, the Gullah women sell their baskets and crafts there. Other places too. Fine hotels, specialty markets."

"Cool. I'll check it out," I say.

Mamie looks pensively at a trio of Native American cedar sculptures on the wall, then swerves her head to look at me. She puts her hands to her head and puffs them out, mimicking her mind being blown. "Oh, my word, Fitzpatrick. How am I just making this connection?"

"What connection, sweetheart?" I want to bite off my tongue for blurting out the endearment that sprang to it. *Another brain glitch. Subliminal. Risky.* But Mamie, who's staring into space, doesn't seem to notice.

She looks at me again. "I mean, I know a fair amount about the Gullah. I studied about them in high school. I made a trip out there on a spring break in college to interview a family for a journalism piece. But just now, talking about their art with you, I've realized the connection with—"

In a flash, I know what she's thinking. "The Native Americans and their art."

"Yass," she cries. "Think how much they share in common. Remember the other day when we were talking about Indigenous people and how they bring their stories and wisdom to life? Both cultures have been intentional about honoring their legacies." She sits back against the banquette as though she swallowed the sun. She's quiet for what feels like an eon. Then slowly, she looks at me. She extends her hand again, but this time she lays it atop mine and wraps her small fingers around it as best she can. "Rob, I want to tell you about my grandfather, Tate Atwater, a Navajo Native American."

First, I'm blown away. Then spellbound.

The plush purple banquette in the Grand Bohemian Lodge has become the king's chambers, and Mamie Morrow my Scheherazade.

CHAPTER ELEVEN

Mamie

Rob and I stroll from the lodge to downtown again. It's dark now, and a million lights twinkle around us. We didn't take the time to change for dinner, and though it's warmer tonight, Rob still looks dapper in his green sweater and scarf. As usual, my outfit telegraphs boho fashion know-how and just-throw-it-on insouciance. But I did apply fresh red lipstick (that's supposed to last twelve hours) using a compact and then gave the mirror a mock kiss and smile.

At the middle of the bridge, we stop to peer down at the rumbling falls. The slap of water against the rocks keeps time with the beat of my heart. Greetings and laughter drift across the evening air. Though others pass around us, I feel closer than ever to Rob, like we've transcended mere partnership, leap-frogged to caring friends, and are now slipping toward romance. I hope he feels the same way. My intimate feelings were kindled when I ripped out my soul by telling him things that no one other than Abigay knew. First, I told him about my mother and the kind of person she is. And then about Grandtate and my quest to get in touch with my heritage. I talked until the candle on the cocktail table guttered low. Rob reacted with such kind and empathetic words; I knew I'd been right to tell him my truths.

Mamie

I watch him now happily taking night shots of the falls with a special camera filter and feel guilty about allowing temptation to best me this afternoon. It happened when Rob slipped out of our restaurant workspace for a bathroom break. A curious and impetuous imp—maybe a haint—had snatched me up by the arm and sent me scurrying around the table to his open laptop. I wanted to see his pictures so badly that I committed an act as bad as reading someone's diary. About to click through the file image he'd saved on his desktop as GBL_Photos_Fitzpatrick_2022, I noticed another file right next to it. *Mamie*, it simply read. I craned my neck toward the corridor at the sound of footfalls on the wide-planked floors. But it was Josh who, without seeing me, turned left and into the kitchen. With stealth I didn't know I was capable of, I opened the file. I froze at the sound of Rob's voice nearby. But the distance and the professional cadence of his voice told me he'd stopped by the gallery and must be talking with Isla. I scrabbled for a glasses wipe, cleaned my lenses, and then zeroed in on the file. Except for the silly photo of Rob and me in the egg that day, the rest of the file was populated entirely with pictures of me. *Only me.* In a host of expressions and postures. All of them were in profile. That's how he'd caught me unaware. He'd captured the curves and angles of my face, my head bent over my computer, my hair down, my hair up, my chin propped on my knuckles, laughing, talking to someone, and, in the last one, intently studying the bracelet in the gallery case.

I could still hear Rob talking with Isla, but just in case, I got myself into a runner's starting position by his chair. For a moment I felt violated. But as I flipped back through the perfectly lit images, I began to feel the personal and loving quality of the photography. Never had I looked so beautiful in my own eyes, as fair and bloomy as a Renoir. Had Rob's mad skills made me more beautiful, or is this how I look when I part the door of my heart?

I heard the singular sound of his rangy gait, the tread of his leather shoes coming down the corridor. I zipped back to my chair. My heart pounding with a feeling I couldn't name, I took up my writing again, my head down, but as Rob settled in and his violetty breath fell around me, I suddenly *had* to consult my touchstone, Abigay. I snared my phone, settled it in my lap, and rapped out a text.

Me: *I hope U R there.*

Thankfully, three dots appear beneath my words and waltz across it: one-two-three, one-two, three . . .

Abigay: *I am. Jake and I are cuddled up by the lobby fireplace with mugs of spiked eggnog. We're so festive! Say hi to Mamie, Jakie.*

Me: *You realize we're texting.*

Abigay: *Oh yeah. LOL. (I imagine her delighted tipsy giggle.) What's going on? R U okay?*

Me: *I am, but you will not believe what I just did.*

Abigay: *You give MSP a peek at your cleavage?*

Me: *What the heck? No! And what cleavage?*

Abigay: *Hush, Bee. You're perfect.*

Me: *We were working and he went to the restroom. His laptop was open, and I sort of accidentally opened one of his private files.*

Abigay: *Sort of accidentally.*

Me: *Well, it was right there across the table from me.*

Abigay: *What were you looking for? Are you afraid he's a perve or something?*

I have to laugh.

Me: *No. But he still hasn't shown me his photos. And I need to see them to make sure we are on the same page about the article.*

Abigay: *Look, Mamie. I'm suffering déjà vu whiplash from a convo about this very thing. One in which you were going to trust him?*

I glance across the table at Rob. He looks up and gives me a tentative smile.

Me: *Yes. Yes. I know! Why does this have to be so complicated?*

Abigay: *Love is complicated and messy.*

Me: *Love????*

Abigay: *Who knows you the best? Me! But I've never known you like this. Dr. Fletcher diagnoses a case of new love. So don't screw it up. Listen up. As far as the work goes, everyone doesn't do things exactly the way you do or exactly when you do them. Stop the obsession and do your part. He will do his. And send me the picture of him you were supposed to send. I love U, btw. Merry Christmas!*

Me: *Love U too, Bossy Bee. Merry Christmas!*

Jakie. The perfect guy for my Bee. I don't often let myself think about what it will be like when she marries him next summer and moves into his small townhouse. She won't be far away and we'll always be best friends, but it will be weird flying solo for the first time in my life. They say living alone teaches you how to enjoy your own company. A single friend from college says she wouldn't be the artist she is if she hadn't learned to occupy her time alone in a fun way.

I give myself a point for coming to Greenville on an assignment by myself but then peek at Rob over the rim of my cup. Of course, I haven't literally been by myself because of Fitzy. That's what I call him in my private thoughts now. And those thoughts are pretty constant. Like the first thing when I wake up in the morning and the last thing when I close my eyes at night.

What will it be like when we get back to Charleston and take up our separate lives again?

I press my hand to my heart where I feel a pang.

On our way to dinner, Rob and I step from the bridge and into the park, now thrumming with tourists. When other people notice the two of us, I wonder if they can tell that we're a few blocks from really falling for each other. I wish he would hold my hand. But from what I've learned about Rob over the last few days, I understand that he doesn't rush things. He's discerning and deliberate. Ahead, a family who appears to be Native American is posing for a photo with the falls as a backdrop. Rob and I step back so as not to photobomb the shot. While watching the family put on their merriest smiles, it occurs to me that, while I've seen people of all races and creeds at the lodge, these are the first Native Americans I've spotted. Suddenly, I'm dying to talk to them, to learn how they feel about the hotel, the art. The showcasing of their heritage. How would Tate feel about it? I'm groping for a conversation starter when respect taps me on the shoulder and gives me pause. I remember how I prefer to view art—alone—and how personal art is. I'm here to write an article about the uniquely themed hotel, not about the people or art it represents.

I almost file the notion away. But what if I wrote a piece about it later? If only I had the missing photo of Tate and me taken in New Mexico or more insight into his life. The wheels in my head are still turning as the family photo is taken, the camera is passed around, and the capture is unanimously approved. The children disperse to scamper up on the wall surrounding the giant bird tree.

I smile up at Rob and take his arm. He stiffens a moment before giving me a surprised smile, but then pulls his arm—and thus mine—toward himself as though escorting me down an aisle. The "aisle" continues up the steps to Main Street, where Rob points out the restaurant on the opposite corner. Steep stairs that have us both reaching for a railing take us to the second-level eatery, where the aromas of rosemary, basil, and garlic fill my nose. Whispers of perfume.

We're greeted and invited to hang our coats on a brass tree near the hostess stand. Rob helps me out of my coat, and I nestle it between two mink coats that smell of clean, cold air. The thought that southern women will parade their furs out on the town or to church no matter how mild the weather twists my mouth into a smirk. But if there's one thing I've learned in the last couple of years, it's that all of us are free to wear whatever we want. Rob tugs his scarf from his neck and hangs it over my coat. A trickle of thrill moves through my chest at the thought of burying my nose in my coat later and maybe smelling a trace of his sandalwood shave cream.

A hostess wearing a pencil skirt and Isla-esque heels takes up two menus and leads us on a circuitous route through a maze of tables. As we turn a corner, I glance back at Rob to see if he's checking out her legs and shapely rear view, as most of the men in the room seem to be, but my perfect gentleman's eyes are glued not to hers but to mine in the jumpsuit. Feeling smugly content as we reach a surprisingly nice—for a last-minute cancellation—table by a window, I give Rob a brilliant smile. Our waitress, who's pretty and bubbly and about four feet nothing, introduces herself as Amanda. She recites the specials, and we order two waters with lemon to start.

Rob asks me a question in the vein of the icebreaker one I'd asked him earlier. "What's the worst date you ever had?"

I grin. "This one so far. With a lame question like that."

His big shoulders shake with laughter, but then he gives me a considered look. "So this *is* a date, then?"

I blush, my face likely reflecting all the shades of a flamingo's wing. "You tell me."

He grins sweetly and reaches his big hand across the table.

"Here are your waters," Amanda chirps. Rob pulls his hand back and takes his glass from Amanda. "How about a cocktail or glass of wine?" she continues before handing a leather-bound list to Rob, as though this is a date and he is the architect of such.

"A glass of pinot grigio for you, Mames?"

My heart skips a beat at this comfy shortening of my name. I give him a silky smile. "Yes, please."

Four women about my age in upscale Christmas sweaters and meticulously tattered jeans are being seated at the next table. Each of them directs gleamy-toothed smiles around the room as though searching for people they know. "Oh, hey!" and "How are y'all?" they call to friends seated at tables. Until they get a look at Rob. On him, their gazes come to a skidding, tire-burning halt. I survey them with a closed-lip little smile, dip my chin, and shake my head as if to say, *That's inappropriate.* They get my meaning because all of them look over my head as though studying the bar area. *Good.*

Oblivious, Rob orders our wines from Amanda and then turns his attention to me in a way that makes my legs wriggle beneath the table. When he extends his hand again, I take it, and our grip comes to rest on the white linen cloth. Though work-worn in places, the texture of Rob's skin feels just right to me. It's as though my hand is a lone glove that's finally found its match.

"So back to whether or not this is a date," he says. "It feels like one to me." He squeezes my hand. "And the best I've had in years," he softly adds.

I narrow my eyes and tilt my head. "I do and don't like the sound of that."

"I hope you *do* because it's the truth." He releases my hand and holds his aloft, then lifts two fingers to his brow. "Scout's honor."

"You were a Boy Scout."

"A Cub Scout. I quit before I made it to Boy Scout. Smoke, though . . ." he says, shaking his head with a fond smile. "Smoke did so well, he stayed the course. Even earned the rank of Eagle Scout. I remember feeling so proud of my big brother." Rob's eyes bear a slight sheen. "I still am."

I'm happy that Smoky is special to him. "I love that." This time, I take his hand and squeeze it, running my thumb over the base of his. I'm still left to wonder what troubles him so much about the rest of his brothers. He studies our hands. Amanda arrives with our wine and a basket from which the clean, yeasty, and nutty aroma of freshly baked bread curls around our heads like smoke. Rob takes his hand from mine, thanks her, and digs beneath the white napkin swaddling the slices to snare a piece. He sets it on his bread plate and passes me the basket. I set it down between us. "The last thing I want to do," he says, buttering a piece of focaccia, "is get hangry."

I laugh as he pops the bite into his mouth, chews a moment, and moans aloud. "Abigay's fiancé, Jake, gets hangry too. I think it's a guy gene."

His eyes flick to mine. "I didn't know Abigay was engaged."

"She is. They're getting married in September when it's not so grossly humid in Charleston. Jake's finishing up law school."

"Well, good for them. Will they live in Charleston?" he asks, and I wonder if he's thinking about me living alone.

"They will. Thank God. We've been best friends since we were eighteen."

He looks me over and points to me with his butter knife. "I bet you're a great friend."

"I hope so. It's easy to love Abigay."

Rob raises his brows, and a fresh smile plays across his lips.

"What are you up to, Fitzpatrick?"

He takes another piece of fragrant bread from the basket and butters it. But this time he inclines it toward *my* mouth. I lean in and eat it from his fingers. He grins and wipes the corner of my mouth with his thumb. A quartet of soft "aahs" comes from the next table. But Rob and I are too into each other to care.

I watch him as I chew the delicious focaccia that's sprinkled with fresh rosemary, willing to bet that his kiss is more delicious. Getting a grip on my emotions, I primly wipe my mouth with my napkin. "So back to the date thing. How could someone like you not have had a great one in years?"

He closes his eyes and presses his thumbs to his lids for a moment. "That topic's off-limits for this date. But I'd love to tell you a *good* story about my friend Seamus."

My ears prick. "I was hoping you'd tell me about him."

He crosses his forearms and rests them on the table. "Seamus is the reason I became a photographer."

"Oh. Wow." Utterly charmed, I raise my elbows to the table and rest my chin on my knuckles. My rapt attention is his.

Rob goes on. "It started in Mr. Gallagher's junior high physics class when I fell in love with light. I was fascinated with the way it changed form. How it had the power to make ordinary subjects more interesting. More alive. You know? It made me desperate for a camera of my own. Mom went behind Pop's

back and bought me a Polaroid for my fourteenth birthday."
The lights dim—must be that time of the evening: the time
for romantic ambiance. The candle on the table highlights the
deepening hollows of Rob's face. "Mom said I had an eye for
details that others missed."

He captures my gaze. "You were right, Mamie. She recog-
nized my creativity. Unlike Pop, she *got me*." Tears of empathy
and gratitude for Rob's self-discovery sting the back of my lids.
"I was right too. It's both genetic and cultivated. I have my
mother to thank for believing in me. And then providentially,
I believe, Seamus came into my life. Or *me into his*. My teacher
Mr. Gallagher, who realized I needed to earn some money, sent
me to see a friend of his who ran a furniture restoration shop.
He was getting on and could use some help, but wouldn't admit
it, Mr. Gallagher said. The day I went there for the first time,
I stood on the street listening to someone inside belting out a
show tune—like, in this huge bass voice. It was "Seventy-Six
Trombones" from *The Music Man*."

"Seamus!"

Rob grins at my enthusiasm. "It was Seamus O'Malley, a
lover of the stage and a gentleman as refined as his English
breakfronts and French consoles. I still get an earworm now and
then when I hear one of his songs."

"He sounds like a neat man."

"He is. Seamus became my mentor and then friend." He
looks at his hands and flexes them. "After school and on Saturdays, while my hands learned the motions of C-clamps, miters,
grooves, and jack planes, I absorbed Seamus's talk of the finer
things in life." My heart twists. *Like my mother and her foster
parents. That's what led her to leave New Mexico and end up in
Charleston.* "And at the end of each week that I spent paint
stripping and steam bending, he'd pay me in cash. When I
saved enough to buy a good camera, I insisted Seamus come

with me to make the purchase." He puts his hands on the table and seems to examine them. "I bought a Canon PowerShot, the nicest one I could afford, and the rest—as they say—is history."

"Oh, Fitzy, I love it. That's a wonderful story."

Rob flashes a grin that looks like it may become permanent. Amanda appears at his elbow in a flurry of ticket shuffling. She scrabbles through her black apron pocket for a pen. "I know you didn't wave, but the kitchen's backing up, and I thought you might like to go ahead and order."

I grin at her. "Thank you." Suddenly, I'm starved. Starved for romance, Abigay would insist, and I've never known my bestie to be wrong about anything of consequence. I look at Rob Fitzpatrick, who's becoming exponentially more interesting. "Since the chef makes the pasta, I'm thinking I have to have some." I turn to Amanda. "May I have the pasta with bacon, tomato, and garlic?"

"Certainly, love."

"We're staying at the Grand Bohemian Lodge. The manager suggested we come here for the pasta."

"Ooh," Amanda croons, and looks from Rob to me. "Are we celebrating a special occasion?"

Rob grins and speaks directly to me. "Getting more special all the time."

My cheeks heat. I used to be a walking thesaurus, but right now, I feel like a stegosaurus, wordless, heavy with falling for this man.

Amanda fans her pinking face with her ticket book before flourishing a pen and scribbling my order. Looking at Rob makes the idea of eating garlic wave a red flag between the menu and me. Since we have established that this is a date, maybe he will kiss me goodnight. My eyelids are heavy with that desire, but I peek at him over my menu while he tells Amanda he'll have the same. *Did he consider the garlic too before ordering?* Overhead,

Norah Jones's sultry version of "Run Rudolph Run" puts me even more in the mood for getting those lips of his on mine. The old "Shoop Shoop Song" about how it's by his kiss that you'll know if his love is real has been an earworm running through *my* mind all day.

With Amanda on her way to put in our order, I sip my wine and try to regain my powers of speech. "So. You're still in touch . . . with Seamus O'Malley?"

"Yah huh. Talked to him today. Told him all about you." He takes up his wineglass and swirls the bowl.

All about me. I love the notion of a man feeling that he knows all about me—especially after such a short time—and really likes me. "You did, huh?"

Rob takes a big sip and sets his glass down again. "Yah. I told him you remind me of a very young Barbara Stanwyck from the movies, this . . . amalgam of energy and fire." His eyes roam my hair from the part to the ends, and I shiver with pleasure. "With the red hair to match. Seamus had a thing for Stanwyck since *Christmas in Connecticut*, so he loved that." *I love that too. And I would love to meet Seamus.* "And I told him that you're talented, smart, and professional with tiny feet—usually in sneakers. I said that not only are you early for everything but that you foraged and brought me coffee almost as good as Dunks' at the peep of dawn one morning." He grins. I manage to smile back, despite the way my heart has grown wings that are flapping against my rib cage. "I said that you are respectful of all people and that it's important to you to help protect their dignity." *Aw, the Native Americans?* "And that you can be fussy when you are stressed."

"Fussy!"

"Yes, fussy," he answers with a grin and a punctuating dip of his chin.

I give him a closed-lip smile of concession. "I guess there's a certain symmetry between hangry and fussy."

He goes on. "I told him that you're the most charming girl I ever met." His eyes first rove my face and then hold mine for three beats of my heart's wings. He toys with the stem of his glass, then lifts his gaze to mine again. "And that you would be way easy to fall in love with."

I sit very still, trying hard to absorb his words and his meaning. Is he implying that he is falling in love with me, or that he should keep his guard up so that he doesn't?

"Pardon the soliloquy," he says, "but I *was* an English major."

He smiles, but I note a chink of disappointment in his eyes, the set of his silky brows. Did I flatten his enthusiasm with my non-reaction to his unexpected words?

Amanda sweeps in with two hot plates, saving me from witless blathering or bursting into tears—I'm not sure which. Quietly, Rob and I pick up our forks and, like a mirror image, twirl a little pasta around them before dredging the strands with fresh tomato sauce and slivers of basil. We chew and exchange cautious little smiles between bites. He has mentioned the L-word. It's out there, probably uploaded to the cloud. We have a lot in common. We've had fun and connected like the polar ends of magnets. And though I've moved on from mere flirting with Rob and have given the L-word a comfy chair and a glass of whiskey, how could real love have made itself at home in my heart in only days? They say people can fall in love at first sight, but what if that's a fairy tale that will eventually implode?

We finish about half our meals with a sprinkling of small talk, and then, at Amanda's insistence, share a ramekin of caramel bread pudding that I can barely taste. A busboy takes our dishes. Rob looks crestfallen. "Mamie, I apologize for not sharing the photos with you yet. I honestly forgot today. It wasn't intentional."

Does he think I think he's holding out on me and that I'm upset about the photos? I capture his eyes. "I know you will. And I'll be excited to see them. Maybe first thing tomorrow?"

"First thing tomorrow." *But what will happen tonight?*

Amanda brings our check, and we ask her to split the amount so we can put it on our expense accounts. Rob says he needs to hit the restroom and leaves an American Express card leaning against a pepper grinder. I watch him go, and he doesn't look as tall as he did on the way downtown. I glance at the name on his card. *Robert E. Fitzpatrick.* I think of how hard he's worked to get from his Pop's home in South Boston to upscale Charleston and start building a career in photojournalism. I feel proud of him. I hope his father is.

Finally, I'll get to see the photos. Oh snap! I forgot to send Abigay his photo. I snare my phone, check for signs of Rob every few seconds, and navigate to our last text chain. In two taps, I add the picture I took of him from my camera roll, and off it goes.

Me: *Bee, here's the photo. Robert E. Fitzpatrick in the flesh. What think you?*

Abigay: (popping right back) *Bee, he's epic handsome! Those shoulders! That grin!*

Me: *I know. I told you! Beeeeeee, he dangled the L-word out there at dinner.*

Abigay: *Wait. Did he say I love you?*

Me: *No, no. But he said he told his friend that I'd be way too easy to fall in love with.*

Abigay: *When they mention it to their friends, that's pretty telling. Let me think . . .*

Rob's sandalwood scent makes it to the table just before he does. I get to my feet as though someone asked for a volunteer to cover a story on the Palace of Versailles. I make myself smile. "Excuse me. I think I'll run to the restroom too."

In a stall, I struggle with my jumpsuit, then sit and, still flustered, try getting to my texts. One bar. Poor service. Someone gives the door a smart rap. "One moment, please!" I call out, loud and shrill.

> **Me:** *Okay, I have to hurry, but we've only touched hands so far. Well, once I put my head on his shoulder. How could he be in love with me?*

Three angry-sounding raps hit the door. The pearly button on my left jumpsuit strap clacks against the rim of the toilet seat. I leap to my feet—like a scalded haint—and grab it, then thank God it didn't fall in. Someone is twisting at the doorknob. Then abruptly, the men's room door across the hall slams. I figure whoever's been waiting has given up and is willing to risk being locked in a room with pee on the floor around the toilet or even a nasty urinal. Yuck-o!

> **Me:** *Gotta go. XO*

> **Abigay:** *Good luck and let me know! XO*

I wash my hands, reapply my lipstick, and fly from the ladies' room so the woman in the men's room won't see who kept her waiting so long. When I get back to the table, my equanimity mostly restored, Amanda's giving Rob our receipts. I take mine, pocket it, and thank her for the great service. "Oh, and Merry Christmas," I call to her, trailing Rob.

"Merry Christmas to you both." Preoccupied with the kiss to come, I hadn't noticed how packed the place had become. There must be sixty people in red tartan, velvet, and sequin wrap dresses waiting for tables, festively garnished cocktails in hand. Rob and I manage to make our way past the reception desk, to the coat rack, and back down the stairs to the street.

Two's company; sixty sardines are a crowd.

CHAPTER TWELVE

Mamie

"It's warmer tonight," Rob says on the sidewalk outside Jianna. "Want to walk the grounds of the Grand Bohemian, maybe check out the Christmas Market on the Green?"

"That sounds great." Looking taller again, Rob smiles down at me and then waggles his fingers for mine. I breathe out a silent sigh of thrill and take them. We cross the park hand in hand. The other guys I've held hands with in the past laced their fingers with mine, but Rob prefers palm against palm, our fingers wrapped around the backs of each other's hands.

The press of his Fitzy palm feels wonderful.

Before tonight, I wanted to know more about him.

Now I find myself wanting to know *everything* about him. His favorite boyhood Halloween costume, if his mom kept his baby teeth, his favorite movie, the novel that had the greatest impact on him, and what he would do on his idea of a perfect day.

I look up at him. "Who was the first girl's hand you ever held?"

"Hmm. Olivia O'Keefe. We were fourteen. Who was your first kiss?" *Kissing is on his mind!*

"Pink Rembert. Sitting in a magnolia tree."

Rob laughs up at the sky. "Pink?"

"Short for Pinkney. Old Charleston name."

"Ahh. A rich boy."

"They're strictly overrated. And Pink was wearing a retainer," I say, scrunching up my nose. "And creepy Spanish moss was all around us."

"Does that mean we won't be sitting in a magnolia?" *He is thinking of kissing me!*

"Not tonight."

He snaps his fingers in defeat. "Okay. What's your favorite color? And don't say pink," he says, lifting our hands to bump them against my shoulder.

"Teal. Like my sneakers."

"You are a sneakerhead, Morrow."

"I know! I am! Love them. I like all the shades of green in nature," I say, spreading my hands in an arc. "Ever thought about how green looks with everything? In every room? Because most people, if they're lucky, see green when they look out a window. Green brings the outdoors inside."

"Do you have a lot of green in your apartment?"

"We do. Well, I mean, I do." I flash on living there without Abigay to talk to in person and push the notion away for the moment.

"I bet your place is pretty."

Is he thinking about coming over when we get back? I try and imagine him there without success. "Well, thanks, Fitzpatrick. So what's your favorite color?"

"The green of the sweater you wore the first day." *He remembered.* "It showcased those eyes of yours." He looks me up and down. "'Course, I like the brighter green of your jumpy thing too."

I snort a laugh. "Jumpsuit! You ninny noggin."

Rob laughs until he has to let go of my hand and run his hand over his mouth. While he's recovering, I ask another question. "What's your shoe size?"

He stops short, hikes up a pants leg, and lifts the toe of one boat of a brogue to rest it on its heel and gives me a smirk. "Twelve and a half."

"Is that all?"

He gapes at me with mock outrage. "Yes?"

"Okay, okay. Nothing wrong with that." I picture us cuddling in bed, his great big feet sticking out, and then quickly banish the thought. All we've done is hold hands. And laugh *a lot*. "You sure are fun, Fitzpatrick."

He squeezes my hand and his eyes grow serious. "You're the most fun girl I've ever been with, Morrow."

Are we with each other, or with with each other? "Thank you."

"It's true. And before we met, I expected you to be stuffy."

"I've never wanted to be that," I say, thinking of my mother before shaking my head and sending her image packing.

Tacitly, we let go of each other's hands as we step onto the Green and move into the bright Christmas lights of the people-packed and white-pine-scented market. Is he wondering, as I am, what people will think if we morph from work partners to a couple who may or may not be falling in love? Then again, there are only a handful of people who even know who we are. I take Rob's arm and he smiles down at me. Carnie and Wendy Wilson's song "Hey Santa!" drifts from outdoor speakers. That's one of the Christmas tunes that Abigay and I love to jump up and sing along to. *Abigay.*

"What size ring do you wear?" He tosses off the question as though asking *my* shoe size. Taking my left hand, he looks down at it. "Such slender, tapered girl fingers," he murmurs.

I peer at my ringless hand, my heart lurching. "Umm, I'm not sure what size. I don't wear a lot of jewelry."

He reaches to run a roughened finger behind one of my ears. "Only the pearls?"

"Mostly," I say, suddenly as shy as a stray fawn. "When you're little, large jewelry can look gaudy."

"You look just right as you are," he says, searching my eyes and leaning into me.

"Mamie and Rob!" It's Isla, popping out from behind a vendor booth that's decorated like a glittering gingerbread house. It's the first time I've seen her wearing boots, and naturally, they rival everyone else's—knee-high and hot pink. She looks utterly smashing with a long-sleeved vintage pink-and-red minidress and tights. "Hi! Good to see you."

Did I just miss a first kiss? "Isla! Great to see you out tonight. You're stunningly poshed up," I say, waving my hand up her outfit to the matching headband holding back her perfectly curled hair.

"I'm headed to a Christmas party at Zen," she says, busting a little move to showcase her outfit. "What are y'all up to?" she asks, eyeing the two of us.

"Oh, you know, just walking, taking it all in, exploring . . . things," I say, and Rob and I exchange sheepish grins.

"Be sure and check out this booth," Isla says, pointing to the one she came from. "A local author wrote a Christmas romance set here at the lodge, the falls. It's selling like tacos." She consults the time on her phone. "I need to scurry, loves, but I have to take your picture! You guys look so happy tonight."

I blush and smile at Rob and then hand my phone over. Isla takes several snaps. And she's off. I watch her go, wishing I had shopped for something smashing like her outfit to wear.

But Rob seems to have eyes only for me.

Our gazes lock, and my heart busts a dance move of its own.

Shopping the market is the last thing on my mind. And tonight, anywhere we go will feel too crowded, too loud, too much. As though reading my thoughts, Rob says, "Want to find a place where we can sit and talk? Besides in a tree."

I laugh softly. "I spotted a bench a little ways down the hill the day I went to get our coffee."

He grins. "Lead on, Morrow."

I'm glad Rob still has my hand as we pick our way down the darkened and rutted slope to the wood-slatted bench. Thankfully, we seem to have the small clearing all to ourselves. Rob takes a seat near one end, but, unexpectedly nervous, I stand for a second to plow through my pockets for a glasses wipe.

"What do you need?" he asks, furrowing his brows.

"Oh, I have smudges on my glasses." I take them off and rub the lenses on my sleeve, which naturally makes the blur worse. But Rob reaches around to get to his back pocket. He pulls out a square packet.

"Where did you get that?" I plant my hands on my hips. "That's just like the ones I use!"

He smiles and says, "Maybe you're not the only alley cat who can forage."

"Ha!"

He shrugs. "I bought a box at the drugstore. Thought I'd keep a fresh one in my pocket every day so you'd have an extra if you need it."

"Robert Edward Fitzpatrick, that is the most thoughtful thing a guy has ever done for me."

He lifts his chin. "Maybe you haven't found the right guy yet."

Breathless with expectation, I plop down on the bench. *Kissing is one thing, and a relationship is another. But if he's talking about a whole relationship, one that continues into our real lives at home . . .* An alarm sounds in my head: *Too soon! Too soon!* I scrub fiercely at my glasses and hold them up to the only light, the giant moon rising above the lodge. Finally, they are as clear as Rob's feelings.

He pulls his mints from a pocket, pops one, and then shakes the package at me as if to say that he'll drop one into my hand if I want it. I do and put out a palm. I sit back against the bench rolling the violet mint around my mouth. We sit there, side by side, looking up at the Grand Bohemian Lodge where we may or may not have fallen in love. The coolness of the mint is soothing. Helps me gather my thoughts. Try and make sense of them. Maybe Rob is only thinking of us being in love and together as a couple. And no further than that.

I turn to him. One look at his handsome face, and his sweetly patient countenance is all it takes to make me know that I could live with that. I scoot closer to him, take off my glasses, and slip them into my coat pocket. Settling myself, I gaze at him again before giving him a couple of slow bats of my eyes, giving in to whatever this is.

He scoots closer too and starts in like he's going to kiss me but pulls back in a way that looks like he wants to make sure it's what I want.

I take hold of his lapels and pull him to me.

My eyes at half-mast, I watch for the moment he closes his. At the first press of his lips against mine, a constellation of stars shoots through my veins. Like his hands, his mouth feels like it's the perfect pairing for mine. All the kisses that came before Rob's evaporate like morning dew on grass. Minutes later, he pulls back, takes my face in his hands, and smiles into my eyes. "I wanted to see what you look like when you're being kissed."

"Oh . . . Fitzy," I murmur, lightheaded and limp limbed. "What do I look like?"

"You look like I thought you would. Like you're falling for me."

The top of my head feels like it might explode from the mush he's making of my brain. Tears swim in my eyes. "What if I am?"

"Sweetheart," he says, taking his scarf and dabbing at my cheeks.

Suddenly, I recall when he slipped and called me sweetheart the night we were talking about the Gullah. This is no slip. This is how he's begun to think of me. I'm certainly not ready to get married, but on the other hand, I don't want to lose this guy. A little hiccup escapes me.

"Oh, Mamie, come here." He puts his arms around me and holds me close to his chest, my head on his shoulder the way it was the other day in town but a galaxy removed. He plants a kiss on my head. I realize the glasses wipe is still in my hand and pull back with a giggle. He takes it and pockets it for me.

"I saw you the other night, you know."

He grins and kisses my lips again, then asks, "When?"

"When you came back into the hotel with plastic bags. I was mad with jealousy because I thought you were flirting with the desk clerk."

"Believe me when I say I've had eyes for nobody but you since our lives began blending into each other's."

"I know. I feel close to you, Fitzy. How has it only been since Tuesday?"

"Let's not count the days or call them by name. Let's just say that day or the other day."

I slowly nod. "I'm realizing it doesn't matter how long it's been."

"*Sweetheart,*" he says, tracing my jawline. "I saw you too," he adds.

I grin and kiss him, then pull back. "What? *When?*"

"When you were hiding behind the big Christmas tree."

"You did not!"

He chuckles. "I did too."

I put my hands to my flaming cheeks. "How embarrassing. You must have thought I was some kind of . . . stalking creep."

"Never. But it was pretty funny. Remember in the car that day when I said if angels came to earth they'd speak with southern accents?" My heart swells the way it had that day. "I meant you. The way you speak."

My heart threatens to take over my entire torso. "I don't know what to say. I'm certainly no angel."

"Who is?" Rob asks as he begins stroking my hair from crown to ends.

As though to prove that I'm no saint, the notion of building my career and getting in touch with the sliver of Native American heritage Tate left to me rudely rouses itself and makes me feel self-centered. I worried that love would wreck my goals and even the assignment. But I'm standing at the edge of its quicksand. If I'm in love, can I still make my goals happen? Rob and I have to get back to work on the article. Our involvement has already slowed the pace of our work.

I shove my worrisome and traitorous thoughts away and look up at the man who I suspect might grow to love me despite my faults. I twine my arms around his Fitzy-sweet, sandalwoody neck.

Tomorrow.

CHAPTER THIRTEEN

Rob

When Mamie and I made it back to the hotel last night, I felt like there was a giant cheesy red heart around us—like a cardboard frame a couple stands inside to have a prom or dance photo taken—and that everyone was staring at us. Granted, we *were* holding hands and wearing stupid-happy grins. Maybe some *were* staring and wishing they had what we appeared to have. What I never dreamed I'd find this week.

At the elevators, Mamie asked if I would look at the painting of the Native American chief with her before we went upstairs. I waited in expectant stillness as we stood side by side surveying the piece, missing the wondrous feel of her palm against mine.

She took a deep breath and let it out slowly. "While I was in art school, I made it a practice to view art alone. It's been a highly personal affair. Other people's observations and evaluations of a piece distract me. But this one . . . I want to share with you, Fitzpatrick." My tongue started to form the words I wanted to say—that I felt honored—but she reached out and placed a finger across my lips. "Wait," she said, "this is important to me." I relaxed my shoulders and arms, realizing that this was a big moment. "I told you about my grandfather, Tate Atwater, and that getting in touch with my heritage was foremost in my mind when I took the assignment."

I looked at her, my brows lifted, not sure if she'd asked a question or was giving me a test. I wanted to make sure she wanted a response. She gave me a short nod of permission. "You did," I said, hoping that if it was a test that I passed it.

She smiled at me and I felt a sense of relief. "The letter said that a photo was included in the box he left me, but there wasn't. The unidentified sender must have forgotten to pack it. And my mother didn't have a single photo of Tate to share with me." She shook her head. "Which is bizarre. The first time I saw this painting, my mind took over and made it into my grandfather's image." She gave the man in the picture a small smile. "It's been a gift of sorts." She looked back at the chief. "Sometimes I recall hazy images of a man with long Willie Nelson–like braids. His hair is black, like my mother's. But his face—I can't see it. And I want to so much."

I studied the chief again and at once understood why the piece was so meaningful to her. "I wish I could buy it for you."

She placed a palm on my chest. "Fitzy, you are the sweetest man on earth." Cool, clean ripples spread across my chest. "This one is part of the permanent collection and not for sale." I raised and lowered my chin as if to acquiesce. "But even if it were, it's too precious to own. If I saw it hanging on my wall every day for the rest of my life, it would become ordinary. Something that caught my eye, like the unemptied dishwasher, or a lampshade, or a beetle on a windowsill."

"I get that."

"And other people should see and appreciate it. Just not with me." She laughed.

I nodded and smiled at her. She gazed at me, her eyes lovely and round. I took her in my arms and kissed her. Then someone punched the elevator button behind us. We broke apart and turned. A couple and two bored-looking teenagers, their thumbs careening over their phones. The family stepped inside and disappeared with the low whoosh and hum of the lift.

We stood in the corridor without pushing the button. Mamie regarded her boots. "I do wish I had that photo of Tate and me, though." Then she looked at me and brightened. "Okay. Tomorrow. Want to meet at eight o'clock for work?"

The reek of booze filled the alcove as three men tromped in. One of them pushed the up button with the toe of a dirty boot. The other two gave Mamie stumbly eyed once-overs. Bigger than all of them, I risked casting a menacing glare in their direction, but they were too plastered to notice. I took Mamie's arm and pulled her aside, hoping the elevator pinged soon.

"The hotel's getting more crowded with Christmas coming," I said.

Her fine strawberry brows came together. "I know! On Sunday."

I wondered if she was thinking, as I was, of how the days were passing, like scenery through a car window. "It may be tougher to find a place to set up our work stuff."

The elevator closed on the drunks. I let out a breath and made a mind map of the lodge. "What about the whiskey bar below Between the Trees? Spirit & Bower? We never did go look at it."

"We didn't!"

"But there must be a bunch of places to sit. And Annelise *said* we had free rein. I doubt it opens until five o'clock, so we'd have most of the day."

She smiled. "That's brill! Be there or be square."

I laughed but then abruptly felt like a balloon with a big hole in it, the air leaking out at warp speed. "May I . . . see you to your room? I feel protective of you now." I glanced at the chief once more for his silent approval and then locked eyes with the woman I wanted to be my mine. "You're precious to me, Mamie."

She let out a small gasp, and her eyes grew shiny with tears. She peeked back at the chief too and swallowed several times. There are times when silence is a sonnet; this was not one of those times.

Finally, she turned her gaze on me, and my eyes belonged to her alone. "You're precious to *me*," she said. My heart swooped so hard in my chest that I almost staggered. But she reached out to hug me, pulling me in tightly to her. "Sure," she said into my shoulder.

Sure? What?

She pulled away and smoothed her hair. "I mean yes," she said formally. "You may see me to my door." *Door, not room.* She grinned and hit the elevator button with an elbow. *She must have noticed the drunk who used his boot.*

I hoped for another kiss in the elevator, but as my dumb luck would have it, an older couple slipped in with a spryness I wouldn't have expected, the man letting the woman enter before him, just before the doors closed. We exchanged polite hellos. Familiarity borrowed my mind. *Are these the folks I saw walking on the bridge the first day? It has to be. But they hadn't seen me. I'd used a telephoto lens to take a photo of them.* When we realized they were getting off on Mamie's floor, the third, we wished each other Merry Christmas, and Mamie and I let them exit first.

Walking the corridor with her door in sight, I thought about how much my feelings had changed since yesterday. I was sure she was the girl I wanted to marry. At her room, I kissed her soundly. "Good night, sweetheart."

She smiled, sleepy lidded. "Good night, Fitzy. Sleep well."

I stood there a minute in front of her closed door with my hands deep in my pockets. I missed her already. Until the right time came to share my whole feelings with her, I expected to face a lot of closed doors. Mamie Morrow is not a girl that anyone in his right mind would have a one-night stand or fling with. *Our timing* is like something from the movies where a guy has to do something rash to win the girl. Seamus liked to play Turner Classic Movies on a thirteen-inch black-and-white TV in the shop at Christmastime, and one of his favorites was the forties film *Holiday Affair* with Robert Mitchum and a beautiful, young Janet Leigh. At the end, the formerly coolly reserved Mitchum dashes onto a departing train to get Janet Leigh back before the train whisks her away to California and from his life. The Janet Leigh character had been engaged to another dude but broke up with him when she realized she was in love with the Mitchum character. And like Mamie and me, the characters had only known each other for a week or so. I'm incredibly fortunate that Mamie doesn't have another guy in her life. If she did, I know she would have told me.

But this is real life, complicated and messy, and we're no movie stars. What grand gesture could I make to prove to Mamie that my love for her is real? I tell myself I won't rush her. I won't risk it all and propose until I feel like she's ready, whether it's this week or not. I can't believe what a chowdahead move I made the other night when I asked her ring size. She looked nonplussed and answered as though we were still playing the getting-to-know-you game. And there'd been no foul. But I can't help wondering if she knew precisely why I wanted to know. *Fuhgeddaboudit, Fitzpatrick*, I told myself.

I plodded into a thankfully empty elevator, remembering what Seamus said to me when I told him I was falling for her.

When I stepped onto my floor, I was singing.

CHAPTER FOURTEEN

Mamie

I wake with a smile on my face. It's almost Christmas, and I'm all wrapped up in romance. That's what I'm calling this thing between Rob and me in my head now: a romance. I think about phoning my touchstone, Abigay. But the pinky-orange light oozing around the edges of the plush drapes in my room tells me it's way too early to place a call to the faraway land of Mountain time.

I pull the covers up to my chin, snug as a bug, and roll onto my side. I grin, reliving yesterday's thrilling moments. *Fitzy.* He's sweet and thoughtful. His gorgeousness is a delicious bonus. I wriggle around under the covers with the thought of all the kissing. Not one boyfriend has ever kissed me so brilliantly, even the few with whom I've exchanged "I love yous," thinking I meant it. The way he pulls back now and then just to smile his delight into my eyes makes me feel cherished. Is Fitzpatrick a summa graduate of some South Boston class in the art of the smooch, or is it his love I'm feeling when our mouths meet?

I turn onto my other side and raise my fingers to my lips to see if they are puffy, giggling about a particularly perfect elevator kiss while reaching for my goat's milk lip balm. I apply a generous smear and consider sending Abigay a text. But when I snare my phone, it's only 7:10.

I open the camera and flip the screen to see myself. "Is that beard burn?" I ask the room, contorting my face to better see a narrow pink swath on my chin. *That's* unprecedented. Rob Fitzpatrick is a *man* in every sense of the word, not a boy. I push out my lips in a pout. If Abigay were up, I'd ask, *Do I look like Taylor Swift?* Or no, wait for it—I push my hair up into a sultry swoop, my chin down—Scarlett Johansson! With a pillow crease on one cheek. *Dream on, Morrow.*

Rob seems to be as much in love with my mouth as he is with the whole of me. I'm grinning at the thought of greeting him this morning in Spirit & Bower when a brisk slap of realization propels me up to lean against the padded headboard. I drop my phone to the bed. Gobsmacked. All this time, I've felt like Rob has been the one outpacing me in this . . . romance.

But the filly just rounded the quarter pole and caught up with the front-runner.

I've fallen in love with Fitzpatrick.

I want to pick up the landline, push Room Service, and send everyone on the second floor a pitcher of mimosas with a note that reads, *Merry Christmas! Mamie Morrow loves Robert Fitzpatrick!* Instead, I hug a pillow to my chest and grin into it until the workday ahead intrudes on my mind trip. I pull a face and open my Google Mail.

Farida's name leaps out at me from the list. Why would the publisher be contacting me so early? I throw my legs over the side of the bed and perch there. I'm about to open her message when I notice the send time. Today is Friday, but the email was sent Thursday. At 7:30 p.m. In a kissing fog last night, I hadn't checked my phone before bed. Farida addressed the note to both Rob and me. Darts of concern sting my torso.

Farida: *Mamie and Rob, two ads have been pulled from the issue at the ninth hour. The parent company wants a*

*fuller spread. Double what you were planning to do. And I
need it by EOD Friday to edit the formatting and get it sent
by the 23rd. Thanks.*

A word that rarely escapes my lips does. I bail from the bed
and throw open the curtains. My phone vibrates in my hand. A
call. I look at the screen. *Rob.*

"Morrow," he blurts out. "Have you seen Farida's email?"

"I have. I didn't . . . check my email yesterday. Just unearthed
hers from an avalanche of others." Why didn't he check his
email last night? Was he reliving our day as I was?

He repeats Farida's words. "EOD Friday. That's today," he .
adds, as though I'm unfamiliar with a calendar. "We could have
worked last night, if we'd known." *But would we have?* It sounds
like he fumbles his phone, and I'm off to imagining him in a
T-shirt and boxers. Messed-up hair. Rugged stubble. I hurry
to the sliding door and fling it open, hoping the white-pine-
scented cold air will clear my head. "Morrow, are you there?"

"Yes, yes. Sorry," I say, shivering not from the cold but from
the fear that his other superpower besides kissing could be the
ability to read thoughts.

"I'm jumping in the shower."

It sounds like he's upset. I downshift into humor. "Don't
jump in, just step in." He doesn't reply but lets out a huff as
though he can't understand why I'm joking at a time like this.

"I'll check on the bourbon bar," he says. "Make sure someone can let me in. I can start setting up my equipment and get
my files pulled up. We're way behind now. Have to ramp it up."

"Well, I'm just getting up, so it may take me forty minutes
or so."

"Forty minutes!"

"Fitzpatrick, women can't get ready as fast as men. *I'm not
going down there without mascara, powder, and lipstick. And my*

second-day hair needs washing. "Have you had coffee? Eaten something?"

"Yah nuh, no time. See you soon."

And he's off. *No way, huh?* After last night's love-washed dialogue, Rob's brusque light-of-day words have me sauntering to hit Brew on the espresso machine and then to the bathroom. In the steamy shower cabinet, I brood about his sudden petulant-sounding attitude. I take my time washing and conditioning my hair, then after drying off, slip into the luxe terry bathrobe hanging on the back of the door. *GBL* reads the monogrammed pocket. I give it a pat.

I take the green cup that matches my headboard and fill it with coffee. Before the mirror, I languidly blow my well-nourished mane dry while imagining Rob stewing in the bourbon bar. Then, sipping my coffee, I build a bun. That done, I smile and dig through my suitcase for my curling iron. As I pull out and sculpt strategic strands, I'm convinced that my coif could rival a confection in a Christmas Bake-Off. I slather on moisturizer and brush on full makeup.

Back in the bedroom, I locate the darling striped hot pink, red, and green Draper James sweater Abigay gifted me before I left and carefully pull it over my head. With a satisfied nod at the clock, I dress in a thrifted long pink wool skirt, socks, and booties. Then a practical and powerful idea occurs to me. I collect my coat and gloves before heading out.

Sixty-six minutes after hanging up with Rob, I pick up my computer bag where I left the hefty thing in Isla's care and am soon smiling at the white owl painting over the stairs that lead down to Spirit & Bower. I give it a wink. *Here's to womanly wisdom.* With my arms full, I open the lever latch on the door with an elbow.

Rob looks up from his computer, his face pale, his hair as tousled as though he's been tearing at it. "Mamie! Where have you been?" He stares at the coffee caddy and bag in my hands. "We're far too behind for you to have made a trip to the coffee shop."

"It's lovely to see you too this morning, Robert," I say to his scowl before setting my things down.

This new behavior from him has made me feel like I've been called to the principal's office by the man who, up to this point, has been so cherishing. "Look, we have to eat if we want to be productive. Are you hangry again, honey?" I set the caddy down on the cedar-topped table where he's chosen to spread out his equipment and then take a seat in the brown leather barrel chair across from his.

He gapes at me, then his belly lets out a lion of a growl. His face flushes. "Okay, okay. In a minute," he says, his voice still grumpy. I pull my coffee from the caddy's grip and take a long sip through the slit in the lid. No longer bamboozled by Rob's attitude but still filled with disappointment, I unpack my things and look around the handsome and cozy space. Pink poinsettias set about make the already arresting Indigenous art and Native American–inspired chandeliers and other appointments look grandly festive.

When my belly becomes the epicenter of an earthquake, I grab the bag and pull out a cranberry walnut scone. I take two bites before rolling the bag back down so the rest of the pastry won't get cold. I'm logging into the Wi-Fi and chewing another bite of scone, which is delicious, when I sneak a peek at Rob. He's staring at me, and not in a happy way. I'm too miffed at him to cry, though I suddenly want to. *Is this our first fight? It came on so fast. But then everything between us has come on fast.*

"May I say something now?" *Do not cry.* I dig my fingernails into my thigh as Napoleon-inspired tears sting my lids.

He shrugs and crosses his arms over his beautiful chest. "Yah."

I search his eyes, and there seems to be a softening there. "I was hurt by the way you spoke to me this morning." Rob's mouth trembles, and just like that I know he still cares for me. I struggle gamely to make my point. "But I really don't think the extra time hurt our schedule in any profound way. We will have the extra pages licked today, and you know it." A traitorous tear rolls down my freshly powdered cheek.

He's out of his chair, around the table, and into the chair next to mine. His mouth works again as he holds out big trembling arms. Sniffing back a deluge of tears, I lean into them and he holds me. "Oh, Mamie. Sweetheart. I'm so sorry," he says, rubbing small circles on my back. "It's just that . . . we were in the homestretch when Farida dropped the bombshell."

"We were. We still are," I say into his sandalwoody neck where I feel safe at home again.

He finally pulls away and takes my hands, holding them and resting them on his square knees. He squeezes his eyes shut. "It's just that I have other . . . things to take care of. I mean, uh, there's, uh, so much I want to talk about." He opens his eyes and then looks down at our hands, shaking his head. "This double spread will take a huge chunk of that time. Tomorrow's Christmas Eve." Seeing this flustered Rob is another first. *What other things to take care of? Is something going on with his family?*

"At least we'll be together," I offer. But prickles of concern rise on the back of my neck. I lick my lips before asking him to look at me. "Is everything okay, sweetheart?"

He smiles and holds my eyes. "It is when you call me sweetheart and look at me like that."

He lifts my left hand and kisses the peaks of my knuckles. I can't shed the feeling that something else is bothering him. Something he's holding back. "Please try not to worry. Remember we were creative partners first. We've totally got this, Fitzpatrick. It will be . . . a piece of Yule log," I say with a snap of my fingers. He snorts a laugh, and I find a steady smile to offer him.

Taking hold of my upper arms—which are still chilly, despite the sweater—he rubs them slowly up and down while studying the collar of my sweater. "I think part of the reason, a lot of the reason I reacted like a louse"—he takes a breath and looks up at me—"is that I was afraid to fail and look bad in your eyes. Everything I do has become about you."

My chest feels like I've inhaled a fistful of Fourth of July sparklers. I take a breath. "I don't know what you'd have to do for me to think badly of you, Rob," I say with every ounce of tenderness I have.

His throat works too, and he takes a hitching sniff. "You are such a calming influence on me."

"I've always been calm. Especially in crisis. Not sure why. Maybe it's because my parents were always yelling at each other when I was little. I just go still and into that mode. Like a couple of years ago when Abigay fell on a nasty street corner and hit the back of her head. We were in a sketchy neighborhood for some weird errand and had stopped at a market before calling an Uber back. She had a bag full of groceries in her arms. Cars . . . just kept running over everything." Rob takes his hands back and rakes them through his hair. "I went quiet, called 911, then put my coat over her and called her name until she roused and said my name."

"Man, Mamie," Rob says, shaking his head. "You are my new hero." I smile. "No, I mean it." He regards my face. My hair. "You are the most . . . wonderful woman I know. You know, in general, not just for that."

"You are wonderful too."

He stares into my eyes, and I hear a click as he swallows. "I love you, Mamie."

A sob swells like a song in my head. "Oh, Fitzy, I love you too."

His hazel eyes widen. "You do?"

Overcome, I nod my head and squeeze both his hands. "I *do*."

He shakes his head as if in disbelief. "You make me so happy," he says. "I never wanted to make you cry."

"Oh," I say as another tear falls, "my emotions are just close to the surface right now." I take my hands back to reach for a napkin, but he beats me to it. I dab under my eyes in an attempt to salvage my mascara.

"I don't know why you bother to wear that stuff. You don't need it."

I toss the napkin over my shoulder and my last ounce of caution with it. I take his hand and lay it against my cheek. "Rob, I *thought* I was in love a couple of times. But it was *nothing* like this. What I feel for you. No matter how quickly it's happened." I breathe a little laugh out through my nose.

"It's real for me too, Mamie," he says quietly. "And me too for the first time. I'm somebody-pinch-me grateful I found you. But it's a lot like free-falling—may Petty rest in peace—exhilarating but scary too."

"I know. But they say fear is the opposite of love. Bee and Jake—" Rob gives me a sidelong look. I grin. "*Abigay* and Jake." I flap my hand. "She and I call each other Bee . . . goes way back."

Rob grins. "O-kay."

"Anyway, she and Jake were going through some stuff last year and were smart enough to consult a counselor. He told them that love is by nature strong. When you're in love, you're secure enough to put the other person first. But fear is weak. Um . . ." I look at the glossy brown ceiling as though the rest of the words might be written there for me and then remember them. "Fear is self-centered. It backs away instead of . . . extending. Makes you unhappy, whereas love makes you happy."

"I get that," he says, looking down again.

I tip his chin up with a finger and implore him with my eyes. "So when we're fearful, let's choose love. And *trust*. We've already, um, wavered there a bit. Haven't we?"

"Yah, we have. Especially me."

"No, Fitzy." I take off my glasses and lay them on the table so that not a single thing is between us. "Me too. Next time—and you know there will be a next time because we're flawed humans—do you promise we'll talk things out instead of being reactionary and locking up our feelings?"

He smiles again. "I do."

"I promise too." We lean in, and he seems to study every inch of my face the way I do his. He sighs and rests his forehead against mine.

"How did you get to be so wise?" he says, close to my mouth.

"I'm not really. Just practical, I think. And an old soul."

Something flickers in his eyes. He pulls back and parts his lips as if to react to something I said. But he looks into mid-distance for a moment before he seems to reboard our thought train. "Mamie. I feel miraculously good about us having this conversation. Maybe couples who . . . fail didn't consider things like this at the beginning of the relationship."

"Likely not." But a fresh wind squall of excitement blows as if through the door when the word "*relationship*" soaks in. I grin. "This is when people change their Facebook statuses to 'in a relationship,'" I say, using air quotes.

"I'm not on Facebook."

"I know," I say to my lap before peeping up at him and confessing. "I tried looking you up before we met."

He grins and shakes his head. "Morrow, you won't do."

I crack up. "Look at you go! Another southernism, an old one!"

He shrugs a big shoulder. "Heard that here this week." Then

his smile fades. "I only want us to be happy. And the way we'll do that is by choosing love and trust over fear."

"We will." I'm quiet for a minute, reflecting on this momentous morning.

He speaks up. "We're a love match. Morrow and Fitzpatrick."

"Well, Fitzpatrick and Morrow, if we go alphabetically."

"I say ladies first."

I pick up my glasses and hold them in my hand. "So. Do we have time to seal this with a kiss?"

He laughs softly. "Yah huh, we do." He takes my face in his hands and massages my cheeks with his thumbs. And though we both have coffee breath, he kisses me thoroughly and long. Everything inside me turns over and sighs.

"Now," he says, "how 'bout one of those dang scones?"

CHAPTER FIFTEEN

Rob

With three scones in my belly and my mind jacked up by the giant cup of joe—compliments of the woman who, incredibly, is in love with me—I plunge back into my editing software. When I've finished setting the white points and black points and color graded the last of the shots, it's time to get behind the camera and capture the extra ones we'll need for the double spread. Mamie's head down over her keyboard, her fingers flying, her bun bobbing. Her energy still slays me. And her glasses make her look hotter than any other sexy librarian type wishes she was. Grinning, I punch up my weather app. It's a cold one today, thirty-four degrees with five-to-ten-mph winds.

"Hey, Mames, sorry to interrupt, but I need to know what additional photos you want for the piece."

She looks up and around, as though she's forgotten where she is. And then, blinking, she takes off her glasses. She grins and seems to remember the Boston speak for "of course." "Yah huh."

I laugh. "Why are you so cute?"

"Hey, mister, stick to the work. We're behind." She holds her glasses up to the light and rolls her eyes. "Ugh." She reaches for her computer bag.

I dig in my pocket and hold a lens wipe aloft as though it's the winning card in a high-stakes poker game. And to Mamie, it must be, because she blows me a big kiss and exclaims, "My hero! Thank you."

My heart goes chowdahead happy, but a small clot of regret at my offensive behavior this morning remains in an artery. She smiles but gets focused on opening the wipe.

"Okay," she says, rubbing at her lenses. "How about we go through the ones you have ready, and I'll make notes about others I'd like to see in the feature? I've been noodling on it, so it *truly* shouldn't take long." She returns her glasses to their perch on her pretty nose. For the first time, I notice it's slightly tilted to one side. I smile to myself. She's perfectly imperfect. And perfect for me.

The door opens and Annelise walks in. She glances at the illuminated overhead fixtures and then at us. "Oh!" she says, her hand still on the knob. "I didn't know you were in here."

"Good morning, friend," Mamie says without looking up.

"Good morning to you both," she says. I turn and say hey to her with a wave of my hand. She stands there looking from me to Mamie and beaming. "I came to do a quick bottle inventory check for Vaughn because the Spirit & Bower manager's out sick. With COVID, no less."

"Oh man," says Mamie. "At Christmastime. Poor guy."

"I know, right?" Annelise replies.

I gesture at the table and our belongings. "It's okay that we're here? Josh let me in. With the growing crowd, it's harder to find a quiet place to work."

"Oh sure, you're fine. I'll be unlocking cabinets and such, but I'll try and be quiet."

"No worries," Mamie and I say at the same time, and then widen our eyes at each other.

"Good. Okay. Oh, Mamie, have you been shopping yet? I mean for something to wear to the ball tomorrow night? A *great* local jazz combo's coming. Instrumental Christmas jazz. We've been so swamped in the office that the shopping slipped my mind."

Mamie sighs and leans back against her chair. "That's okay. And no, I haven't." As she tells Annelise about our doubled workload, I tune out, save my work, then use the time to move my computer over to Mamie's table so that we can study the photos together. Spotting an outlet behind us, next to a rock fireplace with a painting of a giant long-horned steer above it, I plug in to give my charge a boost. I pull the photos up and check the email on my phone while Mamie asks Annelise about her date.

When Mamie's ready, we start through the photos. She praises my skill again—as if I needed an extra ego boost after learning that she loves me—and then taps her pencil on her notebook as she voices her opinion on which photos she'd like to include with an eye toward color. Behind the gleaming bar, Annelise opens and closes cabinets, jingles keys, and scratches with a pencil in her notebook. Sometimes I feel her eyes on us and hope she'll be finished with her task soon. Thank God she didn't come in here an hour ago.

"I feel like we should move from the exterior to the interior," Mamie says. "The way you did when you took the first pictures. We have only the single edited shot of the exterior, the view from the bridge. This one," she says, tapping her screen with her eraser, "with the gorgeous sky." She goes all dreamy-eyed and whispers in my ear, "I loved it when you showed it to me through the viewfinder."

She bites her lip and then looks at my mouth. My desire for her makes me want to chuck it all and whisk her off to an unnamed planet, one where only the two of us could breathe. But I sigh and nudge her boot with the side of my shoe, then tilt my head toward the Christmas greenery–swagged bar, where Annelise is on a stepladder, sliding bottles back inside a high cabinet. Mamie takes a pen rather than her usual pencil, writes the word "sorry" on a napkin, and then draws a heart around it. I smile. She penned the word in manuscript rather than cursive, which surprises me because she's so proper. What other surprises await me from Mamie Morrow?

She gets back to business, assuming her straight-backed, shoulders-high presence. I think of the day she told me that she tended to micromanage and didn't want to be that way in our creative partnership. But I'm happy to let her take over here because she is more experienced and design is her domain. She's decisive and direct. And I find that sexy about her too. She glances at my face, which must look completely smitten, and then blushes. "I'd like to include one of the bronze sculptures at the front entrance."

I glance at Annelise, whose back is turned and who must think I'm Mamie's lackey. But it's not anyone else's business how we conduct ours. We have our rhythm down and are about to slay this assignment. I push back my chair, slap my hands on my knees, and push myself to my feet. "Agreed. Do you have a preference?"

"The elegant warrior with the bow." She holds up both hands as if they are the sculptures in question and looks from one to the other. "I think it's the one on the left. Double-check that, please."

"I'll just go do that now."

"And see if you can recruit a festively dressed couple and a valet. We should depict the genuine Southern hospitality here. Ask them to pretend they've just arrived and the valet's opening the door for them. Oh, see if Marco's out there. He's really nice."

Annelise lets herself out quietly. Ready to head out myself, I select two cameras and loop the case straps over a shoulder. "Fitzpatrick," Mamie says, eyeing me over her glasses, "won't you freeze out there?"

I smile. "Yah nuh. This sweater's warm. And hey, I'm tough." I assume a bodybuilder's stance with my arms showing off my muscles. "Boston winters? But man, my hands."

She starts to dig into the coat pocket she brought down in case we went outside. "At least take my gloves."

I bark a laugh. "Morrow, your gloves wouldn't fit my thumbs. I'll run up and get my scarf."

She bends to look at my feet. "Are your socks woolen? Oh, the cool colorful ones again!"

"I forgot to wash them last night. I was um, distracted."

"I thought I smelled something."

I hoot a laugh at the ceiling and then go over and buzz my lips against the back of her neck. Her hair smells like fresh pears today.

"Ooh, that tickles!" She rubs her arms. "Gave me goose-bumps too."

"You're the most fun I ever had," I whisper into her ear.

She shivers and then pretends to swat me away. But she can't conceal her grin. "You too, me too. Now, get going."

My tasks completed, I'm back inside the lodge, blowing warmth into my fists. I hit the lobby bathroom and then decide to grab more coffee for Mamie and me. "Mamie and me," I repeat under my breath, appreciating both the connotation and the alliteration, and smile around at people like I'm the mayor of Greenville.

I can't wait to tell my mom about Mamie and catch Seamus up too. Seamus added a four-word coda, maybe a benediction, to the phone conversation I had with him about Mamie. *Marry the girl, kid.*

With the camera bags on my shoulder and two cups of hot coffee—Mamie's just the way she likes it—helping to thaw my hands, I'm psyched about showing her the shots I captured. From the start, her praise of my work has been a colossal confidence boost. I love it when she says my work will make her writing shine. With new zap in my step, I head toward the stairwell again. Spirit & Bower. Whoever named the bar situated in the foundation of this place nailed the name of the bar. Obviously, "spirit" is a reference to bourbon, but I'd be willing to bet that the word was also chosen to represent the Native American spirit of kinship and deep bonds of relationship that Mamie described to me. I hope to create those bonds with Mamie.

She hasn't mentioned her grandfather in a few. I wonder if she feels that she's as in touch with her heritage as she's going to be, that she's reached the end of her quest.

If the plan I'm hatching is successful, I'll soon know.

As I tread beneath the elegant black bar sign, the word following "Spirit" in the same spare gold lettering pops. *Bower*. A sheltering place. A place to escape. To hide. Spot-on for Mamie and me today.

I'm grinning when I push through the door.

Though the lights are still on, the room's a dim dungeon because Mamie's gone. My mouth twists in disappointment, but I guess she's probably in the ladies' room. I set the coffees down—mine sloshing and burning the tender spot between my thumb and index finger—and spot a note, a blank page torn from her notebook lying on top of my closed MacBook. I wince and wipe the coffee from my stinging hand and the table, then drop back into my leather chair to read it.

F,
Most of the photos are captioned. Gone for a quick shop with Annelise.
Back soon. XOXOXO.
M.
P.S. Trust moi.

"Shopping?" I ask the room, my voice echoing. At a time like this? But she has asked me to trust her. At her prompting, we practically took vows that we would do so this morning. And I will. I look at the note again and smile at her handwriting—her round printing—that looks the same as it probably did when she was in fourth grade. What a girl.

I upload my photos to my editing software and scan them, trying to see them through Mamie's eyes. Fortunately, Marco's on duty today and was out front along with four other guys, so I was able to make the shot with the couple and a doorman happen for her. I hope the pair I found will be a neat surprise.

In the lobby, families seemed to be arriving and departing in equal measure. It's interesting to think about why some people are dying to get home to spend the holiday while others would rather be here. Makes you wonder what their family dynamics are. After spending seventeen Christmases in a small house with enough boisterous boys to fill a pew at St. Joseph's—with Mom and Pop in the row behind so Pop could thump our ears if we misbehaved—it's nice spending Christmas here at the GBL—as Mamie's taken to calling the lodge—where "all is calm and all is bright," or will be when she gets back.

I stare at my keyboard and run a stupid lovestruck finger around the M key. What if Farida had assigned some other guy to pair with Mamie? What if we'd never met? But if we're meant to be, we'd have found each other another way. Through some, in girl speak, "meet-cute" in Charleston.

My mojo rising, I check the clock on my laptop, take a slug of my coffee, and start editing. I'm reducing the noise in the images when a single knock falls on the door and Isla sticks her head in.

"Sorry to disturb, Rob," she says after what seems like a quick survey of the room. "Where's Mamie?"

"You're fine. C'mon in." *Why not? While you're at it, invite the entire staff to stop by. 'Tis the season!* I think uncharitably. "Mamie had an errand. She'll be back soon."

Isla, looking ruffled for a woman so self-contained, steps in and lets the door close. I'm getting to my feet when she waves me back down. She stands in front of my table, her hands on her narrow hips. "There's been a theft. In the gallery."

"No way." I lean back against my chair as if the news has pushed me there.

"Yes. We're keeping it quiet right now, only questioning staff that have been around this morning."

"When did it happen?"

"Had to have been in the wee hours when someone could take a minute to pick the lock on the case." Her lips form a hard line. She looks at the floor and shakes her head almost imperceptibly. *Which case? Mamie and I have seen how meticulously Isla locks up.* "You guys didn't see anyone lurking around the gallery area when you came down, did you?"

I look toward the door. "I came down first in a rush. Our editor assigned us additional pages for the spread we thought was almost finished."

"That's a good thing," she says, brightening a little, "I mean, more exposure for the hotel. I really appreciate all you two have done. Can't wait to see the article."

"It *is* a good thing," I say, wondering how my mind glossed over the serendipitous side of what I thought was a debacle. *Freaking out takes your eye off the ball, Fitzpatrick.* "And thank *you*. You and Annelise have made it a pleasure."

But Isla seems to have tuned out. She nods and worries a silver bracelet around and around her wrist. Her lips grow downcast. I want to help her. "I was downstairs by seven thirty." I think back. "A couple of people were reading newspapers in the lobby. And Tucker and a woman I haven't met were setting up the coffee bar. He and I exchanged quick greetings. I didn't see anyone else."

Isla's phone buzzes. She sighs and glances at the screen. "Gotta take this," she says, and takes her leave.

I'm staring into space and digesting the idea of theft happening in a place like the Grand Bohemian when Mamie rushes through the door with a flurry of apologies. At the sight of her, my heart lights up like the scoreboard at Fenway after a home run. I turn in my chair and rest my arms on the back of it, smiling like the lovestruck chowdahead she's made of me. With her arrival, the room takes on the smells of sunshine and fresh clean wind.

She loves me. She's *mine*.

And I am hers.

"How's it going?" she asks, throwing her coat over a chair and setting down her things along with a big paper shopping bag.

"Great!" *No more grousing from me today.* She comes to me holding a green gift bag with red-and-white candy-cane-striped tissue sticking up out of it. She wiggles her eyebrows at the closed door and then, taking a seat on my thighs, sets the gift bag on my lap. She leans in and weaves her arms around my neck, crushing the sack as if no matter what's inside it, it could never come between us. "Hello, Fitzy." Her breath smells like chocolate. Under her spell once more, I kiss her firmly but then pull away with a small grin. She takes off her glasses and pulls me in for more. The gift sack crinkles. She tastes like chocolate too. Loud thuds sound against the ceiling, and frowning, we part.

"What have you been eating?" I ask her.

She giggles. "Chocolate truffles—the best! Annelise and I ate a whole bag of them walking back. A small bag. Well, more like a medium bag. Who cares? It's Christmastime."

"Did you bring me one?"

"I did!" she says, reaching into the pocket of her pink skirt and pulling out two. I take the truffles. Soft and warm from her body.

"Oh," she says, sitting up straight and dislodging the now-crumpled gift sack with a flourish. "I have a present for you. Today's Christmas Adam!"

I give her the side-eye. "Christmas *Adam*? Okay, I'll bite."

"It's the day before Christmas Eve. Get it? You don't celebrate?"

Adorable. "I do now." I open one end of a truffle wrapper and squeeze the melty chocolate goodness into my mouth. "Delicious."

"Open your gift so we can get back to work."

I smile, enjoying her anticipation-animated features, and pull out the tissue to reveal a pair of fine leather gloves. The first *new* ones I've ever had. I hold them up, checking them out. "Thank you." *Did she—*

"Wait!"

"What?"

"Is that chocolate on your hand?" she asks, taking my thumb and pulling it away from my fingers to examine the dark spot on the flesh between them. "Don't get it on your glove." She retrieves her glasses. "Oh, is that a burn?"

"Yah. I spilled hot coffee on it this morning. Forgot about it already."

"Let me kiss it, then." She gives the burn a tiny peck. "I have a tiny burn too."

"Where? What from?"

She sticks her chin out and raises it. "Just under here. It's a bona fide beard burn. My first."

"As much as you like to kiss, I have a hard time believing that."

"Ha! Don't let this go to your head, but the boyfriends who came before you were just that. Boys. You're my first *man*. My first tough guy—at least on the outside. And the best kisser *ever*."

I crack up at her calling me a tough guy and run my hand over my midday mug. "I do grow a mean five-o'clock shadow. But seriously, I'm sorry I hurt you."

"Well, kiss it, then," she mock demands.

And I do, softly, before trailing my lips up to her mouth again for another smooch.

When Mamie hops up and smooths her skirt, I pick up the gloves with a sense of unease. I feel like the expensive gift has breached the fabric of our brand-new relationship. When we met, infatuation broke down the lobe of my brain that controls judgment. But I no longer worry about whether my love is real. I'm sure that it is. It's the fear-controlling part of my brain that isn't playing well with the other parts. Maybe Mamie's way out of my league, and what if one of these days she figures that out? Where would that leave me?

She's rummaging through the big bag she brought from town and rearranging things inside it. She looks up. "You do like the color?" she asks, admiring the gloves.

"Yah. Beautiful rich brown." *Rich.* "You were . . . very generous, Mamie."

"The color's cognac. And they were a business expense." *A business expense?* My unease coils. "One of my love languages," she goes on, "is giving friends little happies. And just gift giving in general. And now your hands will be warm when you're working outside. Oh! See the pointer fingers? They're touch tech so you can operate your camera." She consults the clock. "Which, by the way, you need to get back to PDQ, Fitzpatrick."

Though fear continues to prowl me, I have to laugh at the PDQ. "Right. Just let me know what you want."

Mamie treads around the table and opens her laptop. "Let me pull up my design template." She does and then studies it. "Okay." She picks up her pencil and scribbles down four potential outdoor aspects of the lodge, including the stone egg on the bar porch, which surprises me because she didn't seem to like the egg the day of our tour. The day I knew that I loved her. Though so much has happened since then, as anxious as she seemed to be that day, I still wonder if she fell in love with me then too.

Now I need to see her loving smile and hear her girlish laugh. "I'm not climbing in that thing again," I say.

"That will not be necessary," she says with a poorly concealed grin.

"Good thing," I say, deadpanning. I shoulder my camera, put on my outerwear, and tread to the door. I open it and then pause, a gloved hand on the frame.

I look back at her, my fear mocking me. "Later, love."

She smiles. "Later, love."

CHAPTER SIXTEEN

Mamie

I pace the whiskey bar awash in disappointment. I really wanted Rob to have some nice warm gloves. It was a small celebration for me, selecting just the right pair at the men's store. They were the perfect fit. I've held his hands enough that guessing the size was a snap. Then why do I feel I've committed some impropriety? He seemed anxious when I asked if he liked the color. Is it because I said the gloves were a business expense, which I meant as a joke? Does he think I've been playing fast and loose with the magazine's money? Have I given him reason to believe that I'm a dishonest person?

My phone sounds with my Christmas text notification: a jingle of sleigh bells. *Abigay Fletcher*, my screen asserts. *Can you talk?* she's asked. I'm torn. I'm dying to talk with her, but I'm not sure how long Rob's shoot will take. I look at the closed door, roll a mental dice, then push the call button. "Greetings from Co-lo-rah-doh," she says, answering on the second ring. When she doesn't answer on the first one, it's because she's taking a preparatory sip of whatever she's drinking. If it's not yet noon, it's still coffee. That's how my girl rolls.

I take a seat on a barstool facing the door but as far away from it as possible. "Bee," I say. "How's it going?"

"We're sitting in the Eagle's Nest at the top of the mountain in front of a roaring fire. I thought I'd perish from the chill on the lift ride up."

"It's colder there today?" Today's high in Greenville is supposed to be forty-four degrees and windy.

"It is! Thirty-two degrees right now but dropping. And it snowed again last night!"

"Well, be careful up there."

"I always am."

"Apparently, I'm *not*," I say with an eye on the door. "I have committed a glove gaffe."

"I'll need an interpretation."

I tell her about shopping for Rob's gloves and his reaction, or at least the way I perceived it.

"Listen," she says. "I believed it when you said you guys are in love. Love at first sight *does* happen. But after four days, you cannot know the man's thoughts."

"But we're amazingly in sync most of the time. Remember I told you about the trust talk we had? When I told him about your counseling session?"

"One talk. And you were under the influence."

"I was not!" I frown into the phone. "Of what?"

"Euphoria, exhilaration. You know, love drunk."

I sigh. "You're right, you're right, I know you're right." I hear the rumble of Jake's voice, excitement running through the cadence of his sentences. "Do you need to go?"

"Nope, Jake's talking to some people about a black slope they tried." In her voice, I hear her he's-so-cute smile. "But I'm thinking here. Hang on and let me find a quieter spot."

While Abigay's on the move, I hop up, open the door, crack it open to take a peek, and then dare to dash up the short flight of stairs to look for signs of Rob in the lobby. I feel as ridiculous as I did the night I hid amongst the branches of the great Christmas tree. But this time the man's nowhere in sight. I run back to the safety of Spirit & Bower, my breath fast in my throat. "I may not have much time," I tell Abigay.

"Okay. I'm set," she says. "You've told him about your background."

"Right. Of course. About Colleen's character. That I lived South of Broad. But all in brief."

"Okay. What if he's worried about the M-O-N-E-Y?" she says, spelling the word out in a half whisper. Our mothers taught us that talking about money outside the family was "common"—South Carolina speak for uncouth.

The world slips.

"The money? Do you think he wants me *for my money?*"

"No. Nothing you've told me about Rob would lead me to believe that. But if you and he are as serious as I think you are, you're going to have to have another trust talk. This time as in trust *fund*."

"The fund I haven't tapped since I was twenty-three and got a great cash deal on my car?"

"Mamie, I know you've been frugal. It's not like you're out racing fifty-foot catamarans. You shop thrift more than I do. Hush and let me ask you a serious question."

My heart skips. I know what she's thinking and I need her to say it. But why, when the stars seem to have aligned for me, when I've been so blissed out, have things become so complicated? "Spill the tea, Abigay."

"What would you say right now if he proposed?"

"Ooh," I moan. "All we've established is that we are in love. I mean, we've talked about how it takes work to build a relationship. That's forward thinking. Future thinking. But he's said *nothing* about marriage."

My friend digs in. "I have a feeling about this. What would your answer be?"

Clarity breaks like a plate on the floor. My heart beats like a tribe of tom-toms. I have to speak up to be heard above it.

The word launches from my throat, primal and burning. *"Yes!"*

Lavish silence on Abigay's end doesn't mean the call's dropped but that my friend is gifting me with time to gather myself. When she speaks, her voice is gentle but firm. "Okay, darling Bee. Remember what your trustee said when he granted you access to the account when you were twenty-one?"

I nod dully and then speak up. "I haven't thought of it lately. But I do. He would require me to set up a prenuptial agreement when I married." I want to howl. "Oh, Bee, Rob would—"

The door unlatches. I flinch as though the massive horned steer in the wall painting has come to life and is coming at *me*. Rob stands in the doorway, one big shoe propping the door open. He's looking toward the top of the stairs from where a female voice drifts. I'm off the stool and sprinting for the table. Rob calls upward, "Thanks. I'll let her know." Near the table, I fumble my phone and watch it topple and slide along the floor as though making for home plate.

Rob breezes in, holding his camera aloft and looking as triumphant as a Christmas trumpet. "I *have* to get these beauties downloaded so you can see them." He unwinds his scarf and then the gloves. *The gloves. Abigay.* I flash a witless smile before crawling under the table where my athletic phone has come to rest. On my hands and knees, I take deep slow breaths.

Rob's upside-down head appears. "Mamie, what the heck are you doing under there?"

I snare the phone and pretend to dust it off. "Dropped my phone! Be right up."

"Here, let me help you. Don't bump your head." I take his hand and allow him to help me to my feet. "Are you okay?" He regards my hair, where I feel long strands escaping the bun and stealing around my face and neck. "You look a little . . . rattled."

"I—am a little. A touch stressed, I think." I blow hair away from my glasses and eyes, which begin to sting with tears.

He places a big steadying hand on my shoulder. "Go take a break. We'll get this done."

"Okay. I have the first photos captioned and the first paragraph of the piece written. I'll take my shopping to my room and freshen up." I give him a quavery little smile. "Download your photos. I can't wait to see them," I say as though on autopilot.

"Take your time. I can start editing as well." He pulls me in for a hug. I inhale his sandalwood- and violet-breathed essence, wishing I could turn the inexorable clock back a day. He pulls away first. "Oh, I saw Annelise when I came in. Since it's so brisk out—*like Boston brisk*—the staff's ordering in for lunch. She needs to know if we want in. I vote yes."

I try and smooth my hair under his gaze. "I'd like that. Big time-saver too."

"They're ordering an assortment of sandwiches: turkey, pimento cheese, egg salad, and chips and pickles and stuff."

"I'll find her on my way up and tell her we're in."

"Thanks," he says, but then smites himself on the forehead. "I can't believe I forgot to tell you—Isla said there was an art theft early this morning. She asked me who we saw in the area."

His words are still hanging in the air as I struggle to process the news. "*What?* You're *kidding!* What was it?" My mind careens up the stairs, around the curves and angles of the lobby, and to the painting of the chief.

Please, no.

Please, no.

"She didn't say. Just that a lock was picked. So I assume an artifact?"

I nod like a bobblehead. *An artifact, not a painting.* "But a theft happening here . . . I can't believe it."

"Right?" he answers.

And I thought this day had started so well. I have to lie down before I fall down. I collect my shopping bag. Rob glances at it. "Did you find a good dress for the ball?"

"I did, but I can't let you see it yet. It's a surprise."

He smiles but not in his usual Fitzy way. Things suddenly feel forced and false between us. "You are full of surprises, Mamie. Will it make me wish I'd rented a tux?"

It's expensive to rent a tuxedo. *The money.* I have to call Abigay back. "Nope. You'll look perfect in your blazer, your white shirt, I think, and the red-striped tie. Have you taken advantage of the hotel's dry-cleaning service? I've used it twice. Not expensive."

"Nah. But I'll bag up my clothes for the ball and take them to the front desk tonight. See you soon."

He leans in and kisses me on the cheek. "I love you, Mamie."

I realize doubt had crept into my thoughts, so I implore him with my eyes to remember those three words. "I love you too, Rob." I feel his gaze on my back as I leave the room. How have we devolved into Mamie and Rob again?

And why is love such a mercurial, mood-hoovering, mucky mess?

With a short but grateful nod at the painting of "my Grand-tate," I step inside the elevator and lean against the wall. Alone at last with my cyclonic thoughts. Annelise said the sandwiches should be here at one o'clock. I thanked her and said, "Chat soon," before she could engage me in conversation. *Abigay.* I have to get to my room. I have to call her back. She'll be waiting.

In the bathroom, I take a look at my appearance in the mirror and want to burst into tears. I yank the elastic hair tie and bobbies out of my hair, and then toss my smudgy glasses on the vanity. *Abigay.* I take my boots off, lie on the bed with my phone, and pull one side of the blessedly fresh and hotel-crisp duvet up and over me. I think of the day that I starfished here, meditating on the box that Tate Atwater left me, and realize I've forgotten to carry the arrowhead in my pocket as I'd planned to each day. And the other treasured item from Grandtate's box, a talisman that has laid quietly in the sock compartment of my suitcase. Could I dare to wear it? Taking up my phone, I place the call.

"Abigay?" I ask, surprised when she answers on the first ring.

"Dearest Bee, what's going on?"

Tears roll from the corners of my eyes and into my ears. I give a great rattling sniff. "I've come undone."

"Are you in your room?"

"Yes, finally. Lying down."

"Good." She takes a long breath and then insists that I do too. "I've been noodling on this thing, and it occurred to me that you and Rob are in the quote, unquote seventh-inning stretch of the assignment."

There's no reason to remind my friend that this is Rob and not my former boyfriend, Brett, the baseball boy, as she called him, because I know that she's about to use the analogy to impart some great Bee wisdom.

"Think about it, Mamie. It's like the interval of the game when baseball devotees need to stand up and stretch, regroup, assess the game, talk trash about which players need to get their heads in the game, rev themselves up, or calm themselves down. Renew their hope because there's still time, or stress because there's too little of it left. Decide to leave because it's not going well for their team, or stay until the end out of loyalty. Or *maybe* hang in there for the possibility that a miracle could happen."

"A miracle . . . Rob and me . . . We could be a miracle."

Abigay goes on. "I believe you are."

I hiccup a grateful sob at her words.

"And it makes sense to me why it's at this time in both the assignment and the romance that both of you can expect to experience conflicting and confusing feelings. So much was already riding on the assignment for you both, but then you went and fell in love and raised the stakes . . . like, exponentially. This is no ordinary romance. It's a *rocket ship romance*."

Strains of the Sade song "No Ordinary Love" play in my head. More tears coast my cheeks, but they are tears of relief and renewed hope. "Thank you. Thank you. You are saving my sanity here, maybe my life."

"So you're going to bring it up and lay it out there. You'll know the right time."

"I will."

"Good girl. And one last word of advice? Let the man eat before you do it."

CHAPTER SEVENTEEN

Rob

W hen Mamie sweeps back into the bar with a server's tray, it's hard to say which I'm hungrier for: the sight of the lunch or the woman. Both will nourish me. When she left me this morning, obviously upset, the thought of it being about something I did or said made my chest hurt. If more regret lodges around my heart, I'll need an angioplasty.

But now she's smiling her confident and sexy Morrow smile and looks completely refreshed. She's changed into the outfit she wore on our first day.

I'm absurdly in love with every facet of her.

She lays the tray down on the table behind ours and comes to me, draping her arms around my neck and placing kisses in the canyons behind my stick-out ears. I remember the day on the banquette when she said she thought they were cute, and I grin. Her Mamie scent, flowery again, acts as a chaser of gladness and washes through me. I reach up and hold her forearms. She leans her head next to mine.

"I apologize for earlier. One of my low patches. But I took a fresh shower and fixed my makeup and hair. I even lay down for a few minutes and talked to Abigay. She always knows what I need to hear."

I wish *I* knew what she needed to hear and what Mamie felt

came between us in the first place. Did she pick up on my feelings about the money she spent on the gloves? I close my eyes as she kisses me and hope that one day I can give Mamie the kind of support that her first best friend does. *If I become her husband, I want to be her best friend too.*

"Abigay's a great friend" is what I say.

"She is."

"Come here, pretty girl," I say, taking her hand and pulling her around to face me. Her hair is down again and curling. I like that it doesn't look like the spiral curls you see on most girls these days. The curls are natural looking. I'd had a mint a few minutes before so I'm confident about taking her face in my hands and pulling her down for a kiss. The smile she gives me afterward satisfies me as though lunch is already in my belly.

"Ready for a sandwich or two?" she asks. "I brought plates and napkins."

I stand and stretch my arms and back. "Sounds great. Thanks for bringing all this down. I'll just run up and wash my hands. Anything else you need?"

She regards the bottles of water, and a playful gleam forms in her eyes. "You know what I'd *really* love? A Coke, a *real* Coke, with ice. I haven't had one in years."

I shake my head. "Man. I haven't either, not since the pandemic trounced going to theaters."

"Oh, my word, crushed theater ice," she says in the same reverential tone in which she spoke of the chocolate truffles.

"Hey, I had a protein bar earlier. But why don't you start eating and revising your work and I'll go? I'll see if I'm on my foraging game today."

"Team Rob!" She picks up one of the sturdy Chinet plates and makes a tambourine of it, striking her thigh and then pretending to rattle it. "He's awesome," she says, swirling and pounding the tambourine like Stevie Nicks on a stage. I chuckle at her enterprising spunk. She dips her chin. "I can't wait to dance with you tomorrow night."

"That *will* be fun." And then as though I need a reason to kiss her again, I do, lingering until she bops me on the head with her tambourine. "Be back soon," I say.

"Okay," she says, and swirls some more, her skirt swishing around her. "Later, Fitzy!"

Somebody pinch me. "Later, Mames."

As I pass the gallery, a uniformed policewoman and half of Isla behind a column catch my eye. I guess the missing artifact has expanded to a police investigation now. For the first time, I wonder how valuable the stolen piece is and whether or not it will be recovered. There are a lot of people coming through the lodge every day. But I wouldn't think early in the morning. Could it have been a staff member? Or someone staying here? Will they start questioning guests? I feel bad for Isla having to deal with this, especially at Christmastime when she needs to take off and be home with her family.

In the men's room, my thoughts turn to Mamie and her tambourine dance, and I find myself humming Fleetwood Mac's "The Chain." Last night, I had a dream about her in stages of undress. Though everything was gauzy and veiled, I woke up realizing how relatively pure things have been between us. Because it's wintertime, I haven't seen her in anything but long sleeves, skirts, or her jumpsuit thing. It's like she's an almond tart in a bakery window that I can see but can't eat. But my eyes have memorized her face and hands, her long graceful neck—for such a petite girl—and the hollow of her throat. When she wears her sneakers instead of her boots, like today, my eyes are lucky enough to feast on her slender ankles and the little brown mole on top of her foot just where it meets her shin. Every centimeter of those sweet places is flawless in my eyes.

How could she not be perfect all over?

If my dreams come true, I'll know.

Mamie's my first love, and it would be amazing if she were my last. I've never dated anyone so fun and sweet, so charming and bright. A man could be happy with a woman like that for a lifetime.

A smiling older couple, probably fiftyish, is seated on the bench outside Between the Trees. I nod to them, and it occurs to me that neither Mamie nor I had good marriage role models. It was Mom who was the linchpin in my parents' relationship. She was born a sweet, cheerful person and I feel like she was determined to stay that way, despite Pop's philandering. We boys were her life. She loved us well and unconditionally. Still does. As I head into the restaurant in search of crushed ice, I make a mental note to call her tomorrow.

Between the Trees is in full lunch-service swing. The beat of the Taylor Swift song "Christmas Tree Farm," which seems to loop the lodge playlist every hour, fills the space with cheer. Large tables of friends or family toast each other with glasses of wine or beer. I hope Tucker, who alternates tending bar in the lobby and the restaurant, is behind the curved black leather-sided bar and can score Mamie some crushed ice. Despite the Christmas music, the refrain from "The Chain" plays in my mind again. I remember reading that the band members wrote the song during a low patch—to poach Mamie's expression—hoping the bond between them—the chain—would keep them together, no matter what. I want a Mamie-and-Rob chain.

"My friend Fitzpatrick," calls Tucker from behind the bar, where three people are eating or having drinks. I step to the counter between two empty stools. Tucker makes a fist for mine to bump against. "How's it goin', man?" He lays a black cocktail napkin in front of me on the bar.

"Excellent, thanks." I remember that Tucker's a baseball fan. "Mamie and I are at the top of the ninth on the article."

"Awesome." Tucker polishes a glass with a white cloth and gives me a sidelong look. "I hear you're . . . gettin' along well." My empty stomach tightens, whether from the anticipation of a full-blown grilling from the guy or that of the fish whose aroma wafts the space.

"Dude, it's mostly professional. Mostly." I lean forward, my arms on the bar. "Look, things are good between us. But I haven't been to her room, if that's what you're thinking. She's a very traditional girl." My face heats, and I look around to see who may have heard the conversation.

Tucker checks a server's ticket and pours two glasses of red wine. "Ah well. That's admirable, I guess. Self-control."

"So who's talking about Mamie and me?"

He chuckles. "Oh, everybody. The staff talks." He shakes his head. "The things we see and hear. But you two are the hottest topic since the rich recluse in 434 checked in six weeks ago." Tucker scans the room and then looks back at me and pitches his voice low. "They say she orders up two bottles of wine a day. But nobody's seen her come downstairs. Anyhoo, it's the girls who're all excited about you and Mamie. Whitney started a cash Christmas bet that you would leave here in L-O-V-E."

I might as well smile. "What's the pool up to?"

"I hear seventy-five bucks. Everybody's ponied up. The first to confirm that you're in love takes all."

The only way to put an end to this grapevine game is to nip it now. "Tell Whitney you just won the pool, man. It's love. From the horse's mouth."

Tucker's face stretches into a grin. Dollar signs flash in his eyes like a cartoon character's. "Ah-right!" He slams a hand on the bar. "A drink on me!"

I chuff a laugh. "Thanks, man, but I'm not much of a day

drinker, and I have a ton to do this afternoon. But Mamie's got a craving for a *real* Coke over crushed ice. I figured the restaurant might offer crushed."

Tucker, whose eyebrows lifted at the word "craving," twists his mouth and shakes his head as though I'm missing out.

"You figured right," he says, and slides back a stainless lid on a bin. "Crushed we got."

"She'll be happy, then. Thanks."

"No sweat. Comin' right up."

I hold up two fingers. "Two, please. I've got a hankering too."

Tucker cackles and lays a second napkin down. "You got it." He pours the sodas in large glasses and sets them in front of me along with two straws that I slide in my pocket. Tucker tips me a wink. "Enjoy. Hey, I'm a fan of love as much as anybody. A victim myself."

I chuckle and pick up the glasses. "Have a good one."

I'm heading back to Mamie when new regret pummels me. Coke sloshes over the edge of one of the glasses, but the black cocktail napkin absorbs it. What have I done? Mamie's going to have a bird when she learns about Whitney's bet. The things I said to Tucker will only make it worse. Why did I open my big mouth at all, like I was some slick player? I break out in a cold sweat. Part of me wants to find Whitney and tell her to keep it on the down low. But if "everybody," as Tucker said, knows, what good would that do? Annelise and Isla probably know. And Tucker's probably telling someone what I said right now.

I stand outside the door of Spirit & Bower, fragmented. Part of me wants to come clean with Mamie now. How many summit meetings have we had about trust? And now I've betrayed hers again. We have to finish this work today. Another part of me wants to try and forget about the whole dang thing with the bet so I can do my best work—and that's for Mamie's sake.

Mamie. From the horse's mouth . . . What a jaded jerk of a line. At least I defended Mamie's honor by telling Tucker that she and I aren't sleeping together and that she's a traditional girl. Good thing we'll be down in the whiskey bar this afternoon and not around the lobby, where the staff might like to settle back with a tub of popcorn and watch us.

When we were kids and I had bad dreams or thoughts, Smoke told me to picture the bad things inside a balloon and myself with a bow and arrow. He said that when a bad thought popped up, I should pretend to shoot the arrow, pop the bubble, and conquer the fear. Channeling the great bronze warrior out front, I do that now to my fear of Mamie learning about the bet. *Zing!* A hopeful new idea takes the place of the fear and prods this "horse."

Maybe this thing is not as big of a deal as I've made it out to be.

Maybe I won't need a cardiologist after all.

Holding the Cokes in one hand, I open the door before the maybes and the ice melt.

Mamie greets me, all smiles. "Fitzy! Thanks for the Coke." I hand her the glass I didn't spill from. "And you found crushed ice. All my dreams have come true!"

I grin. "I said I'd slay the foraging." *What I didn't say was that I'd make a horse's arse out of myself and betray your confidence in the process.* I fling another arrow at the thought. *Her dreams. I wish I knew what those look like for the future. For our future. I have to make that a priority when we talk tonight.*

She takes a sip through the straw and falls back in her chair as if swooning. "Yum-mo!"

I take a sip too, and it's so good I bob my head twice. Mamie bobs hers too. Then, as though we'd rehearsed it, we end up banging our heads like the guys in *Wayne's World* do to "Bohemian Rhapsody," and then cracking up. She whips off her glasses. "We've gone slap happy," she cries between laughs.

"'*Bohemian* Rhapsody,'" I gasp, clutching my stomach.

"Oh no!" she says, and laughs until she's grabbing for napkins and wiping beneath her eyes.

I heave a breath, settling down. But the release feels good. "I can't believe you like that movie."

"You said I was full of surprises. Truthfully, I haven't seen the movie, just the old SNL skits on YouTube. Hey, are you not starved?"

"Yah, I am." I turn to the sandwich tray, from which I snare two sandwiches—one turkey and one pimento cheese—and then a bag of chips.

"I tried to wait to eat, but I sort of cheated with chips," she says. I grin and take a big bite of a sandwich. We eat in companionable silence, and fueled again, I feel incrementally better. Mamie daintily wipes her mouth with a napkin, then balls it up and pitches it at the trash barrel. "Two points."

This girl. I cannot lose her. Mamie starts collecting our plates. I stand. "Here, I can do that."

"No, sit. I've got it. Since we've nailed down the aspects of the lodge we want to use, do you mind if I work on the article while you're editing? Then I can go back and finish the captions after we've reviewed the photos."

I take a seat and use one more napkin before touching my computer. "Not at all. Good plan." Mamie weaves around the space cleaning up, her moves deft and economical. I could sit and dwell in her loveliness all day.

But the bet rears up before me. Why is love so fickle? It's infinitely more complicated than I thought it would be. Sometimes it feels like one of those amusement park tower rides. One moment you're rising to the top, filled with excitement and expectancy and reveling in the view from on high, and the next you're plummeting, your heart in your stomach. And why do I keep making the same stupid mistakes over it? I hope with Mamie it's because our time on assignment is hurtling by.

I know she's the one.

The conviction is rare and fine, and I believe it only happens once in a lifetime.

I want to make it official between us now.

I don't want to wait until we're back in Charleston and caught up in the busy distractions of our lives as we knew them. Before we were us.

Carpe diem, Fitzpatrick.

"Ooh," Mamie says, her voice sending me back to stare at my computer screen as if I'd been doing it all along. "Know what I'd really love?"

"Another Coke?"

She grins. "No, goob. I'd love to watch you edit a photo. See how it's done."

Thinking of sharing what I love to do with Mamie makes me smile. "I'll save a few for you." I take my mints from my briefcase and offer her one before taking one for myself. Mamie watches me work mine around my mouth and does the same with hers. Her grin is so big that she has a hard time keeping hers in her mouth. I know what she's thinking because it's what I'm thinking.

"Can we smooch *before* we start working?" she finally says. "I need to concentrate on the writing. And you, Fitzpatrick, are temptation itself." Grinding the rest of her mint with her molars, she stands and swallows. "In fact, we should work across the room from each other."

I laugh out loud. "Across the room?"

"I'm *serious*. And I'm putting in my noise-canceling earbuds in case Annelise comes in again."

Rob

No, not Annelise or anyone else who was in on the bet. Isla's likely still embroiled in the theft investigation, so I doubt she'll come in. But I'm left to wonder who Tucker's talked to since I ordered the Cokes. Hopefully, he worked the early shift today and has headed home. I should come clean about what I said about Mamie, and the sooner the better.

Now she slinks over and perches on my lap the way she did this morning after she bought me the gloves, her smile demure. Our kiss is slow and lush. I adore her and still want to make it up to her for the way I reacted when she gave me the gloves.

When our mouths part, I look deep into her green eyes. "Mamie, I need to tell you how extraordinarily warm and helpful the gloves were this morning. They were a super thoughtful gift. I mean it."

She bends to touch her forehead to mine. "That makes me so happy."

"*You* make me so happy."

I kiss her again. But seconds later, she springs to her feet. "Now to the far side, I go."

"Just don't go to the dark side."

"Ha," she says, gathering her things. True to her word, she moves to the other side of the bar and a table near a portrait of a Native American man wearing a vibrant feathered headdress. She sets up with her back to me, and I watch as she moves her head from side to side to insert her earbuds, her beautiful strawberry hair swinging with her movements.

Head in the game, Fitzpatrick, I tell myself, and pull up my editing software once more.

CHAPTER EIGHTEEN

Mamie

At four o'clock, I hit send on an email to my editor at the magazine, the completed article attached. Since I've versed her on the new deadline, I'm confident she'll send her revision notes ASAP. I stand and do a series of shoulder rolls before glancing back at Rob, who's still head down over his computer, his mouth downturned with concentration, his shirtsleeves rolled up. My double take makes my hair swing. His forearms. Oh, my word. They're not as swole with muscle as Brett's batting arms were, but they seem the perfect size for Rob. How could anything about Rob Fitzpatrick be anything but perfection? I want a close-up view of those arms, but I don't want to disturb his concentration. I hope he's almost done with the photo editing. We have to be out of the bar by five.

I want to go to the ladies' room, but I have to walk right past him to get to the door. I slide my chair quietly up to the table and head that way. Rob looks up and flinches, knocking a pen off the table. "Are you almost done?" I ask softly, and move to look at his screen. He smacks a few keys and swiftly closes the laptop. *Is he gatekeeping something?*

Color moves from his collar to his hairline. He clears his throat. "Yah. All done."

My brows want to come together, but I manage to arrange

my face in a bright affect. "I thought I'd run to the restroom before we look at the photos," I say, willing my eyes away from his table and from his arms, which are lightly covered with smooth, soft-looking dark hair. The color fades from his face, and as though the blush were contagious, it blossoms onto mine.

Rob stands and surveys his workspace. "I need to go up too. I'll be right behind you." He smiles tightly. "Did you submit the article?"

"Just did. My editor has it." I look at the clock. "If we don't get your photos reviewed before five, we'll have to find another place to do that. And I'm sure I'll have to make revisions when I get her notes back."

"Right. Maybe the library will be quiet. People will probably be headed to happy hours at that time."

"Right. See how calm and flexible we are?" I grin. "I like us."

"I like us too. See you in a few."

When he doesn't smile or use an endearment, my sus level ratchets. What's he up to?

Upstairs, where Kacey Musgraves's "Glittery" strews musical festivity around the lobby, I see Isla and Annelise, who both appear to be with clients in the gallery. They glance up as I go by, Isla solemn faced and Annelise with lifted brows and a jubilant smile. With our time crunch, I don't have the time to parse either reaction, and I refuse to let them wriggle their way into my mind.

When I've refreshed my lipstick and left the restroom, I turn toward the bar stairs again. Rob, who must have already been in and out of the men's room, catches up with me. *On what planet does a woman ever beat a man coming out of a restroom?* "Hi there, beautiful. Ready to bring this project home?"

Home. Things were so simple before I left Charleston. Before I fell in love.

"I am." I smile at him and then give myself a quick lecture.

You are not the man's handler. As long as his part of the work gets done, it's not your business what he does on his computer. But why did he blush and shut the lid down the way he did? He reaches for my hand and I give it to him. As always, his palm feels exquisite against mine, and that puts a damper on the doubt that has been like a phone that wouldn't stop ringing in my head.

We head down the stairs. "Want to go through the edited ones first, then look at the one I saved for you?" he asks.

"Sure. That's fine."

In Spirit & Bower again, I peer at the clock and wonder if my eyes are bleary with computer fatigue, or if what they say is true and I'm going love-blind. "What time is it?"

He grimaces and scratches his shoulder. "Forty-nine minutes 'til we get the boot."

"I cannot see worth a flip." I pull off my glasses; the edges are smeary. At least I'm not losing my sight. "My glasses need cleaning." Rob's big hand starts into his pocket, but I pull a lens wipe from my skirt pocket with a flourish. "I actually have one today." Then it dawns on me, and I hold my glasses aloft. "These are kissing smears!"

Rob laughs. "Sorry about that. You may have to start taking them off because I'm obsessed with your lips and my box of wipes is running low."

Obsessed with my lips. "I like *that*, Fitzy." I clean my glasses, slip them on, and the world's clear again. If only a tool existed that could make emotions, thoughts, and motives clear.

The minutes careen by. We take a quick seat at Rob's table, and as he opens his laptop, his editing software fills the screen. "The stone egg. It looks terrific."

"Thank you. It was a challenge because of its dimensionality. I wanted to show its openness, the thing that draws people to sit in it. I got shots from several angles, but thought this one was the best. What do you think?"

"It looks very inviting—just not for me," I say prissily.

His shoulders quake with laughter. "Right. Okay, next." He pauses, his fingers on his trackpad. "I *should* save this one for last, but I'm dying for you to see it." He scrolls ahead, then leans back to watch my reaction. It's the shot of Marco welcoming the guests at the entrance. The older couple that Rob has situated in profile is smiling at him and is as festively dressed as I'd hoped. The attractive lady looks smart in a red coat, a shade or two darker than mine, a matching wool cloche hat, and black velvet gloves. The gentleman is dapper in a hunter-green blazer with a denim shirt and Scottish clan–red tartan slacks. His posture is like that of a palace guard. "Oh, Fitzy, it's a *beautiful picture*—so full of life and joy and festivity. Who wouldn't scramble to make a rezzy and be welcomed here like that?"

Rob sighs happily and holds a frame made of his big hands around my face as if to capture my expression, then kisses me through it. "Do you recognize them?"

I study their faces as best I can in profile. "*May-be*. Did we ride up in the elevator with them one night?"

"We did. Anyway, they're the Joneses, Betty and Gary, and super nice. They drove down from Winston-Salem to explore Greenville and spend Christmas at the lodge. Oh, and to celebrate their sixtieth wedding anniversary."

I shake my head. "That's like *breaking news* these days." I smile at the Joneses' images and note the way their faces seem to glow before studying the rest of the photo. "Enchanting. Fitzpatrick, you are amazing."

My compliments must have struck deep. With pursed lips, Rob shifts in his chair, dips his chin, and murmurs a short "Thank you." I go on. "I had a younger couple in mind, but I think you found the perfect pair. This photo will draw more sophisticates to the Bohemian and those who may be art collectors, which the management will appreciate."

"A win-win. If we always tackled all our assignments as a team, you'd be president of marketing."

I laugh lightly because I'm sure he's joking. But my thoughts ping the corners of the room. From what fount did that idea spring? A journalistic partnership? Rob and me in business together? We're compatible, our skill sets and visions complement each other, and we're building trust. But he's leaping continents ahead. We have a boatload more to consider about our *personal* relationship. And as soon as possible. The days are galloping toward Monday.

"Let's bounce, Fitzpatrick," I say, and then slide my chin from left to right. He grins and advances the screen to a shot of the library. I stare at the image. "You made it look so big! It's . . . like a real estate photo that makes a Barbie Dreamhouse–sized kitchen look cavernous. How did you accomplish that and still manage to make it look cozy and inviting?"

"Barbie Dreamhouse. Ha! Your imagery slays me, Morrow. So to make the library look larger, I used a wide-angle lens with a sixteen-millimeter focal length. That's probably more than you wanted to know. But how the room's decorated is what makes it look cozy."

"Huh. Yeah, the masculine palette works well in there. And the fresh flowers are a softening juxtaposition. Ooh," I say, taking a closer look. "You got the corn maiden. Thanks for that."

"You bet."

I picture the beaded maiden from Tate's box where I placed her on a shelf in the apartment kitchen. Abigay and I thought she looked charming there with our odds-and-ends collection of blue-and-white dishes. "It will appeal to women and little girls," I say to Rob.

We move through more photos, sometimes pausing to relive the memories of when he took them: the bronze warrior; the great lobby fir (which I still can't believe he caught me hiding behind), on which Rob has used a filter to make the ornaments appear to twinkle; the handsome whiskey bar filled with convivial patrons and poinsettias; the luminous exterior sunrise shot from the first day; and a view of the falls from a porch table at Between the Trees, in which he's brilliantly captured the impatient quality of the water.

"The photos are spectacular!"

"Thank you, sweetheart. I've been meaning to tell you that the warmth of the gloves helped me steady my hands."

His words are like a Brahms sonata to my ears. "I'm so glad."

Something stirs inside me. *Brahms?* A lullaby. There's a memory buried there. Tate wouldn't have listened to Brahms. Or would he? It still makes me sad that I didn't learn more about him. I look down, away from Rob and the photograph, hoping it will help me unearth a recollection, but my eyes fall on the time. "Snap. We have to be out of here in fifteen. What's left? The purple banquette! You got it, didn't you?"

"Yah huh." *Of course, he did. How could I doubt his thoroughness?* "I think they should," he says as he moves to the next frame, "put a plaque on it with our names."

I forget for the moment about our time crunch and snuggle closer to him. "Yah, they should. If velvet tufting could talk . . ." He laughs, and I kiss him on the corner of his mouth before looking back at the photo and pointing at the screen. "Now, who are the people?"

"Oh, decorator clients of Isla's. They're here looking for prints from the gallery. They were tickled, in their words, about being in the magazine."

The gallery. The theft. "Have they made progress with the investigation?"

"Not that I know of. They seem to be playing it close to the vest. Somebody said it was one of those big necklaces."

A gust of cool, bright air sweeps my mind. Earlier a concern had drifted into the part of my brain where unspoken things are stored. I'd worried that the thief might have taken the beautiful bracelet that I thought looked so much like the one from my grandfather's box.

Rob tilts the laptop screen so we can see the photos more closely. "Here we go," he says, suddenly as happy as a dog with two tails to wag, "this is the one I saved to edit with you. To show you what I do."

The art theft slides from the front burner of my mind to the back. "Yippy skippy!"

He chuckles at my expression and taps my nose with a finger, then slides a graphics tablet and digital pen from his briefcase. "Okay. In most photos, there are elements you want to stand out for the observer, and others you want to de-emphasize, make them fade into the background. When you look at an image, your eye is drawn toward the lighter areas of the scene and away from the darker ones. I use a method called 'dodge and burn' to guide the viewer's eye. Dodging lightens and emphasizes objects or areas, and burning darkens and de-emphasizes them." On the screen, Rob indicates the table behind the banquette and the cedar wall sculpture above it. "These aren't relevant to the theme of the banquette itself, so I'm going to burn them." With a series of strokes on the pen tablet, he darkens the objects so they seem to fade into the background. "Same with the agate sculpture, but not as much burn."

I watch, mesmerized, as he dodges the banquette itself so that it pops and then does the same with the people on the bench. My mind returns to the photo of the couple at the entrance. "Fitzpatrick . . . the photo of the Joneses you showed me first. Did you dodge their faces to make them shine?"

He slowly smiles. "Nuh. That's the natural glow of lasting love. No photographer could replicate that."

I turn to him. "What a beautiful thing to say."

"Thank you, Mames." He kisses my cheek and then trails his lips to the lobe of my ear. The wings my heart grew the night of our first kiss flutter and grow strong beneath my sweater.

I take a shaky breath and shove my longing aside. "Fitzy, what are we *doing*? The article! We're so close to the end now."

He grimaces. "I can't help myself. Loving on you makes me lose my mind."

I sit up straight and motion for him to do the same. "C'mon, Fitzpatrick. We can do this." I turn my attention to the computer screen. The *banquette*. I study the photo carefully. "Now what about the women's purses? And that shopping bag on the floor? Should you burn them too?"

"You're a fast study, Morrow. You drive." He nudges the laptop my way and lets me burn the bags so that they don't catch the eye at first study.

"Fitzpatrick," I whisper, "this is magic. Who knew?"

He grins. "All photographers."

I give his shoulder a little shove and then shift to face him. I trace the curve of his face with my fingers. "I'm so grateful Farida hired you. Not only because I'm crazy about you but because this article is going to"—I throw up my hands and sweep them wide—"make one *cannonball* of a splash. Farida said you'd make my words shine." I place a hand on his chest. "And you have. You are."

He moves a hand up to press into my side and pull me closer. "You make my *soul* shine," he says.

In the chiming silver moment, I understand that my heart, wings and all, belongs to Rob Fitzpatrick. He leans in for a kiss, and my lids lazily close. A clamor sweeps into the bar. We jerk to attention, our floundering hands struggling to land in businesslike poses as Josh troops in through a back entrance, trailed by Whitney and Tucker.

"Well, hey, guys," Josh says. "How's the project going?"

"Hello." My voice comes out as husky as Lauren Bacall's in an old film noir. I clear my throat. "Very well. We're pretty close to being done."

Rob recovers his powers of speech. "Sorry we're still here so close to opening time."

"I mean, it's cool if you stay a while," Josh says, "but it may get loud in here."

Whitney, who's grinning like Lewis Carroll's cat, looks around at the other servers. "Couldn't Mamie and Rob set up in the break room? I mean," she says slyly, "unless they want to take it upstairs."

I glance at Rob, who has begun clenching and unclenching his jaw. I assume it's because of Whitney's calculating remark, which didn't surprise me because something I've learned about her has spoken volumes about her impetuous character.

Tucker says, "Hey, hey, Whit. That's enough."

"Use the room," Josh says, looking at the other staff members and rolling his eyes. "None of us will be getting a break tonight."

I nudge Rob's leg under the table with mine. "We could do that," I say as a half question for Rob and half answer for the server. Rob replies by closing his laptop and getting to his feet. A bevy of laughing women enter the bar. We gather our things, and Josh kindly offers to show us to the break room. Rob goes ahead of me and seems to avoid Whitney-the-walking-smirk as assiduously as I do. She won't ruin our evening.

We step into a corridor. To the right, I can see into a private dining room, from which Christmas music softly tinkles. People dressed to the nines are merrily gathering around an on-trend rattan bar in the back. Along the length of the white-cloth-draped dining table is a runner made of fresh magnolia and white pine with flourishes of pheasant feathers and red ornaments. Someone slips from the crowd and trumpets, "Mamie Anson!"

Rob turns to stare at me, his brows lifting and then coming together as my stomach does a backflip. I answer, "Hello, Pink. It's been a long time."

CHAPTER NINETEEN

Rob

J osh turns back and sees that Mamie has stopped to talk with the man who called out to her, so he simply points out the door of the break room for me before heading back toward the bar. My mind is so blown, a nod of thanks is all I'm able to muster. Mamie *Anson? Who is this guy?*

Mamie pipes up. She extends her hand in my direction. "Rob, this is Pink Rembert, an old friend and neighbor from Charleston."

"It's uh, Pinkney now," the guy booms.

I extend my hand. "Rob Fitzpatrick," I say as Pinkney, formerly known as Pink, whom I suddenly recall was Mamie's rich, retainer-wearing first kiss, studies me and pumps my hand.

"Pinkney. Nice to meet you."

Mamie's smiling up at me. But I stand there in the blue shirt I washed last night and ironed this morning, feeling like a rube until the man's eyes travel the curved highway of my girl's frame. My hackles rise until they must be visible on my back.

Oblivious, Mamie speaks up. "I am a journalist now. Rob's a photographer," she says, and lays a cool hand on my back. My hackles recede slightly. "We're here to cover the hotel for a Christmas issue of *Charleston Á La Mode* magazine."

"Nice. You always were good with words. Where'd you end

up going to school?" He folds his arms over his chest. Gold cuff links wink below his suit sleeves. If he's married, he's not wearing a wedding ring.

"Thank you. SCAD. I studied fine art before earning a master's in writing. What about you?"

"I'm a Duke man." *Translation: I'm kind of a big deal.* "I'm an architect with my dad's firm now."

"Good for you. I'm sure your dad's happy."

Pinkney smiles and rocks back on his heels. Whiskey fumes gust over us. Then, almost toppling, the guy reaches out to clutch the doorframe, his face magenta.

"Oh yes, he is. He is."

The Duke man is short with platinum blond hair and glacier-blue eyes. At his throat is a pink bow tie. I bet it's a superfluous signature tie and that he has a drawerful of them in a fancy dressing room. Even his cheeks are pink. But it looks more like chronic alcohol flush than what my mom calls roses in your cheeks. Like the ones in Mamie's.

Pink beams at her now, his dignity recovered. He tweaks his tie. "Are you in Greenville now?" he asks. An older woman in a multicolored bouclé suit—I know the style because my mom would point it out whenever Kate Middleton wore one on TV—clips around the door of the private room and sidles up to Pinkney. Simpering, she brushes something from the shoulder of his suit before taking his arm.

"Mother, look who it is. Mamie. From Tradd Street."

"Well, my gracious!" she exclaims, recognizing Mamie. "Mamie dear, how delightful to see you."

"Hello, Mrs. Rembert. It's very nice to see you as well." Mrs. Rembert's piercing eyes the color of her son's rivet me.

As the woman seems to inventory my attire, Mamie says, "I'm so pleased to introduce to you Robert Fitzpatrick." *Pleased to introduce?* I guess you can't wash South of Broad out of the girl.

"I'm very pleased to meet you, Mrs. Rembert," I say, Mamie's marionette.

"Quite," she offers. "Will you be joining the party then?"

Pinkney asserts, "No, Mother. Mamie and *Robert* are journalists here on an *assignment*. I was just asking Mamie if she relocated to Greenville."

Mrs. Rembert titters and gives her son's arm a little shake. "Well, I could have told you that, son. Colleen and I still play bridge once a month. Mamie has remained in the Holy City."

"Right-o," Pinkney responds.

His mother's gaze bookends Mamie and me. "I must tell your mother that I saw you at the Grand Bohemian with . . . *Robert*, and looking so . . . well."

"Thank you, Mrs. Rembert," Mamie says, and then to my surprise, smiles up at me and takes my hand. "Rob and I have a deadline to meet this evening. Will you please excuse us?" My hackles flatten and my shoulders rise.

Mrs. Rembert sputters, "Oh my. Yes, of course."

"Merry Christmas to you both," says Mamie.

"Merry Christmas, Mrs. Rembert and . . . *Pink*," I say as Mamie tugs at my hand. We turn in the opposite direction and make for the break room.

"Merry Christmas" trails after us, followed by a "Did you see the—" from the ridiculous Mrs. Rembert.

In the well-appointed staff break room, which nevertheless reeks of leftover sandwiches and bug spray, a combo that doesn't inspire confidence, Mamie leans back against the door and hoots with laughter. I stand silently, waiting. *Did she not pick up on my feelings of confusion and unease?* She finally lets out a great breath. "Whoo! Remember me telling you about Pink? I can't believe I've run into the Remberts at the GBL! Awful, aren't they?"

"Yeah, I remember. But it took me a minute."

"This computer bag is digging a trench in my skin. Man, it stinks in here. So much for the glamorous life of a journalist, huh?" She glances at me and then shrugs as if she can't deal with any more drama, then makes her way to the big table at the room's center and starts to set her bag down. But she swoops it back up into her arms. "This surface is unacceptable. Gross! Can't people clean up after themselves, or would that be asking for too much adulting?" She shakes her head and scans the kitchenette along one wall. "Let's find something to clean it with." She fixes her green eyes on me. "Want to help?" When I don't answer, she finally seems to notice my reticence. She looks at the door. "What? I thought you'd laugh too about what happened out there with Charleston society's finest."

I run a hand through my hair. "When were you planning to tell me?"

"What, for Pete's sake, about my torrid love affair with Pink-*ney* Rembert?" She snatches paper towels from a dispenser above the sink and lays them out on the counter. "Here, let's set our bags on this until we can clean the table." She raises her bag with an "oof" and sets it on the counter. I set my leather satchel beside it. She rubs her arm and looks over her glasses at me. "C'mon, Fitzpatrick. Will you at least find an outlet? See if there's one near the table?" She crouches down and opens an under-sink cabinet. She pivots to me, a plastic cylinder of Clorox Wipes in one hand. "Okay. Okay. What is it?"

"When were you planning to tell me your real last name?"

"Oh, my word," she says, standing and smacking her forehead. "I didn't think. *Truly*, Rob. That's what's bothering you?"

"Didn't you think I'd be mildly curious about hearing

you called by a name I've never heard? You could have been divorced or something, for all I know."

She sets the wipes on the dirty table. "No, no, no. Anson is my last name, my real one. Morrow is my middle name and my mother's maiden name." She props her fists on her hips. "*Nobody* calls me Mamie Anson anymore. Pink just did because I haven't seen him in, like, ten years. And you know how I love alliteration. Mamie Morrow makes me feel all shiny."

"I'm just nonplussed that you've kept it from me."

"Rob. Sweetheart. We've barely known each other for a week. People can't cover every detail of their lives in that time. I wasn't intentionally keeping it from you. It *truly* hadn't entered my mind."

"Your name isn't exactly a minor detail."

She huffs a sigh and begins ripping Clorox Wipes from the container, scattering them along the table. "Okay, Rob. I'm sorry I failed you there. But look at the clock. Can we perform a postmortem of my behavior after we finish work?"

I close my eyes and nod several times in reply. She turns and attacks the grime on the table. *She's right. We don't have to talk about it now. But how many other things that she considers minor is she still holding back? And then I'm sucker punched right in the glory of my self-righteousness.* I hang my head. *I haven't laid down all my cards with her either. But my stuff depends on timing, on other people, and on how things pan out the next day or so. Soon she'll know everything.* "Here," I say, reaching out for the wipes. I'll do that."

"Well, thank you. This stuff's murder on the cuticles. Oh, there's an outlet. Let's sit at this end of the table." She slides a chair out and examines it. "Hope these aren't nasty too."

"I'll wipe them down."

"Thanks," she says with a small smile. "Oh, there's a sawed-off wooden wedge there in the corner. A doorstop. Okay if I crack the door open for a bit? Too bad these basement rooms don't have windows."

"Really," I say.

Mamie props the door open. But minutes later, the brassy and shrill racket from the private room propels her to close it again.

When we're finally situated at the table, she looks at me and places a palm over the back of my hand. "You know what?" she says gently. "You don't have to stay while I write the captions. You could take a break. Go upstairs and get some air. I could text you when I'm ready for you to approve them."

Maybe she wants me to leave. And I wouldn't blame her if she did. But no way I'm leaving her alone down here in this place. "Yah nuh. You're stuck with me. We're a team. A wicked good one. *Morrow* and Fitzpatrick."

"That's nice," she says shortly, but keeps her eyes to herself.

"I've got a couple of protein bars in my bag. Want one?"

"Please and thank you." We start on the bars and Mamie readdresses her work. "Here goes," she says as though it's for her benefit. But her hands falter on the keyboard. "Rob. I don't want to start our night with this name thing hanging over our heads."

I swallow a bite of the bar and then give a great sigh of relief. "I don't either. It's just . . . how can we move forward without communicating better than we do?"

"We can't," she says.

My circulatory system reverses. *What have I done? Have I driven her to the point of giving up on us? The way she introduced me as Robert to the Remberts, like she was trying to dress up a chimp, chafed me. But then she took my hand, and that felt like an affirmation, proof that she's with me. If anyone disapproves, they can take a flying leap.*

Mamie rolls back the wrapper on her bar and takes a big bite. *Am I that insecure? Do I still think I'm not good enough for her? I need to talk to Seamus, the real father figure in my life. The one who's honest and reliable. The one who's never failed me.*

In the spirit of communication, I feel like I should offer Mamie something I'm free to divulge now. "I haven't told you about something either," I say to the top of the table before giving her an oblique peek.

Her straight shoulders sag. "Oh, Rob," she says as if she's thinking, *What now?*

"Whitney started a bet. About us. That we would fall in love before leaving here."

Mamie props her elbows on the table and plants her chin on her folded hands. "Fitzpatrick. I *know* about the bet."

I press my lips into a firm line to keep my mouth from gaping open. "You do?"

She takes a quick look at the big black-and-white institutional clock on the wall. "I overheard Whitney and the part-time desk clerk—I can never think of her name. Oh well. They were talking at the vanity in the ladies' room, not knowing I was in a stall. The other girl said that watching us cuddle was like being in the middle of a great new romance novel. *And* that you are incredibly hot, by the way. The bet was Whitney's idea. Silly and high schoolish, I know. But it still felt disrespectful. I stayed in the stall, toying with the idea of bebopping out to mess with their heads, but finally decided to blow it off." She smiles. "I did flush the commode, though, and they hightailed it out of there." She takes another bite of her bar.

I have to smile at her pluck before going grim again and facing up to my confession. "I agree we should blow it off at this point. We're bigger than that. But, Mamie, *I'm* the one who confirmed the truth about us falling in love. To Tucker when I was getting our Cokes."

She chews her bite for an agonizingly long time and then swallows. "I know."

I almost drop my last piece of the bar. "How?"

"Tucker told me this afternoon when I saw him on the way to the ladies' room. Before you made it upstairs. He was real sweet and apologetic about it but also glad to know that we had defined the relationship. Well, to be literal, *you* did."

"I know. I'm sorry. He put me on the spot. I thought it would nip the whole thing in the bud. But I was also trying to be a cool guy and ended up being an idiot."

"But you're *my* idiot. And I'm sure I'll get a chance to be yours one of these days."

Relief makes me crack up. Then I take her hand. "Mames, you amaze me. You couldn't be more wonderful."

"I don't care who knows that I love you. I'll tear into Between the Trees later. Jump up on the bar and let the room know we're in love. Like the head cheerleader at a pep rally with a megaphone. Not that there's anyone left who doesn't know yet," she says with a grin.

"So we forgive and forget and go up there tonight with our heads held high. Then make out on the banquette."

"Ha! Yah huh," she says. "I like the way you think."

Our status quo restored, Mamie opens her caption template. She hears back from her editor with notes on the piece but decides to plod through the captions before tackling the next task. But when she looks at my finished photos again, her inspiration geysers. "Robert Edward Fitzpatrick! These pictures would give Ansel Adams a wicked bad case of imposter syndrome."

"Woman," I deadpan, "don't tempt me with your Boston speak. It could lead to distracting behavior."

She grins. "But we're going to be . . . the next big thing in Charleston."

"Only in Charleston?"

"Planet wide!" she says, creating a giant sphere with her arms and hands.

"Okay, then."

I watch the template as Mamie populates it with keystrokes that become letters, letters that become words, and words that become sentences infused with imagery that flows from her creative mind. Most captions you read are parched and technical, matter-of-fact, but hers are insightful with little surprises that will send the reader back to take another look at the photos. She said my photos would make her words shine, but her words reflect a glow that will make the reader linger over the pages, hand the open magazine to a friend, and say, "Read this."

On our first day she told me she couldn't stand someone reading over her shoulder, but now that she's in her element, she seems to like me being here to support her. I think she's growing into her best, confident, and happy self. I hope we both are. With my insecurity, I seem to be lagging behind.

When she's halfway through the photos, she stretches her neck and looks at me. "Want to take a short break, or work straight through dinner and, as Tucker says, 'Get 'er done'? Our night together would be longer, and we could really relax."

"I'll do you one better. How 'bout I go grab some tacos? We can't stink this place up any more than it is."

"Brilliant!" she proclaims. "And two more Cokes?" She pops up as though she's been submerged. "I'll go this time."

"No. No worries. Let me go so you can keep working." I put my hand on the head of my bobbing cork of a girl and push her toward her seat.

I rush upstairs to grab my scarf and gloves and take a whiz before heading out to get the tacos. When I stride from the elevator, checking my weather app, it says the temperature is dropping and going below freezing both tonight and tomorrow night. There are even snowflake symbols on those daily pages. When I called my mom last night to check in, she said Boston had gotten sixteen inches from the recent storm. But Kwame at the front desk, who wishes me a good evening, says, "We don't get excited about a prediction of snow in Greenville. A dusting is about it." His voice goes low, and he makes his eyes shifty. "Those snowflakes on the app? It's a conspiracy to make us keep looking for updates." I laugh and agree with him. "See you later, man."

Crossing the bridge to downtown, my belly makes bearlike growls. I can't wait to feed it a taco. I wonder if they will be part of Mamie's and my meet-cute memories. I picture us at some random stovetop making tacos together, Mamie in a pretty vintage apron, tied to show off her slender waist.

But where would that be? I want her more than anything I've ever wanted in my life, even photography. But I can't make a home for her in a garage apartment that smells of must and the occasional whiff of motor oil. Or drive her around in an old Nissan with coffee-stained cloth seats. She was raised in a mansion South of Broad, while my financial status still treads water. When it comes to learning each other's truths, finances are a hot-button topic. I have to breach the subject with her. My mom taught us that talking about money outside the family was uncouth. Refinement and good manners were a big thing with her, and she had her work cut out for her with a couple of my brothers. But I'm a man now, and half the money management responsibility in this adult relationship will be mine.

I reach the colored-light-swagged taco truck and stand in line. In front of me is a girl with strawberry hair, but its color could never compete with that of my girl's. *Mamie*. We've talked about my upbringing more than hers. The things she's told me about Colleen and the kind of mother she was, and is, makes me sad. But it also makes Mamie all the more extraordinary in my eyes for her blithe spiritedness.

I rub the fine leather of my gloves together. When she gave me the gift, it made me wonder what a magazine pays a features editor. And though she and Abigay share the rent on a two-bedroom apartment that's part of a house in a hip neighborhood near downtown, the rent can't be cheap. But if Mamie has the jack I think she has, uncouth or not, I can't propose until I get some perspective.

A thing like money can't come between us.

I want her to be mine. *Soon.* We could date for a year and get to know more about each other, but why wait? The almost instant bond that formed between us is remarkable and rare. I want our forever to start as soon as possible.

Some guys are yukking it up in line, and I think of my brothers again. I can just imagine the way they'd freak out about me marrying a rich girl. I believe my mother would understand and approve, but Mamie's might not. I wonder how she views romantic love. Did she ever really experience it?

I step up, next in line now, and think of Mrs. Rembert, who is probably still at the lodge. With *Pinkney.* If she and Mamie's mother are good friends, Colleen could be as awful as Mrs. Rembert. If she learned we were getting married, she could make things tough on Mamie. That would crush me like a soda can beneath a semi tire. She and her mother are not close. If they've been in touch since we've been in Greenville, Mamie hasn't mentioned it. But she's a grown woman. Her mother should allow her to live life on her terms.

Back at the lodge with a warm plastic bag of tacos that are making me salivate, I'm hoping I don't run into the Remberts. I don't spot them in the lively lobby crowd. But though it's well past gallery closing time, I can see Isla, who appears to be packing up her things for the night. I hope they've solved the theft, but the bent stem of her neck tells me otherwise.

"Hi, Rob," she calls as I pass on the way to get the Cokes. "May I have a word?"

While my empty stomach clenches, my tongue begins forming the automatic Boston y-sound at the beginning of "yah huh," but I catch it and upshift to the formal "Yes, of course." I'm embarrassed to be standing in a crime scene and with a bag of stinking tacos. I try to telescope and make myself small—which is impossible—so I position myself behind a pillar between the gallery and the lobby. "What's going on?" I ask.

Isla's fair-skinned but today she's, like the song says, a whiter shade of pale. "Rob, this hasn't been announced, but one of the pieces that was taken"—*There was more than one?*— "was the silver-and-turquoise bracelet that captivated Mamie so."

The taco smell wafts from the bag. My legs threaten to fold. I spread my hands wide. "Isla, I swear on my life, there is *no way* that Mamie had anything to do with this. Her character is sterling. She was still upstairs that morning anyway." I stare at Isla, trying to read her reaction, and I see her making a similar assessment of me.

Finally, she lets go a breath. "Okay, Rob. I had to ask. There are few suspects."

Dread makes my scalp feel too tight. "Please. *Please, Isla.* Don't mention this to Mamie."

This secret I'll keep to protect the woman I love.

Despite the fluting of Christmas music, Isla's silence swells until it drums in my ears. Finally, she answers. "I won't. But know that the investigation is still hot. I'm hoping that with the loose lips around here, the local news doesn't get wind of it."

My ship can't sink.

In the break room, Mamie's back and neck are a comma over her computer. I go in and set the two Cokes and the bag of tacos quietly on the kitchenette counter. The room that feels as if it knows no day or night still smells of lunch leftovers and a trace of Clorox. But a new scent, effort, now meets my nose. Mamie types on but straightens a bit and holds up a wait-a-sec finger. Her face is nearly the pale of Isla's. *Isla.* The bracelet will not be part of my thoughts again tonight. *Watch, Smoke, I'm letting an arrow fly, brother!* My mind clears of the worry. But I sit uselessly wishing there was something I could do to help Mamie reach her goal. I could rub the knots from her shoulders, but that would likely be too distracting.

Abruptly, she looks up at me, and color washes into her face once more. "Fitzpatrick! You won't believe it: the captions are done, and I've revised a third of the article. It's looking good."

"Congratulations. That's huge progress."

She sits back and does a series of shoulder lifts. *Snap, crackle, pop.*

I raise my brows. "I bet that felt good."

"It did."

"Do you want to break for some early dinner"—I grin and hold up the bag—"or what passes for it?"

"I'll wait a few. But please go ahead, sweetheart."

"Ready for your fresh Coke?"

She falls back against the metal chair, her limbs splayed. "Yes. I'd love it. Thank you so much." I punch a straw into a cup and carry it to her. "Would you mind or feel comfortable"—she raises a shoulder—"giving me a little shoulder massage?"

I'd had the heart of a lonely man, but now everything has changed, everything's different. "At your service, my lady," I say.

"Oh, Fitzy, I always knew you were a prince." She fishes through her bag, retrieves an elastic hair thingy, and puts her long hair up and out of my way. I move behind her chair. Her shoulders are so small. Not bony. Sweetly rounded and firm. Wondering if she played sports, I carefully use the pads of my big thumbs to apply pressure to the points that I know hours of computer work can slay. "That's fabulous," she murmurs.

Despite steeping in the smells of the room, Mamie's hair smells of lemons. And honey. I bend low to kiss her along the part and then move down to her ear. I like that her jewelry is minimal. Her pearl earrings are likely real. She says she wears them every day, so I assume they're her only pair. Maybe I should have mentioned that to the curator. Why would a woman, a reputable and professional writer with a style as spare as Mamie's, steal jewelry, even if it was made by Native American craftsmen and reminded her of her grandfather? It would be like a nun getting a tattoo.

Mamie moans, practically cooing. I'd love to hear that coo for the rest of my life. I take the earring between my lips. She gives my cheek a light get-away swipe of her nails. "Hey, hey, I'm projecting an eight o'clock submission. *Latest.* If you keep that up, I won't make it." Grimacing, I give her upper arms one last squeeze. "That was so relaxing," she says, smiling up at me. "You put me to rights."

"I'm happy it helped."

She takes a long sip from her straw. "Oh, my word, nectar of the gods," she says before addressing her computer again. She wakes her sleeping home screen with a key tap. "I've been picturing Farida pacing in her stilettos, waiting for my email. Checking her phone every five minutes."

I laugh. "She probably is. But don't rush the rest."

"I won't. You know what? I think I *will* take a minute to eat a taco, though. They smell good."

"Keep your seat. I'll get it."

I forage for a couple of paper plates and plastic forks, score some that look clean, and plate two tacos for Mamie. "These can be our appetizers," I say, "but I want you to have a good meal tonight."

"That's sweet. You nurture me, Fitzy."

"I want to."

She smiles around a wolfish bite of taco. "I feel that. How 'bout we nurture each other?"

My phone clock says 7:25. The swift hands of the ugly wall clock agree. Its tick is loud enough, but its tock is jarring. I remember that inexorable sound as I closed in on the last questions of an exam at Fisher College. The tocks of this clock almost drown out everything. The sustained muffled roar of the party down the hall. The tapping of Mamie's fingers on her keyboard. The crinkle of a taco wrapper when she takes a bite. The crushed ice as it melts, shifting and settling in our cups.

I scarf my second taco and check my email. The word I'd hoped to receive earlier today has finally raised the population of my inbox by one. It's an enthusiastic reply. But again, something I will be telling Mamie later. I sip on my straw to stifle a tooth-baring grin, and then compose a grateful and graceful response that would have sent my English professor into rhapsodies of delight.

Mamie pushes back in her chair with a great screech of metal. "It's a wrap!"

"What? Already?"

"Yep. I just proofed it and attached it to an email bound for the boss. Want to be the one to hit send on our project?"

Not only am I a good sport, but I'm also her biggest fan.

"Sure." At the rap of my finger on the send button, the momentous job zips away as if it had been a fly.

Mamie gets to her feet. "We did it, Fitzpatrick!"

"We did it together. Morrow and Fitzpatrick."

"No more business talk tonight, mister," she insists. "It's time to celebrate!"

I hug her and whirl her around. She kisses my cheek and I pout. "No lips?"

"Not with *this* toxic taco breath."

We add our trash to the leftovers of others in the big barrel and then, as if we had discussed it, I pull the huge trash bag from the can and Mamie ties it off. "It's the right thing to do," she says as I drag the bag into the hallway. We gather our things from the break room.

"I say try and leave a place better than you found it."

"I like that. Boy Scouts?"

I smile. "Treasa Fitzpatrick."

"I can't wait to meet that sweet lady," she gushes, then gives me a double take. "I mean, I hope to meet her one day."

You will if my plans pan out. "She'd sure love you," I say aloud, and hold the door for her.

When we enter the hallway, we're bombarded with music from the private room, where the party is still going strong. Mamie raises a shoulder and gives her sweater a sniff, then makes a face. "That stink had a presence. I hope it's not in my pores."

I laugh. "It's not in your *pores*."

"Still, it's early enough to take another shower and change."

"Don't change too much," I tease her.

She grins. "I won't."

"I'm showering again too."

"Then we'll be ready to par-ty! Do you realize tomorrow is the first day that we don't have to get up early?"

I think about the smoldering hot iron I have in the fire for tomorrow. But an effusive "Yah" is what I say. Then, "Hey, I know a party we could probably crash."

She cracks up. "Yah nuh, Fitzpatrick."

CHAPTER TWENTY

Mamie

When Rob and I have made our way up again, I blink like a mole that's just surfaced from a hundred-foot earthen tunnel. In the lobby, I realize how shallow my breathing must have been and breathe deeply, expanding my rib cage. My reward is the scent of newly freshened floral arrangements. They're lush and creamy, sharp and quick, and as soft as a sweet memory. Rob and I smile at each other, and he takes my hand as we move toward the elevators through fewer people than usual. I wonder if he's thinking about our time together tonight. I have to catch Abigay up on the day when I get to my room. But after that? I don't want to think about anything but being with Rob and letting off steam. We *could* go out to eat. It's not that late, though it feels that way, but I want my guy all to myself. *In a manner of speaking.*

Kwame's at the front desk. He nods and smiles at us, and thankfully, not in a smarmy or knowing way. The news that we've finished the project sends up new bottle rockets inside me. I whisper to Rob, "Do you care if I tell him we met our deadline?"

"Are you still planning on jumping up on the bar in Between the Trees tonight?"

I shove him to the side with my hip. "Not sure yet."

He throws his head back and laughs. "Go ahead and tell him. I'm proud we're done too."

"We finished the article!" I shout to Kwame.

He grins and claps once. "Hey, that's *fantastic* news."

"Thank you," Rob and I say in tandem, and then laugh because the laughter feels so good.

"Are you coming back down to celebrate?"

"You bet," Rob says.

"Let me buy you guys a drink. I insist."

"You're on," Rob says.

I'm reminded that Kwame, who's from Ghana, told me his name means "Saturday" in his native language of Ghanaian.

Tomorrow's Saturday, so I think I'll pick up a little happy for him.

When I make it to my room, burdened by my weighty computer bag, I tip the little owl a wink, step across the threshold, and jettison the bag on the plush carpet like a teen with her backpack on a Friday afternoon, the promise of a no-telling-what-might-happen adventure and homework-free weekend stretching before her. A thrifting trip with her bestie? A great date with her boyfriend? I may have even let out a whoop loud enough to be heard in the lobby.

My phone rings. Abigay Fletcher, the queen of impeccable timing.

"Bee," I say, "you got my text!"

"I did! I hoped to catch you before you got in the shower."

"How is it going with *you?*"

"Oh, you know . . . your meh Christmas Adam snuggling with the love of your dreams. One crackling and sifting birch fire. Two old-fashioned cocktails with cherries and orange slices. Three rich cheeses on a board. Bing Crosby crooning away. Watching the snow fall on aspens through floor-to-ceiling windows."

I drop to the bed, cracking up. "Love, love, love it!"

"Back to *you*, my dearest, most brilliant Bee. I am so, so proud of you. What an accomplishment! You made your deadline while cuckoo banana pants in love. Most people can't put one foot in front of the other or string a coherent sentence together in the throes of new love."

"Ah, thanks, babe. You're right. I need to take a minute and let the accomplishment sink in. I think Rob's bringing out the best in me."

"And you in him."

"I hope so. He seems to think we should go into business together . . . like a package deal, journalist and photographer."

"How do you feel about that?"

"Not sure yet. It has potential. I guess we would pool our resources. Now, Abs, don't get salty with me, but I still haven't breached the subject of the trust fund."

She sighs loud and long. "I'm not . . . going to shame you. I'm just concerned. It's not a pleasant subject, and I know you don't want to get into it with him tonight, but soon, okay?"

"Okay," I say. "You're right, you're right. I know you're right. Hey, topic shift: Is Rob my boyfriend now? I was thinking about the word a few minutes ago."

"Well, are you considering terms? What do you think? You're the walking *Webster's Dictionary*."

"Don't forget thesaurus."

"Right."

"I mean," I say, thinking aloud, "we've defined the relationship, but not the nouns. I haven't referred to him that way yet. It sounds . . . I don't know . . . juvenile somehow. Rob is so different, so manly."

"So what is a boyfriend?" she asks.

"A constant male companion with whom one has a romantic relationship. Or a piece of clothing designed to be oversized and comfortable, i.e., a boyfriend cardigan."

"Seems to me Rob is both those things. Romantic and comfy to be with. And definitely oversized." We laugh together. "I can just picture you swallowed up by one of his sweaters."

"Ha! So I declare that he is my boyfriend and therefore I am free to address him as such."

"Do it, Bee!"

"Oh, I miss you! Did you guys decide to stay in Vail for Christmas?"

"I'm thinking we will. But either way, I'll see you Monday afternoon at home."

Home. As much as I love our apartment and living with Abigay, suddenly Rob feels like home. "Yes, Monday, for sure. Can't wait to see you. Chat a minute tomorrow?"

"Of course."

We end the call, and I plug my phone into the built-in lamp charger before leaving a trail of clothes on my way to the bathroom. Once inside, I stand in the shower, hot water sluicing my shoulders and back, and imagine the remnants of my muscle and mental fatigue circling the drain.

In the bedroom again, I sit on the bed in my undies, making eyes at the pretty box waiting by my suitcase. Not only did I find a great vintage dress downtown for the ball tomorrow night, but I found two other items that should make Rob Fitzpatrick a very happy man. Tonight's the night to wear the slinky red dress that is *so* not me but seems fun and fitting, pun intended, to wear for our celebration. I slip into the dress and then open the fresh paper and leather-scented box. I hold up the pair of peau de soie red heels, grin, and give them a smacking air *mwah*.

Love be a lady tonight.

CHAPTER TWENTY-ONE

Rob

My luxury hotel room feels as lonely as Tom Hanks's deserted island in *Cast Away*. I haven't resorted to naming and communing with inanimate objects, but I long for Mamie.

When I washed back onto my island, I tugged off my taco-reeking clothes and stuffed them into the dry-cleaning bag bound for the hotel laundry service. Maybe tacos won't be a fun couple's memory for us after all, but with time it may be a funny one. *One day at the Grand Bohemian Lodge, we ate tacos in a smelly-to-begin-with break room and ended up stinking to high heaven. Your mother was afraid the stink was in her pores,* I might tell our children.

I had one of the best showers in memory, brushed my teeth as though it were National Dental Care Day instead of Christmas Adam, then changed into the green sweater that's been chilling and freshening on my balcony for two days and a pair of soft, old mustard-colored chinos. Comfort clothes. I'm glad Mamie's a casual kind of girl and that I can feel free to wear the clothes I have.

I take a seat in one of the two chairs in the room, thinking it's not good for a man to live alone. I pull on a pair of socks. Everywhere things are paired: bookends, bat and ball, head-lights, chopsticks, pen and paper, twins. As small feet pound the hall outside my door and high-pitched laughter rings, my thoughts turn to children and one day being parenting partners with Mamie. She would make such a lovely and energetic mother. And that's extraordinary because she was raised by someone who probably should never have been a mother in the first place. Colleen. I know I'm judging her by reputation, but what would it be like to be the woman's son-in-law and have her as a grandmother to my children? Should we enter into marriage knowing Mamie's family deck is stacked against us? And would Mamie come to resent me for it? That would be a whole quiver of arrows to my heart.

Missing her again, I'm ready to celebrate our project triumph with her. I knew she'd take longer than me to get ready because I'm learning that even minimalist girls roll that way. I smile, picturing her applying pretty red lipstick, and remember to pocket a fresh sleeve of mints. I check my phone because she said she'd text me a five-minute notice when she's on her way down. But so far, no word.

Pacing the swirling pattern of the bright green, gray, and white carpet, my eyes move to the straight lines of the contemporary furniture. I decide to risk trying to reach Seamus in the time I have left. I haven't contacted him since he sent me the great line that's probably from an old movie: *Marry the girl, kid.* Of course, I haven't told Mamie what he said, but it would be cool if I could somehow work it into my proposal. The clock tells me my old friend won't be at the shop now, but I have his home landline number. I picture the avocado-green relic as it rings in South Boston.

Seamus picks up after six. "This is Seamus O'Malley speaking."

"Sea-man, it's Rob."

"Robert Edward Fitzpatrick, you fine Irish mick, how are ya?"

I snort a laugh. "Hey, you fine mick yourself. If I was doing any better, Red Bull would be pounding me."

"Well, that's excellent. You married yet?"

I howl a laugh. "Not yet, but I'm working on it. How are you?"

"Getting along. Don't get old, kid."

"You're not old."

"Yah? Please explain that to my breath-snatching sciatica."

I sober. "I'm sorry about that."

On his end of the line, a TV blares with a clatter of bells and strains of bouncy Christmas violin music that I can't place. "Hold a moment, will you, Rob, and let me turn this shrieking TV down?"

"Yah huh." I toggle to the home screen to make sure there's no word from Mamie yet.

Seamus collects his clunking receiver again. "Say, I forgot to tell you. I finally finished the last piece you worked on before defecting south. I'm scaling back the shop and pondering selling the side wing to a persistent purveyor of musical instruments. The guy's in here nattering at me every week."

Is Seamus thinking of retiring? I wince at the notion of never winding my way through his showplace of a shop again: where old-timey fans send the soothing scent of lavender oil to sweep the air; where crystal chandeliers cast dancing light over the English chests and Chippendale chairs I polished while in high school; and where in college, I often left my few-hours-a-week refinishing work with chemical-stained hands and the occasional abrasion, but always with the best kind of tired.

Seamus goes on. "I've been thinking of what to do with pieces I decide to let go. I know you don't have room in Mrs. Aiken's garage place, but when you move—and it will be soon because you're gonna light up the world as a photojournalist—you might wish to have them."

My chest warms like it did when Mom rubbed Vicks VapoRub over it during a bashing bout of bronchitis. But my throat thickens. "Thank you." Pop never believed in me or made me feel the way Seamus does. I was his weird kid, the quiet boy who chose education and culture over a do-your-eight-and-hit-the-gate job and beers with the boys every night the way my brothers did. Abruptly, the Christmas music on Seamus's end makes it to the tip of my tongue. "What are you watching?"

"*Meet Me in St. Louis.* For the fortieth time."

"The Trolley Song." *Decent movie. But girly. I bet Mamie likes it.* I'm reminded how much we don't know about each other and how much I want to learn. "Good for you. Should make you feel festive."

"Yah. Always," he says, and then picks up his dangling thread of antique talk. "So let's see . . . I'm thinking about four pieces that you restored. The Hepplewhite mahogany sideboard, the English bow front server, the Irish tea table . . . and the New England cherry highboy with the fan carving. I *could* rent out space in a storage facility. Or how would you feel about me finding a buyer for them? I could easily get you three or four apiece. That's at least twelve grand."

I gulp the winter air. "But . . . that's . . . *your money,* Seamus!"

"What the heck do I need it for?"

My limbs suddenly feel as heavy as the highboy I'd labored over for weeks. I forget how to move. "Seamus, you can't just—"

"I can just. Indulge an old man. The Lawsons in Beacon Hill might snap them up tomorrow. Or my online clients, the Remberts of Charleston, could be interested. They're decorating *another* beach home, this one on Kiawah Island. You been there yet? I hear it's beautiful." My mouth has grown parched. *The Remberts?* But Seamus goes on. "I bet the missus would chomp at the bit for them." He chuckles. "She does ride a high horse."

The riot this talk has made of my brain gets me moving again. I lick my lips and slide the door closed, then lean against it, grateful that Mamie hasn't texted me yet.

"Mamie knows that family," I murmur.

Rob

"As a native Charlestonian, I'm sure she does." As if set to do so, my phone vibrates. But Seamus is still on a roll. "The Remberts are major players in the antique and art scene. The missus was a *Calhoun*. Excellent clients too, the Calhouns. Mrs. Rembert accumulates bits and bobs from all over the country. But just between you and me and the lamppost, I think she's a reverse hoarder . . . if that's a thing. Not of Tupperware and broken TV trays, but of fine things. Like she's going to take them with her when she kicks the bucket."

As he cackles, I catch my reflection in the mirror above the desk. My face is as slack as a stroke victim's. Maybe I should call the front desk. Ask, "Is there a cardiologist in the house?" But I try and compose a nonchalant tone because Seamus has always been able to read me. "Uh, sure, Sea-man. Sell them if it would be easier for you not to have to store them."

"Rob, you've been like a son to me. And I know what the cash could mean for you, helping establish yourself in your career, starting a new life with that pretty lady. If I can sell them, consider the money a wedding gift."

I could buy Mamie a ring. I swipe my damp eyes with the back of my hand and sniff back tears. "I hope you know . . . you've been like a father to me."

"I know, kid. I'll phone my clients tomorrow and likely be in touch after the holidays. Merry Christmas, Rob."

"'Have Yourself a Merry Little Christmas,' Seamus."

He ends the call with a clunk of his ancient avocado receiver. I lie back on the bed and release a fifty-pound sigh of relief. To get ready for the evening with Mamie, I slam a mental door on the remaining thoughts about the money but continue to marvel over Seamus's benevolence. His fatherlike love for me when I've needed it most.

Minutes later, I sit up and smooth the back of my hair, and then open Mamie's text. *Hi there, handsome. Are you ready for me?* At once, I feel like me again, and the man that Mamie Morrow loves. My mouth forms the smile of a smitten chowdahead.

Be down in five, lovely, I type. I stride to the bathroom, wash my face, and dry it.

My iron in tomorrow's fire just took on a compadre.

I'm at the front desk signing away my laundry bag with Marco when Mamie walks around the corner from the elevators. There's an audible hitch in Marco's inhale. But my breath has left me. The word "walk" is a weak verb choice for the way the woman moves into the lobby. Eartha Kitt's silky "Santa Baby" swoops the air—*boom-boom boom-boom*—and Mamie's every step is in sync with the music. She alternates between leveling her green gaze on me and dipping her chin, a small smile on her red lips. Two couples, whiskey glasses screwed into their hands and chatting in front of the great fireplace, fall silent at the sight of her. But this woman bears little resemblance to the Mamie I've come to know. Our romance has to remain wholesome. For now. And the last thing I need is this siren's call to the mission-driven but vulnerable Odysseus in me. But any woman who shows up for a celebration with her love wearing a sexy new red dress deserves a jaw drop of a reaction or rush of compliments. I have to say *something*. But if it's in my vocabulary, it's firmly stuck there.

CHAPTER TWENTY-TWO

Mamie

The elevator opens at lobby level. I step from it in the chic red heels that already feel pinchy in the pointy toe boxes and fold the filmy wrap that came with the cocktail dress over my arm. I felt stunning in the outfit upstairs, but now, about to face Rob and whoever else is in the lobby tonight, I feel a little insecure. The dress is so fitted there's no room for pockets, so I'm carrying the small clutch that I packed on a whim.

As my discomfort nibbles at me, I decide to spend a moment hoping for a silent confirmation from the grandfather figure I've made of the chief painting. Since no one's around, I whisper, "What do you think of my outfit, Grandtate? Do I look glam or like a scarlet woman?" I peer down again at the strapless, fitted bodice that reveals the skin of my chest (sans evidence of cleavage), shoulders, and arms, and then look back up at Grandtate. If only I had known him and his perspective on how culture has changed the way most women dress. "It's fine, right?" The chief's hooded eyes don't change, but I detect a slight rise in the vertical wrinkle at the left corner of his mouth.

Or maybe it was only a shadow.

Either way, he's banished my inner critic. I blow him a kiss and then clip toward the lobby in search of my love.

I draw near to Rob, who's standing next to the registration desk. Marco, who's attending it tonight, does an about-face and slips through the door behind the desk. Rob tilts his head and looks down at me. I wait, my thoughts dipping and darting like swallows. A smidge of a crease forms between his brows. And then in his hazel eyes, surprise seems to make fast friends with admiration. He gives me his I-have-no-words smile and inclines his hands. I set my clutch on the registration desk and take them, my heart rising like fresh, fragrant dough. His voice comes out lower than usual, husky. "Mamie, you look gorgeous, sweetheart." Cool, clean ripples spread through me. Leaning in, he gives my cheek a sound kiss and whispers close to my ear, "I love you."

I stand on tiptoe and pull him in for a hug. "And I love you."

"Would you like a drink?" Rob asks.

Norah Jones's "Run Rudolph Run" replaces "Santa Baby" and revs my pony engine. I collect my clutch. "Ab-so-lutely. Let's get this party started."

He grins and offers me his sweet arm. We make our way to the bar, on which someone (it must be a team of nocturnal elves because there seems to be something shiny and new here each morning) has placed trios of pre-lit bottlebrush trees in every shade of green along its length. "Oh, I love those," I say as Rob and I take two barstools. "Abigay and I meant to get some for our place this year." Rob smiles tightly, then slips his arm around me. But I feel his hand falter as though it's unsure where it should go. When I turn a smile on him, his hand regains its momentum and comes to rest around my shoulder.

Tucker's behind the bar and unloading a dishwasher, his glasses opaque with steam. He waves a hand in front of his face, and I feel a rush of affection for him. The staff has been so good to us, despite the one hiccup—that has become a nonissue to Rob and me—and I feel that we've made friends here. Only one other fortyish-looking, well-dressed twosome is seated here, the man one seat away from Rob and his wife on his other side. With satisfaction, I notice the same Rifle Paper Company monthly planner that's in my computer bag propped before the woman. I wonder what will be scribbled on the pages of the weeks and months to come in mine. The couple seem to be comparing calendars and discussing their children's schedules, he from his phone, she from the planner. I smile to myself and relax into Rob's arm. How smart to turn a mundane calendar meeting into a date in such a special and festive place. I bet those two rock as parents.

Tucker has come to chat with Rob. I study Rob's profile for a moment, imagining him as a dad one day. I feel like he'll be a good one. With utter certainty, I know he'll be nothing like mine, nothing like his.

I greet Tucker, and his eyes throw sparks at me. "The lady in the red dress! Y'all goin' somewhere fancy tonight?"

I hadn't looked beyond his gorgeous face before, but now I take in his casual dress. Rob Fitzpatrick would look terrific wearing a big burlap potato sack race bag. "Nope! Just to Tucker's bar," I say.

He grins and slaps two of their signature black napkins on the agate bar.

"First, a complimentary champagne. I've been given orders—pun intended—to serve you a glass in celebration of finishin' your magazine story." He pulls two flutes from behind the bar. Rob smiles at me, but that brow crinkle appears again. As Tucker pours, I whisper to Rob, "Kwame, that sweet guy. Tell you later."

Tucker presents our glasses. "Congratulations, Mamie and Rob."

The calendar woman peers around her husband at us with big question marks for eyes. She smiles at me and tilts her head. "Are you getting married?" she asks sweetly. As the M-word hovers in the air and drifts around the bar, Rob looks at me with raised brows and gives a small helpless shake of his head. I purse my lips in a grin and shrug as if to say, *This is on you; say whatever.* I know if I answer the woman, I risk blathering on about the obvious but as yet unvoiced conversation that's pressing in on us.

Rob half turns to the woman as if to avoid her eyes, raises his glass, and simply says, "Sláinte," before taking a big sip. The woman twists her mouth to one side and takes the stem of her wineglass as if to lift it, then says something to her husband and sits back against her stool again. Other merrymakers are taking seats around us.

"Well played, Fitzpatrick," I whisper. "A verbal poker face." He lets go a breath that ruffles a pile of cocktail napkins on the bar. Then he turns to me and takes my hand. He rivets my eyes with his. In their gentle hazel depths, I sense a momentous message: *Wait, Mamie, wait.* And then, *Trust me.* I swallow and close my eyes as if to hold the secret words in my heart, then smile at him and kiss his cheek. He turns my face and kisses my lips. The way we seem to have learned to read each other so quickly fills me with wonder. And his *kiss.* His kiss. Is bliss. *This one* makes me feel effervescent, brimming and spilling with gladness and a sweet assurance.

We sip our champagne. My eyes fall on the windows beyond the bar. The night is cloudy. The Greenville winter has settled around us, and the cold nights have pressed the perennials back into the earth. Movement in the glass has me searching the reflections for me and Rob, the way I'd done before when I wondered if we looked like a couple. My bare skin above the bodice of my dress and on my arms looks no more indecorous than other women in the lobby. I toss my hair and then turn my focus to our body language in the glass. Rob's sipping his champagne and gazing at my profile. We have morphed into a couple. My reflection beams back at me.

I pick up my flute, but then something small and white and close to the window catches my eye. "I think I just saw a snowflake!"

Rob looks at me. "Where?"

I lean my head against his and point. "Right there."

"Yah. I see more."

I'm off my barstool. "Oh, my word, can we run out and look?"

He chuckles at my eagerness. "I guess we better."

I hurry to the edge of the lobby porch overlooking the restless falls. Rob comes to stand behind me and wraps his arms around my torso. I cheer as snowflakes drift down. They float sideways, looking fluffy and indecisive, as if they know they belong farther north and are falling here by accident. "It hasn't snowed in Charleston in so many years, I'd forgotten how beautiful it is," I say with a wistful longing.

After a few minutes, the flakes stop falling. But the magic isn't over. It's here in this night, in this place, and in this man. I turn around and lift my chin. Rob leans down to meet my lips and, closing his eyes, begins to kiss me, his mouth tasting of champagne laced with violets. "Mm," I murmur.

"Mm," he murmurs back. But after a moment, he pulls away. "Sweetheart, there's something you should know."

Oh no. "What?"

"It's *brick* out here." He shivers and shoves his hands into his pockets.

"It's *what*? Brick? Does that mean 'cold' in Boston?"

"If you're a Southie, it does."

I laugh and tug him back inside, thinking of Boston and the

picture he'd shown me of his family. I wonder what their family Christmas looks like and if they're missing Rob now.

Inside, it's toasty, and someone has turned up the music. Billy Squier's rocking "Christmas Is the Time to Say I Love You" throbs from the speakers. The bar's almost surrounded by new arrivals, some of them dancing, all with glasses in their hands. My heart lurches. "Rob, are our spots still open? I left my bag on the bar."

"Yah, I can see it. It's fine."

I squeeze his big bicep. "I *love* that you're tall." We weave our way through the throng and back to our places, where I give my bag a little pat. Tucker's hustling, but another bartender has joined him, a woman I've never seen before. She's carrying five glasses of wine, and I marvel at her dexterity.

Tucker stops in front of us, pinpoints of sweat popping from his forehead. "Hey, guys. Did you wanna start a tab?" I look at Rob. But he defers to me.

"Whatever the lady in the red dress wants."

I grin. "Sure. And I think I'd like . . . an old-fashioned. With three celebration cherries, please."

Rob nods heartily and raises two fingers. "Just what I wanted. Make that two. But mine with one cherry and orange peel, please."

Tucker says, "Ha. You think I'm goldbrickin' back here? Orange peel is a Tucker's bar requisite."

"Touché," Rob says.

We laugh as Tucker says, "Be right back," as jolly as Old Saint Nick himself, and continues delivering his goods. I finish my champagne and waggle my shoulders to the music. The acrobatic female bartender slides a small wooden bowl of Chex Mix in front of Rob.

"Thanks," he says, but she moves on without comment. He shrugs but then takes a loose handful—because a whole handful for Fitzpatrick would mean the entire bowl—of the snack and pops it into his mouth. "Sorry," he says around a bite, and pushes the bowl to me.

I smile. "Poor baby, are you starving?"

He turns to me. "Like zee wolf."

I giggle. "Let's get you some real food."

Tucker sets two highball glasses before us. "Cheers, y'all."

I lift mine to the light and smile at the cherries. "Perfection! Hey, are we able to order food from the bar?"

"Of course," he says, and pulls out a couple of menus to lay in front of us. "Darla—she's our fill-in person—will take your order, okay?"

"Sure." We sip our cocktails while giving the menu a once-over.

"Okay," I say, "what looks great to you? And you can't say the whole menu."

"Well, in that case, I'm going for the Carolina coastal shrimp and grits from Anson Mills—how 'bout that?" He looks at me. "Anson." I just smile because we've put our squabbling and grievances behind us. He reads the rest of the description. "Anson Mills stone-ground grits and tasso ham. I haven't tried shrimp and grits yet."

I put my arm around him and give him a little side hug. "Hey, when in Carolina! Go for it. It's so yummy, you'll never want to go back north." I keep a finger on the entrée I have in mind. "Pour moi? The Ora King salmon with parmesan-chive grit cake, charred broccolini, and fennel sauce vierge."

Rob spots Darla and raises a finger. "I swear my mouth is watering," he says.

"Oh, mine too."

Darla nods at him and delivers wine to three guests before making her way to us. "What would you like, sir?"

"Oh, I'm Rob, and this is Mamie."

"Hey," she says, and eyes us coolly. Rob gives a small shrug of a big shoulder. We place our orders and ask for more Chex Mix. "I'll put that right in."

We pick up our drinks, and I grin at my guy. As fiddle strains of someone's clever riff on "Auld Lang Syne" dives and swoops from the speakers, I'm reminded of the short time we have left together and of the magic bubble we've been living in where time is measured in seconds, minutes, and hours instead of weeks and months. *Do not go there, Mamie. Wait.* The wooden snack bowl makes me think of the larger one Tate left me. I picture it in the apartment where I placed it atop the microwave. *Home. Is that now in Rob's sweet embrace?* The savory scent of the fresh Chex Mix the server sets down hits my nose. My mom made that a lot. I collect a handful from the bowl. But she made it cheesier because that's how I liked it. How have I forgotten the good things about growing up in my mother's home?

Tucker comes over and sets his elbows on the bar. "I bet you're worn out," I say.

"Dude, we've been slammed. I'm plumb tuckered."

"Ha! This drink is awesome, by the way."

"Glad to hear. Hey, will y'all be at the big feast at Between the Trees on Christmas night?"

Rob looks at me. "I guess we kind of forgot about that."

"Do we need a reservation?" I ask.

Tucker says he'll check the list, and he comes right back. "You're already on the book. A seven o'clock."

"We are?" I ask. "How?"

"Mr. Reagan blocks off a few tables for special guests."

Rob's eyebrows shoot up. "Wow. That's so nice."

I smile and shake my head in wonder. "Are we like players now?" I whisper.

Rob's expression is thoughtful. "We could be someday."

Morrow and Fitzpatrick. Stranger things have happened.

I excuse myself to go to the ladies' room. I'm almost to the door when my big toes let out piercing shrieks of protest. Oh no. The lovely shoes. *Beauty is pain, Mamie,* I hear my mother saying as she brushed the tangles from my long hair. At eight or nine, I'd taken her at face value. All the curling iron burns and poky hot roller clips I still endured. She was right. What else was she right about? My now-mincing steps make me think of Farida's stilettos and Isla's lofty stacks. *Buck up, babe,* I tell myself as I open the door.

Back in the bar, I settle onto my stool. My toes tingle and sigh.

"Are you okay? You look like you're in pain," Rob says.

I pull a face. "I am. It's these heels."

"Silly girl. Did you wear those for yourself or to look good for others?"

I grin and dip my chin. "I wore them for my boyfriend."

CHAPTER TWENTY-THREE

Rob

I 've wanted to be a lot of things.

A T-Rex when I was three.

Batman at four.

An Oompa Loompa stirring chocolate at six.

Huckleberry Finn at eight.

A Red Sox player at ten.

A Navy SEAL at twelve.

A photographer at fourteen.

Mamie's boyfriend the day I met her.

And incredibly, I am. The word never sounded better than when it fell from Mamie's pretty southern lips.

Miraculously, her favorite place, the purple banquette, is all ours. After the wicked spectacular meal we shared at the bar, which made me a member of the shrimp and grits club for life, we left the noise of the bar with glasses of wine and looked for a comfy spot to relax together.

Mamie, who remarked that she's such a lightweight that, at this point, it's *get hydrated or get hammered*, ordered a carafe of water from Josh.

This side of the tall banquette faces the gallery rather than the bar and offers us more privacy. But the sight of the gallery sends a stealth bomber to my mind: Isla's ridiculous suspicion of Mamie. But telling myself it's not our problem, I shoot it down.

Josh delivers the carafe and sets it on the cedar-and-iron cocktail table in front of us. Mamie drinks a full glass of water and then shivers. "Here. You're cold," I say, wishing I had my blazer to give to her. I take the fancy wrap that goes with her dress from her lap and go about trying to drape it somewhat gracefully over her shoulders.

"Thank you, sweetheart," she says with a smile. "Though I can take pretty good care of myself, I *do* love the way you tend me."

I grin at the word "tend" and shake loose two mints.

She rolls hers around in her mouth, but then pockets it in her jaw. "Oh, Rob, I think I'm too full to kiss right now. Can we *talk* for a while? I love it when we find out new things about each other. I always feel closer to you then."

I realize at that moment that we don't even know each other's birthdays. The laughter of children rings from across the lobby and reminds me that it's still relatively early. There's still time to talk now and kiss later. "Yah huh."

The song "See Amid the Winter's Snow" begins to play. "I love that beautiful song," Mamie says with wistful eyes. She lays her head back and listens for a minute, and I remember how hard she worked today. She needs time to chill, and I'm happy that she can. When the song ends, she looks at me and says, "Wouldn't it be fun if it snowed, like really snowed?"

"Sure," I say with a smile, though after growing up in Boston, I don't care if I never see more than a dusting again. "When's your birthday, beautiful?"

She gives me a double take and then rolls her eyes. "December twenty-fifth."

"Man. *Really?*"

"Yes, but I wasn't going to tell you because I thought you'd hustle out to get me a gift."

I grin. "That remains to be seen."

She twists her mouth. "Okay, so when's yours?"

"July fourth."

"*Get* out of town. You made that up."

I laugh. "I did *not*. Want to look at my driver's license?"

"As a matter of fact, I do," she says with glee all over her face. "I want to see if your picture is as bad as mine." *She's so dang cute.* I lean forward to get to my back pocket and then slide out my wallet. "Wait," she says, holding up a stop sign of a hand. "I don't want to see any other items you might have in there."

I give the contents a mental rifle through. "I assure you there's nothing you don't want to see. Here, look for yourself," I say, and toss it into her lap.

"Wow," she says, unfolding the worn leather and then sliding my license out of the clear plastic frame thing. "This is gold, Fitzpatrick. One hundred and ninety pounds. And six foot three! I suspected so. Do you know that you're a foot and an inch taller than me?"

"I do. That's the one redeeming feature about those shoes," I say, gesturing to her feet, "I don't have to lean down as far to kiss you. Your boots work better than your sneakers, though."

"Ha. I don't think you have to worry about seeing these heels again. I'll thrift them when I get home. But they sure are pretty," she says, giving them a longing survey. The mention of her thrifting reminds me that we *have* to talk about money, but I sure don't want to bring it up tonight. "This picture of you is absolutely *breathtaking*! Nobody's photo looks this good." She gives me a sidelong look. "You weren't flirting with the DMV clerk, were you?"

I make wide eyes at her. "Who, me? Flirt?"

She laughs and flips to my signature on the back. "You write like a serial killer in cursive."

I want to fall on the floor laughing my Boston butt off and

almost do. "I know! It's terrible!" I say when I manage to blow out a breath. *Oh girl, what's next?*

She holds the wallet away from me and gives the contents another scan. "Wait," she says, her voice stern. "Just what the merry Christmas is *this*, Fitzpatrick?"

My belly full of food lurching and my face growing hot, I think of what might have been stuck in there for years.

I look over at what rests on her palm.

It's a glasses wipe.

I hide my head in my hands, my whole being shaking with relieved laughter. "Morrow, are you trying to kill me?"

Laughing too, she leans into my side and smooches my cheek. "Let's always have this much fun, Fitzpatrick."

I smile. "Let's."

Mamie comes back from the ladies' room practically limping. I wish she'd take off the high heels, but she's way stubborn. Drawing closer, she stops in front of me and places a hand on her hip. "Mind if I join you, handsome?"

"Well, I *was* waiting for my girlfriend. But you *sure look fine*."

She smiles as if our article just won a Pulitzer and primly takes a seat next to me. Then, when she crosses her legs, I get a look at the knees I've strenuously avoided ogling all evening. "I love being your girlfriend."

I'm crazy about her. "I love it too."

She picks up her wineglass and takes a sip. "I still don't get why you haven't had a great date in so long. Remember the night at Jianna when you told me that?"

"I *did* in high school and college." My heart grows leaden. I've needed to bring up an ugly truth about my family and have dreaded doing it, but she's gifted me with a segue. *Here goes, sweetheart*. I hope this doesn't make her question ever getting involved with me. "When I told you about my brothers, I didn't tell you the worst of it. But it's like this . . . Hindenburg-sized thing hanging over my head."

"Then you need to get it out. Now. Tell me."

I turn to her. "The men in my family are cursed, Mamie. I call it the Fitzpatrick curse."

She looks at me and nods twice, then takes a long sip of wine. She holds up an index finger, then opens her pocketbook and pulls out a wipe. She cleans her lenses as though clear-sightedness will help her hear what I'm telling her. Taking a breath that seems to raise her shoulders three inches, she says, "I'm listening, Rob."

Demoted again to "Rob," I close my eyes a moment before speaking. "My father was a hardworking man, a good provider. He and my mother loved each other . . . Guess they still do in their ways. But Pop had an eye for the ladies." I survey Mamie's face for a sign of distress, but her countenance is still smooth. "When my brothers were old enough, they figured out that he was stepping out on Mom. If *she* knew, and I don't see how she didn't . . . I mean, when he came in late, strong perfume and a mixture of bar smells—cigarette smoke, booze, and the close press of strangers—would make its way to the living room, where we were watching TV, before he did. Mom always said the same thing. 'Frank, your dinner's on the stove.' Us guys would silently mouth along with his reply, 'Not hungry, Treasa.'" I look beyond Mamie. "Now that I think about it again, that made us what? Pop's co-conspirators? Co-dependents?"

Mamie touches my arm. "No, sweetheart, just *boys*. Captives, really, of your parents' dysfunctional marriage."

I close my eyes again and let out a grateful breath. "This one time? We were watching a *Bonanza* rerun in the semi-dark when Pop came in. I saw some dark splotches on his face. I stifled a gasp, afraid he'd been in a fight. But Roger kicked my foot and hissed, 'That's lipstick, ya dolt.' With those four words, I understood I was never to mention it outside the family. And I haven't, Mamie. Only now, to you."

"Because you trust me," she says with a reassuring dip of her chin.

I take a long pull of my wine. Both of our glasses are almost empty.

"I do. But there's more. Every one of my brothers has followed Pop's example, Mamie. Even I"—I hold my palm to my chest where a pang lodges deep—"was tempted to cheat on a girl I dated senior year, Kerrie, but I couldn't go through with it. Now my brothers—they're all married except Smoky—cheat on their wives. Smoky's engaged, and I've talked with him about being faithful to her. I'm sure you can tell the two of us are tight."

A small smile surfaces through the hurt on Mamie's face, the hurt my sweet girlfriend feels for me. "I sure can."

I smile. "I'm sure there are people in the old neighborhood who remember Mom as Pop's doormat, but she has a great circle of friends—sweet ladies—who support her. See, Mom believed in the sanctity of marriage. And being Catholic, she would have never divorced him. I think she just forgave him. Over and over and over. I hear his philandering days are over, and I thank God for that. But I wish Mom could have had a life that included the true love of a husband. She deserves so much better." I search Mamie's eyes and find nothing but love and understanding there, so I go on. "I want to be the husband that none of the others has been. I want to leave a legacy of the lifelong love of a good woman for *my* children. But I have high hopes for Smoky too."

Mamie leans her shoulder against the banquette. She reaches for my hand and holds it palm to palm with mine as if simultaneously giving and drawing strength. I didn't intend to spill the part about being a husband on her, but my mouth became a water bubbler lifting a fresh arc until I put a toe on the pedal. "And what about your dates?" she asks. "Remember when you told me you haven't had a great one in so long?" She sips her water and seems to give me time to switch to a different sort of conversation.

I pick up my wineglass, forgetting that it's empty, and set it down again. "I had two girlfriends in college. Nice girls I went to high school with. A lot of us ended up at Fisher because we didn't want student debts. Since then, and before I left the city, I was so busy working, my dates were fix-ups of my brothers' doings. A few of the women were pretty—not in your league, of course—but nice-looking and sweet. I met this one woman that Cy set me up with at a movie theater. Luna was her name. Halfway through the show, she started climbing on my lap! I got up, spilling a bucket of popcorn all over the place, and then got the heck out of Dodge."

Mamie flashes me an I-can't-help-myself grin, but then forms a fighter's scowl and pretends to box the air. "I bet I could take her."

I shake my head and laugh a little. "Bet you could." I take her soft, pretty hand and run my fingers over her pink nails. "But those girls' nails were super long, witchy looking . . . and painted all these garish colors. I like short nails on a woman. Natural looking, like yours."

She admires her hands with a smile. "I'm wearing gel polish. Bubble Bath is my signature color."

"You like bubble baths?"

"*Love* them. I read in the tub. My paperbacks are all watermarked."

I picture her relaxing in a tub, the bubbles ebbing her chest, the cute toes I'd rubbed pressed against the opposite end. But the image washes away as I'm wrenched back to the Fitzpatrick curse, and my face goes wry. "Mames, *I'm* the one to break the curse. Maybe with Smoky's help. But what if I can't? What if it's, like, genetic?"

Mamie strokes my hand. "First, there's no such thing as a curse. And second, the legacy your father left is not in your genes any more than . . . that disgusting taco smell was in my pores."

We share a laugh of relief, and I feel closer to her. Hopefully, Mamie's the last woman I'll ever have to date. I drink my water down as Josh appears. I'd felt like Mamie and I were alone together in the snug and warm cabin of a small craft, but he must have been keeping an eye on us.

"How's it going?" He looks from me to Mamie. "Would you like another glass of wine?"

"One more," Mamie and I say at the same time, and Josh grins.

"Two wines it is." He looks at Mamie. "*And* I'll bring you some fresh water."

"Thanks bunches," she says.

"It's pretty dead already, so I'll probably shut the bar down at ten. But the lobby will be open." He us gives us a confidential smile. "We keep two unopened bottles of white and red in the little fridge under the bar for special guests who want to hang out after closing time. If you decide you want another glass, feel free to take it."

"That's nice of you, Josh. Thank you," Mamie says.

Josh leaves to start our order. I check my phone. It seems like we've been talking for hours, but it's only been forty minutes. Feeling as shored up as a man can feel, I decide to take a break and hit the men's room. But once inside, I realize I haven't heard Mamie's story. It's lain between us like an old roll of film that no one has thought to develop.

The lobby must be clearing, locals headed home, guests to their rooms. Even the music seems to know the night is wrapping up because the songs are more chill, the words rounder, softer. Mamie finally takes off her shoes and, wincing, pulls her feet under her, and then tugs down the hem of her dress. She drinks her water, then sets it down without making a sound as Karen Carpenter sings the purest rendition ever of "Silent Night." When it's over, we lift our freshly poured glasses of wine. "To you, Mamie Morrow, for listening to my family story and still loving me."

"I do love you, Fitzy," she says, her eyes glowing like the first stars of a black night. But she doesn't offer me her story. I stand up. "Let me rub your tortured tootsies, sweetheart."

She makes big puppy-like eyes at me. "Re-a-lly? Do you know how *intuitive* you are, Fitzpatrick? And *incredibly* thoughtful. I like that about you."

I grin at her compliments because I realize that, when someone tells you they like something about you, it's directed to your inner self. When they say they love something about you, it's usually about your appearance. I hope to spend my life naming for Mamie the things I like about her.

There's a small chair near the gallery. I pull it over to the banquette, take a seat in it, and pat my thighs. Mamie grins and untucks her feet. She stretches out her lovely legs, tugs her skirt down again, and rests her feet on my lap, then lays her head back and closes her eyes. At once, I'm back on the bench with her, down the hill from the lodge where I asked her to close her eyes before I kissed her for the first time. But every kiss with Mamie is like the first time. If my dream comes true, we have a mine of delightful discoveries to look forward to.

While rubbing away at the curves of her feet, I think of the day in the whiskey bar when I massaged her tense shoulders. That was before I had seen her chest and arms, much less her bare legs. And there *was* the band of creamy tummy skin I saw beneath her cropped sweater the first morning. I give myself a quick lecture. *Okay, Fitzpatrick, picture her swaddled head to toe in snow gear.* But when I find myself staring into the headlights of her knees, my composure takes a hit. I try reciting all nine of Santa's reindeer but come up with only seven before moving to the essential steps of camera maintenance. By the time she's cooing, I'm calculating the number of stadium seats per section at Fenway. Pulling and stretching out her toes, I summon my willpower and form a new mental picture. Seated on Mamie's left and right, respectively, are her mother and her parish priest, who clutches a lie detector kit in his gnarled hands. Mamie's head lolls against the velvet, her feet and legs boneless.

"Mamie. I've never seen your toes before, but in my studied opinion, they look swollen. You aren't getting back in those shoes tonight."

She flutters a languid hand. "Oh, I'll be *fine.* This is just too fabulous, Fitzy."

I close my eyes, rub her heels, and count the doors along my floor. Mamie's floor is the same. I wonder what the third floor's like and if the rumor of the woman holed up in room 434 is true. The Christmas music shuts off and the lights dim. It must be ten. The lobby is as quiet as a field of cairns. Does the mysterious woman come out at night when no one's around? My neck prickles at the thought of the cackling ghost woman in *The Shining.* I couldn't sleep for a week after watching it, and my older brothers gave me the business about it.

I'm getting creeped out. My hands go still. "You still in there, sweetheart?"

Mamie shifts, opens her eyes, and gives a little yawn. "Hi, Fitzy." It's the first time I've seen her yawn, and even that's cute, the way she wrinkles her nose. "You are the best medicine. Great hands."

"I'm glad I helped." And grateful to have her to talk to again.

Sitting up, Mamie crosses her legs and, mercifully, lays her red wrap thing over her knees. She picks up her glass of water and drains it. "I think," she says, hydrated again, "I'm ready to tell you about my family. But it's short because my father left when I was so little."

I take her hand and give it a reassuring squeeze. "I'm here." Her fine brows begin to move toward a tiny wrinkle between her eyes. But she gives me a tight, determined smile and begins to speak.

"My earliest memory is of sitting on the steps of our wide front porch with a Little Golden Book and watching a horse-drawn carriage full of people go by. The clip-clop of hooves. The odor of horse manure. I think I was two. Some of the carriage people would take pictures of me and I guess the architectural aspects of the mansion. Back then—you know, when the Internet was newer—nobody thought twice about taking pictures of other people's children. And my second memory is of making benne wafers with our housekeeper, Gladiola, at the kitchen table. I stuck my finger in the batter, and the sweet, nutty flavor spread over my tongue.

"Gladiola was sweet and gentle like that batter. She was my safe place—she and the little telephone closet under the stairs—when my parents started shouting at each other. Her shout was louder than his. But he cursed. A lot. I know that must have affected me, but I don't know how. I didn't have a sibling because I doubt my parents made love much before my father left. Maybe that made me seek out one close friend.

Someone who kept my secrets safe like a sister would have. Even now, it's been Abigay." She smiles. "And now you."

I offer a small smile of encouragement and kiss her hand. "Thank you for sharing those memories with me. They help me see the way those early years shaped you. And the ways they could have shaped you but didn't. I know your mother was stern. But from the things you've told me about her, she is also strong. I think you have her strength and maybe your grandfather's."

Mamie takes my face in her hands. "You may be right. Oh, I do love you, sweetheart."

"And I you," I say as she kisses me again. "Remember the day in the car when you told me you were an old soul?"

"I do."

"I studied the theory a few years ago." I hold Mamie's eyes. "Because I'm an old soul too. I think we may have found each other because we're kindred spirits."

"Kindred spirts," she says, as if tasting anew the term most people pass around as casually as platters at a table. She's quiet for a moment, and her gaze moves up to the large pink geode on top of the banquette. "I like the term 'kindred spirits.' It seems broader and more . . . profound than soul mates. And like something Native American people would espouse."

"I feel that way too."

"I wish I had grown up knowing Tate. His thoughts and feelings."

"I know, baby."

"I'm getting woozy," she says.

"Yah, we need to sleep on it tonight. I have some stuff to take care of tomorrow, but would you like to have breakfast together at Between the Trees?"

"I want to sleep in for a little while, but then I'd love it. Oh, and I'm going to try and get a massage or facial later at the spa downstairs."

"Nine o'clock for breakfast?"

"Perf."

We stand and she reaches for a shoe.

"Mames, you can't get those on."

"Well, I can try!" She holds onto my arm and shoves her foot inside. "Nope. Not happening," she says. "I'll carry them and wash my feet when I get to my room."

"Now, that's a plan that can walk."

She smiles and takes my hand with her free one. As we make our way to the elevators, I remember the meal vouchers lying on the chest below the TV in my room. "I forgot to tell you—Vaughn Reagan gave us some GBL dining vouchers the first day."

She flips me a look of surprise. "*That* was super generous. Guess he gives them to all media guests?"

My doubt concerning Mr. Reagan's motive shrivels and disappears. *Media passes.* "Guess so. We could use one for breakfast and the rest for the big feast Christmas night."

"Oh, my word," she says, doing a little hop of a skip on the wide plank floor in her bare feet. "Christmas is the day after tomorrow!"

I grin. "And your birthday."

"Well, let's not make a big deal out of that."

"But wasn't it hard growing up sharing a birthday with the baby Jesus?"

"Sometimes. I got used to it."

We'll see about that. My plans for tomorrow fan before me like a royal flush. I'm betting that the first task I'll tackle can be accomplished before nine. The rest can wait. I have all day.

CHAPTER TWENTY-FOUR

Mamie

I've just stepped from the shower and slipped into a fresh GBL robe when my phone rings and my Christmas ringtone, "All I Want for Christmas Is You," fills the steamy air. It's Abigay, who texted me last night and asked if I was up for a call this morning. I sip from a little cup of fresh espresso and then swipe right to answer. "Good morning, Bee. Merry Christmas Eve! I'm putting you on speaker so I can get ready while we chat."

"Merry Christmas Eve, Bee. We *miraculously* scored seats on the early nonstop." She pauses as the ubiquitous warning message not to accept baggage from someone you don't know sounds from her end.

"That's so great, and you're at the gate already," I say, throwing my head forward to wrap my hair in a towel turban.

"Yup. Jake's getting us the biggest coffees he can find."

While wiping the steam from the mirror, I remember Rob's Dunks desire and how sweet he'd been about the substitute I foraged for him. "Good. Well, it is a season for miracles. Guess who scored two canceled appointments at the Poseidon Spa here in the GBL for late morning: a massage *and* a facial!"

"Yay! You so deserve that," she says as I pick up my moisturizer and then put it down, remembering that the facialist will be cleansing my skin.

"Thanks, Abs." I run two drops of bonding serum through my hair with my fingers and then comb it through.

"While you're all relaxed and rejuvenated this afternoon, I'll be navigating the teeming aisles of Harris Teeter."

With the massage in mind, I decide to forgo my earrings. "Smart. But ugh, I feel ya. At least you and Jake can tag team it."

"There's that," she says as I pad into the bedroom imagining the fun of tag teaming tasks with Rob.

A new shiver of excitement runs through me. "How great is it that we're both in love at Christmastime?"

"So great."

A second announcement rings out in a woman's cheery voice. "Merry Christmas to those who chose to fly with us this morning. Delta flight number 2655 to Charleston, South Carolina, will be boarding shortly."

"Gotta fly—ha-ha—and here's Jake just in time."

We end the call, and I find the green jumpsuit Rob loves in the closet. On a whim, I decide not to wear the predictable cream sweater underneath but instead pair the bright green with a lighter color in the palette. I choose the sage sweater I haven't worn yet and lay out my clothes on the bed. I give my hair a quick blow-dry, dress, slip into my teal Allbirds, and then apply my lipstick.

Breakfast with my love awaits.

I step through the lobby amidst the now-familiar scents of evergreen, peppermint, coffee, and fresh baking drifting from the restaurant. At once, a driving rain pelts the large windows. I forgot to check my weather app, and the ferocity of the rain takes me by surprise.

Annelise rounds the corner wearing a pretty work dress and

her hair in an elaborate updo. "Hi, Mamie. It's been a minute since I've seen you."

"I know! What are you doing here on Christmas Eve?"

"I live out in Simpsonville, a suburb, so I brought my dress-up clothes and am hanging out here until it's time for the ball." She spreads her hands. "Using the time to clear off and organize my desk before vacation."

"Smart idea. I *love* a fresh workspace. Your hair looks gorgeous. Did you have it done?"

She smiles and turns her head to and fro for maximum effect. "I did it myself."

"I wish I could do that. I'm all thumby bumbly when it comes to styling my hair beyond a basic bun."

"Yours always looks beautiful, Mamie. That natural luminous red."

"Thank *you*. I'm on my way to breakfast with Rob, so see you at the ball?" It seems like forever since Annelise first told us about the event.

"Yes! Drinks and heavy hors d'oeuvres at six o'clock. I want my boyfriend to meet you both."

"Me too. See you there!"

Rob's already seated at a cozy corner table in the restaurant. I grin, remembering it was me who has always been the early bird. I feel like Rob has helped make me less rigid and regimented. Beyond the windows, the rain picks up. Undaunted bright umbrellas bob and weave along the suspension bridge under a weighty, cloud-scudded sky. As I draw near to Rob, I see that he's drinking coffee, his eyes bolted to his phone on the table before him. *What is fascinating him so?* Afraid to spook him, I softly say, "Good morning, Fitzpatrick." He starts and swipes his screen closed, then turns in his chair to check me out.

"Good morning, *Morrow*. And hello, my favorite outfit."

I step behind him, and holding onto the back of his chair, I bend to buss his cheek. I allow my lips to linger there. "Somebody didn't shave this morning," I whisper into his ear and, with satisfaction, watch the chill bumps respond and rise on his neck.

He reaches for my hand and grins. "I'm saving the fresh shave for tonight."

I squeeze his hand and then move toward my chair. He jumps up to pull it out for me. Before sitting, I stick out a ta-da foot for him.

"You're back in sneakers! Smart girl." He shakes his head. "You should have been arrested last night for committing a footwear felony."

A woman who's seated at the next table looks at Rob for two beats before turning away and whispering something to her daughter. *Let 'em talk.* I take my seat. "Did you save the shave so that we can dance cheek to cheek?"

"Something along those lines," he says, a gleam in his eye. "The service is slow this morning. The minor league team must be playing."

On each table is a fresh petite bouquet in a rustic apothecary bottle: a single red rose, a spill of white snowdrops, and a sprig of holly with berries. I smile. *The work of the elves again.*

"Let's get you some coffee," Rob says, and waves to the only visible employee behind the bar. The man nods, then turns and says something to a woman hidden behind him. It's Darla. I'd assumed she was a relief bartender, but apparently she's waiting tables too.

Darla smiles stiffly, picks up a couple of menus, and heads our way. She lays the menus before us. "Will you be having coffee?" she asks in her flat tone. She doesn't look me in the eyes but just beyond my right shoulder.

"Good morning. Just decaf for me, please." Darla moves off. I read somewhere that people who have trouble making eye contact often suffer from neuroses or guilt. I wonder what Darla fears. I feel for her because fear can be crippling. I look at my handsome boyfriend and smile again. "I had made espresso this morning, and I don't need any more caffeine because"—I make a little finger drumroll on the table—"guess what I have this morning."

"A massage."

"Yaass, *and* a facial." I glance through the window. "This weather must have precipitated cancellations."

Rob grins. "No pun intended."

I chuckle and hold up my menu. "What do you have your eye on?"

"The steak and eggs, baby."

I grin. "I knew it! I'm looking hard at the ciabatta french toast and maple bacon."

Darla reappears with a small pot of decaf coffee for me. "Here you are."

"Thank you so much," I say, seeking her eyes, but she still doesn't give them to me.

"I believe we're ready to order," Rob says to her. After we've placed our order and the server has moved on, Rob raises his hand in a wave and smiles at a senior couple seated at the most sought-after table for two in the restaurant, the one in front of the fireplace. "That's the Joneses I was telling you about," he says. "The ones in the photo and who are here celebrating their anniversary."

They look so nice. I smile and give them a little wave too. Betty returns the wave, her eyes widening with what feels like a warm and special smile.

I sip my coffee. "Abigay and Jake are flying home today. They're cooking Christmas dinner for both their sets of parents and Jake's sister tomorrow at his apartment."

"That's ambitious," Rob says over the rim of his cup.

"Indeed." I fiddle with my black napkin-wrapped silverware bundle and try to imagine my mother and Rob's parents and brothers sitting down for dinner together. We have our work cut out for us. I unroll the bundle and lay the napkin across my lap.

"I have news too," he says. "Isla asked to look at my photos of the lodge. Maybe she'll buy a few to be made into prints for sale in the gallery. Of course, I'd need Farida's permission."

"Fitzpatrick! That would be wonderful. The tourists would love them, the locals too. Congratulations, sweetheart."

"Well, it's not a done deal. But Isla said she had time to meet with me this morning."

Darla arrives with our breakfast and sets large white plates before us. "Will there be anything more?" she asks the salt and pepper shakers. Five words, and my mother pops into my mind again. Rob thanks the server as my thoughts return to a conversation with Abigay.

"The other day," I said to her, *"I felt myself arching one brow in that creepy Mommie Dearest way of hers that stopped me in my tracks when I gave her sass. Am I becoming my mother?"*

"No way," she answered, before giggling helplessly at my *Mommie Dearest* reference. *"I mean, as you know, most women become their mothers in one way or another when they get older. But your character is nothing like Colleen's. And Mames,"* she said, and then paused. *"Maybe it's time you recovered the good memories with her. Those are the parts that should surface in you."*

"You're right, you're right. I know you're right," I said.

I pick up my knife and fork, grateful for a moment to my mother for instilling good manners in me, and cut a piece of the French toast. "Have they solved the theft issue?" I ask Rob. "I haven't had my ear to that ground in a while." His eyes are glued to his plate. He plows into his steak and eggs like it's his job. I smile and shake my head at his gustatory gusto, and then take my first bite. The flavor of the special bread combined with syrup explodes in my mouth. Rob looks up at me. "What?" I ask.

"Nothing. I didn't ask about the crime." He smiles tautly and picks up a piece of bacon with his fingers.

I point repeatedly at the toast with my fork. "This is the best French toast I've ever had in my life."

"I'm glad." He reaches for the ketchup and pours a puddle next to his breakfast potatoes. His phone buzzes with a text, and he nudges it next to his plate with a pinky finger. He smiles at the phone, but then, his head still down, ignores the echo buzz. *What's he up to this morning?* Since it's my birthday tomorrow *and* Christmas, I'm going to assume it's gift-related biz.

The rain lashes the windows as I finish my breakfast. "Hey, Fitzy, I want to hear more about old souls." I look at my phone and grimace. "Ooh, but I don't have much time."

He lays his knife and fork across his plate, wipes his mouth, and smiles. "Oh, we have plenty of time to talk about it later. But I do feel like there's a lot there for us to unpack and lean into as a couple."

A couple. I smile. "I've always liked the number two because my sweet first-grade teacher, Miss Sadler, called it the swan." Rob laughs and nods at me as though I'm the most adorable thing he's ever laid eyes on. "Would you mind if I left you to settle up so I can run upstairs before my appointment?"

"Yah huh," he says. "But give me a sweet kiss first." He points to his chin. "You have a little spot of syrup right here."

"Aah!" I dip my napkin in my water and dab at my chin. Then I can't help but join him in a laugh. I hop up, and because we're the last people in the restaurant, I scurry around the table and plant a big one on him. Then I leave him but turn back as I hear his text alert again. He's sitting there gaping at his cell, alternately frowning and smiling, both hands gripping the table as though, if he didn't, he might float away.

CHAPTER TWENTY-FIVE

Rob

I sit in the restaurant. My table has been cleared and cleaned, but my mind is a vortex that makes the turbulent rain seem like a delicate spring shower. I stare at my phone again, afraid to touch it in case the whole message from Seamus had been a hallucination. Then, filled with a rush of emotion that can follow a great shock, I drop my head to my hands and hold it, still processing, praying. I shed a few tears then. Fat ones that spill down my cheeks. For the first time since I met Mamie, I'm glad to be alone.

I wipe my face on the collar of my sweater and get a grip. I didn't realize my friend even knew how to text. But that means he's still learning new things, so he isn't getting old as fast as he believes. I rise on shaky legs, make my way to the bar, and call out, "Is anyone there?"

"Yes, sir," the voice answers before materializing in front of me as the bartender. "The restaurant's closed . . ." But when he takes a look at my face and recognition enters his eyes, his face becomes a mask of concern. "I'm sorry, Mr. . . . Fitzpatrick. What may I get you?"

"Just a glass of water, please."

"You got it." He adds a little ice to the largest-size glass and then fills it with water.

I pick it up and take a big gulp, then look the bartender in the eyes. "Thank you. Would you mind if I hung out in here a few more minutes?"

"Of course. Take as long as you need."

"Thanks, man."

I walk back to the table, take a seat, and notice that the guy has moved from the bar to the hostess stand. From behind it, he pulls out stanchions and velvet ropes and cordons off the entrance. I look out at the rain. The kindness of strangers. And the miracles of Christmas. When I feel like I have it together again, I pick up the phone and reread the text. Receiving it was a hinge moment: the second you hear news that could change your life forever.

The title of the text consists of a single word: *SOLD!* And then Seamus's message:

Are you sitting down? Old Mrs. R. came through in a big way. She wants all four pieces. I read her eagerness and finessed the price to 5K apiece. We got you twenty grand, my boy. She's wiring me the money today so that she can receive the shipment in time for her annual New Year's Eve soiree. When I have it, I'll wire it to you through Western Union there in Greenville, unless you'd rather me send it to Charleston. Be back to you today.

Merry Christmas, son.
Yours truly,
Seamus

I swallow around the giant lump in my throat and down the rest of my water. My friend has changed the course of my life, not once but twice. I haven't found the right time to bring up the subject of money with Mamie. But with the amount of money that's now at play on my side, I could help set us up in business together, if she decides that's what she wants. My mind whirs on. I could sell or donate my beater of a car, and with the income from my photography work, I could buy a more decent set of wheels. And if Mamie agrees to marry me, I could put some of the jack together with the rent I'm paying now to get us into a bigger apartment after we're married. But more important than anything, I can buy Mamie a ring. It won't be anything flashy, but Mamie prefers minimal jewelry, and knowing her, she'd love whatever I could afford.

I'm meeting with Isla at eleven, so I need to run upstairs and freshen up. I step over the ropes and leave the restaurant, then stand waiting for the elevator. I murmur to Mamie's chief in the painting. "If she says yes, I'll devote the rest of my life to making her happy."

In the elevator, I'm still processing the last twenty minutes. Oh man, it occurs to me, the poetic justice! Mrs. Rembert virtually handing over $20,000 to a man she snubbed. Should I tell Mamie? I could just add the jack to my account, the way I would the sale of a print. After our talk that night in the break room, I know that the Remberts don't mean anything to her. It's not like she would spend the rest of her life imagining the fine antiques I helped refinish, squatting in the Remberts' beach house.

Smoky. I've meant to call him anyway, but a conversation with my brother feels freighted, urgent now. In my room, I watch the relentless rain and smile, thinking of Mamie safe and snug and pampered in the spa, then pace the carpet again, stopping to check my texts for word from Seamus or Isla, or the person I'm thinking of as my ace in the hole, the biggest iron in the fire.

I thumb through my phone and to my favorites contact page. I ring Smoky, who I hope to catch enjoying forty-eight hours off from his firefighter duty. Everyone who meets him finds his name unbelievable. Sometimes he good-naturedly shows them

Rob

his driver's license. I think about Mamie looking at mine while the phone rings. He answers the call with, "Little bro! I thought you'd fallen off the earth. How are yah?"

"Hey, bro. Sorry about that. I've been busy here for a minute. But I'm good, really good." I hear the low rumble of men's voices on Smoky's end. "You on duty?"

"Yah. A twenty-four straight. But then I'll have forty-eight off for Christmas."

"That's great, man. You spending it with Angela?"

"Yah. *And* her family, but it should be a good time. We'll go by Mom's first and eat something, you know, like, appetizers. I gotta have a bite of her wicked stuffing. Pop's good. Behaving himself. Staying home at night."

My mouth waters at the thought of Mom's stuffing, and I briefly miss being there myself. Seeing Mom. And even Pop. "I have some news, Smoke. I'm in love."

"Yah?" He coughs and then chuckles. "Who's the poor girl?"

"Yah, you chowdahead. Her name's Mamie Morrow. And she's actually from a wealthy family."

"Weal-thy? What's she want with the likes of you?"

"Bro, seriously. She's crazy about me. I'm proposing."

"Dude."

"Yah." I swallow and then give my brother a recap of my time in Greenville.

"An instantaneous connection," he says when I'm done, stumbling over the word. "That's beautiful. I can't wait to meet her."

"The thing that's gnawing at me is, we haven't discussed her money. I mean, I know she must have, like, a trust fund or something."

"A *trust fund baby*? Like Lindsay Lohan or something?"

"One hundred and eighty from that. Mamie likes to live frugally and minimally. She's down-to-earth and kind and giving.

225

But two people who're thinking about a future together should talk about finances."

"Agree."

"So if she doesn't bring it up, should I do it before or after I propose?"

"Kid, that's tough." He pauses until I wonder if the call has dropped. When he speaks, his words are measured. "I think you should man up and do it *before* you propose."

"Thank you, Smoke. I kind of wanted to know you were with me. That you, you know . . ."

"I know. Keep me posted. And Merry Christmas, Rob."

"Merry Christmas, Smoky. Be safe."

CHAPTER TWENTY-SIX

Mamie

S tepping from the sanctuary of the tranquil and beautiful
Poseidon Spa, I move past the hallway that leads to the staff
break room. Vive la différence! But reflecting on the brilliant
services I've just had sweeps the memory of that room away. I
can't say which of my services was more sublime. I move in an
aura of calmness and harmonious balance, my body as loose
jointed and relaxed as a newborn at its mother's breast.

I open the door to the lobby and reflexively bring a hand to
my cheek. My face feels pure. Energized and glowing. I hope to
catch Rob and see if he notices a difference in me. There are few
people about: a father and son filling cups at the hot chocolate
bar, and a woman reading a book in the library. I don't see Rob,
but Marco's stationed at the front desk. "Merry Christmas," I
say to him. "I can't believe it's Christmas Eve."

"I know," he says. "Merry Christmas to you, Mamie."

I peer around the space. "It's so dead today."

"The weather may be keeping the locals away, but the guest
rooms are only a third full."

"Wow! Really?"

"No worries. We're expecting a hundred people for the ball
tonight. The bar will be slammed by five thirty. They're setting

up an extension to one side for when people come out to get their cocktails during the ball."

"Nice. I'm excited! Are you working all day?"

His face becomes a beacon. "Just half. Kwame's back in at one o'clock."

"Good for you! Hey, I'm thinking of doing a little shopping, maybe grabbing a bite of lunch."

Marco leans over the desk to look out the front doors. I follow his gaze. "Looks like there's a lull in the rain." I hear Rob's r-dropping, fast-paced, and deep voice, and it sounds like it's coming from the gallery.

Then I ask, "Hey, Marco, can you hang on for a minute?"

The phone rings. He puts a ready hand on the receiver and smiles at me again. "I can until one."

I laugh as he picks up the phone and then make my way toward the gallery. Passing the purple banquette, I give it an eye-batting grin. From there, I spot Rob's silky dark hair and shoulders rising high above the back of a Lucite chair. In a second chair, I'm afforded a view of the lower half of a woman wearing a long skirt and flats. Her chair is turned to face Rob. Freezing in place, I frown as he leans forward. He isn't looking at his camera or laptop but at something on a tray in his lap. I move behind a pillar, trying to get a better look at the woman.

It's not Isla.

It's a striking-looking person I've never seen before. She laughs and reaches out to touch my boyfriend's arm.

My jaw and shoulders tense. I have to get out of here. Get some air. Try and parse what I've seen. Bustling back to the front desk, I look back at the gallery and almost run into the great fir tree. But I'm done with hiding. "Marco," I call out before I even reach the desk, "where do you recommend that I go?"

I'm not sure what my expression looks like, but he narrows his eyes at me. "Are you walking? I just checked my weather app, and more big rain is coming. But it's supposed to stop around five. And then get cold tonight."

"I'm walking if you have an umbrella I can borrow."

"You bet. There are a bunch of golf umbrellas out by the valet stand. You're welcome to one. Are you a reader?"

I feel my smoothed and nourished forehead wrinkling. "Well, ye-es. I am."

"Okay, your best bet is our nationally renowned indie bookstore, M. Judson Booksellers," he says as though he owns the place. "It's fun, especially for readers, but they also have good gift items."

"Sounds great. And a café nearby?"

"Oh, M. Judson has an in-house spot called Camilla Kitchen. They serve snacks and sweets and specialty teas and coffee."

I think back to the day Rob and I strolled around downtown. "Is it in the tall building behind the city Christmas tree?"

"Yep. That's it."

"Thanks." With one last look back toward the gallery, I push through the door. I pat my pocket for my credit card and, finding it there, head to the umbrella stand beneath the entrance overhang. I select a green-and-white striped one that looks like it could cover a bison and rush out into the rain. I stop halfway across the bridge to look at the falls. The river has swollen to its banks. The water roils and churns and tosses spray into the air. The rain picks up again. Big drops make a tom-tom of my umbrella. I quicken my pace. By the time I reach Main Street, my clothes are mostly dry, but my sneakers are sodden.

At the bookstore, I mount the stately steps of the old building. An entrance room leads into the bookstore proper.

Umbrellas lean against a wall or lie on the tiled floor on which a big safety mat has been placed. I toss my big honker amid the neat one-click models and make straight for something warm to drink. My sneakers squeak along the wood floor, but newgrass Christmas music plays and drowns out the sound. A couple of kids in elf caps dance in an aisle to a fiddle solo.

I breathe in rosemary and vanilla and smile for the first time in an hour. I join a short line in front of the broad and garlanded Camilla Kitchen counter, then use the time to survey the open space. Books of all colors fill floor-to-ceiling shelves and predominate the display tables. But almost everywhere I look, something charming pops: funny cocktail napkins and mugs, mixing bowls, funky and fetching dish towels, trendy coaster sets, and cool art prints. At my hip is a collection of grabby cookbooks on a display table. I choose *Sweet Soulful Baking*, a collection of cake recipes, for Gladiola, whose favorite show is *The Great British Bake Off*.

Now next in line, I can read the drink menu. The specialty drinks are delightfully named for novels! I set my cap on Dark Pines, a latte with brown sugar and cardamom. The kitchen staff are heads-up and genuine. "Where's the rosemary I'm smelling?"

"Oh, our homemade shortbread. Ah-mazing. Here, try a little piece," says a woman in a vintage apron who appears to be about my age. She hands me a sliver, and I chew it thoughtfully. The sweet is perfectly balanced with a hint of salt, and the rosemary's inimitable piney notes step forward.

"*Unbelievable*. Thank you. I'd like a piece for now and a small bag to take with me, please."

With my cup in hand and a small handled shopping bag pushed up my forearm, I browse the other side of the shop. The latte is delicious. Coffee table books! I love the look of a stack of three pretty ones with an accessory on top. I think of Rob and a future home, but my daydream screeches to a halt. Who was the woman sitting with him in the gallery? The two seemed pretty chummy. My head tells me that Rob adores me and that there's a perfectly acceptable explanation. But my heart inches toward my throat. The secretive texts. The message that affected him so deeply as I was leaving the restaurant. And a tête-à-tête with a mystery woman? The Fitzpatrick curse! What if it's real and he can't break it?

I heave a sigh and pop the square of shortbread in my mouth. It's time for another lecture to self: *Mamie*, I tell myself as I chew, *you know good and well he wouldn't be sitting in the lobby before God and everybody if something had sparked between him and the woman. Enjoy your shopping break and relax. Don't let this ruin your morning of bliss.*

Validated, my shoulders finally lower. I trail my fingers over glossy romance covers. My heart feels lonesome for Rob's smile, his arms, his kisses. I slip my phone from my pocket and send Abigay a shorthand text telling her what I'd seen. If she's still in the air, she won't get it anytime soon, but knowing that she'll see it soon makes me feel better.

A beautiful pink-and-white cover, *Old Roses and English Roses*, brings my mother to mind. I'd forgotten how Mama loves roses. Abruptly, I feel small and mean for abandoning her the way I did after she revealed to me the awful truth about Tate. The news presented in her flat five-words-per-sentence and maddeningly matter-of-fact tone hurt me deeply.

But it occurs to me now that if she hadn't spilled the story or handed over the box of Tate's things, I never would have known that I had a grandfather who loved me, to whom I was special.

I never would have felt drawn to learn more about my Native American heritage and Tate's legacy.

I never would have been so viscerally compelled to jump at an assignment that required me to spend Christmas at the Grand Bohemian Lodge.

And likely, I never would have met Rob Fitzpatrick and fallen in love with him.

I pick up the book of roses and tuck it under an arm. I'll take it to my mother as a belated Christmas gift. As my upper arms prickle with chill bumps, I know I've made the right decision.

Although I've never been one to upholster my laptop in stickers, a basket of cool bookish ones by the register calls my name. Shuffling through them with another woman who says, "How cute are these?" I lay aside for myself a chunky sticker that reads, *BIBLIOPHILE*, one with a quote from a favorite literary author, Oscar Wilde, and another that simply exclaims, *I LOVE BOOKS!* I smile to myself because once again I'm proving that I'm more open to change. While the woman at the register wraps and bags purchases for the man in front of me, I shrug and select a few more. When I uncover one with a smiley sunshine and the words *IF EVERY DAY COULD BE AS COOL AS SATURDAY*, I remember Kwame and realize I've found the perfect little happy for him.

At least my umbrella's easy to spot. At the door, I meet people coming in with dripping umbrellas and swiping at their wet clothes. I take a big breath, hold my big shopping bag close to me, and head down the steps.

But only one block farther, I'm sitting in a diner with my hands around a bowl of rich and hearty tomato basil soup. My phone vibrates. *Fitzpatrick* lights up the screen. "Hello, Fitzpatrick," I say.

"Well, *hello, Morrow.* Where are you?"

"Oh, I've been doing a little shopping. Now I'm eating soup."

"You've been out in all this rain? Man, I'm watching it through a lobby window, and it's really coming down again."

"I borrowed an umbrella. What's going on in the lobby today?"

"Not much. They even closed the Christmas market for the day. I've been taking care of some business."

I frown into my soup. "You certainly have been busy."

"Mamie, if you're casting a line, this fish won't bite. I have surprises. But all will be revealed on Christmas Day, aka Mamie's birthday. Now, trust me."

"Hang on and let me take a few spoonfuls of soup?"

"Yah huh." I make noise with my spoon. I've promised Rob that I would trust him over and over, but flags of doubt keep popping up. I know my family issues are at the root of my trust issues. It isn't Rob's fault. I love the man with my whole heart and have no choice but to trust him. I eat some soup. If we get married and take vows, there'll be no turning back. "Yah huh," I say again, "I trust you." He laughs. "I have a couple of secrets up my sage sweater sleeve too. I hope you didn't go crazy over my birthday, though."

"Not crazy. You'll see."

"So your day's been successful."

"Yah. And profitable."

"Will Isla sell prints of your photos in the gallery?"

"She will. She looked at all the photos I took of the lodge and decided it would be easier and best to choose ones we didn't use in the article."

"That makes a lot of sense."

"Right? No conflicts. No infringements. No harm, no foul. I'll have the photos printed and framed at home, and then ship them up here. The gallery will take a thirty percent commission on any sales. A win-win, I say, and I'm grateful."

"That's terrific, Fitzpatrick."

"Thank you, sweetheart. I miss you. Are you coming back soon?"

"I am. Wait for me in the lobby?"

"Yah. Be safe. I love you."

"I love you." I finish my meal, pay my check, and head out again. Holding my packages high, I head into a torrent. Gusts snatch at the huge umbrella, but I cling to the wobbling handle and take careful steps. At the bridge again, rain pelts the umbrella like rice thrown at a wedding. I make it halfway across.

And Rob is there at the end.

Running to meet me.

Then his arm is around me, holding me tight against his side while he wrestles the umbrella handle with his free hand. We trot past the battened-down market booths toward the hotel, my gifts jostling up and down, and finally bump through the doors. We stand inside, catching our breath and regarding our bedraggled state.

Kwame moves through the registration office door to stand at the desk. "Is it still raining?" he asks, and then watches as we dissolve into helpless laughter.

CHAPTER TWENTY-SEVEN

Mamie was anxious about the condition of her packages but not panicked the way she might have been a week ago. I sat on a lobby sofa with her so she could look through her shopping bags. Tucker—already there at a quarter to three and in full-command mode, steadily supervising the double bar setup and directing the catering team to the pre-function room—took one look at us and kindly brought over a couple of bar towels.

Now my phone vibrates with a call.

My heart gives an extra thump, and I'm on my feet.

Mamie's shuffling through what look like stickers . . . but looks up and gives me a distracted smile.

I hold the cell in both hands and look at the screen.

It's my ace in the hole.

I stride toward the library, hoping no one is there, and answer the call.

"Tom, hello!"

I stand in the library, looking out the windows. The Reedy River is full and tumbling up and down its banks; the sun slides out from behind a patch of clouds. My heart fills with complete calm, and I utter a prayer of thanks. All my hopes, all my research, and all my plans for Mamie's birthday surprise are coming to fruition. Mamie's sitting quietly, her head back against the sofa. I stop by the bar and ask one of the relief bartenders for two glasses of water.

"Hi," Mamie says, smiling at the water and at me.

"Hi, sweetheart," I say, handing her a glass and trying to imagine her expression when she opens my birthday gift tomorrow. "How did your purchases fare the rain?"

"Oh, fine, thank goodness. The extra white paper the bookstore stuffed in the bag took most of the hit because the paper they wrapped around the gifts was barely damp." She drinks some water. "Here, look what I got."

I love the way her eyes light up as she shows me the gifts she found for others. The stickers are cute, and the books she bought for her mother and her housekeeper, Gladiola, are really nice. "So are you proud of me," she says, "for getting my mother a present? It'll be belated, but still."

I quietly take her hand and search her eyes. "Are you going to take it to her yourself?"

"Well . . . I think *so*," she says, her eyes searching mine back.

"What will that look like?"

"I'm not sure how she feels about what happened after all this time. But I think I'm ready to face her again. Without . . . you know, rancor."

"Are you going to ask her to forgive you?"

Mamie's eyes fill.

"Oh, love," I say, "I didn't mean to make you cry."

She dabs at the corner of her eyes with the bar towel. "You didn't. But that's what I've been thinking about. Forgiveness."

I pick up my water and smile gently. "Then I'm *extra* proud of you."

She gives me a wobbly smile. "Thank you, my Fitzy."

I take the roses book, careful not to mess up the jacket with my big fingers. "It may be about roses, but it's a beautiful olive branch."

She surveys the cover again. "I hope so. I'll wrap it beautifully when I get home." *Home.* As she rewraps the books in the dry paper, I feel a new pang—this one in my sternum—at the idea of not spending my days with Mamie the way I have since the day I stepped into her car. I have to propose. I have to marry her.

Mamie looks at me. "I'm not sure if I should call her first or just show up and surprise her."

"Who?"

"Colleen, ya chowderhead."

I howl a laugh that makes a caterer turn her head with a frown that quickly turns into a smile. "If you're going to call me a knucklehead, you're going to have to pronounce the Boston equivalent right. It's *chowdah*, as in the best soup in the country."

She grins. "Chow-*dah*-head then. I'm talking about calling first or just showing up. At Tradd Street."

If it was Monday and Mamie had said yes to my proposal, I would ask if she wanted me to go with her, meet Colleen, and tell her that we're engaged. But that would probably be way more than the woman could stand. "If you're asking me, I advise calling first and just saying you'd like to come over."

"Yes. That's what I'll do."

"That takes courage, Mamie. But with your sweet sincerity, I'm sure it will go well." She eyes my face with an odd little expression, but then squeezes my arm. Despite the people treading back and forth between the bar and the pre-function room and Tucker issuing commands with the unperturbed air of a brigadier general, I put my arms around her and hold her for a while, smelling her hair. Loving her.

We part when the jazz combo troops through the front

doors. Five middle-aged guys dressed in tuxes and carrying their instruments in cases. The largest one must be an upright bass, but its case has wheels. Brill, as Mamie would say.

"I realize this is one ninth-hour chowdahead of a question, but do we have tickets to this thing?"

She laughs again and collects her things to carry them upstairs. "I got them the first day."

"I should have known. Hey, I'd love to pick you up at your door like it's a real date."

She gives me a sus side-eye, but then smiles. "I'd love that."

We head upstairs to our own rooms to rest. From the bar, I hear a bartender say, "Look. The rain is over."

CHAPTER TWENTY-EIGHT

Mamie

My makeup pretty perfect and my updo not bad for my inexperienced hands, I stand in my undies and survey the vintage boho bargain lying on my bed. It's turquoise brocade with a rich chocolate-brown faux-fur collar and cuffs. Rob should be here in ten minutes, and I cannot wait to see him. Shivering with excitement, I carefully slide the dress over my head and then manage to do up the zipper in the back. I stand before the closet door mirror. The dress falls just above my ankles. I know my footwear choice will be just right. They will be true to who I am and not for the woman in the felony-provoking red heels.

I want to carry something that makes me feel connected to Tate, but what? Remembering the beautifully arrayed and framed arrowhead collections in the pre-function room, I look through the little pouch of arrowheads that Tate left me, and holding them in my hand one by one, I think of my grandfather once doing the same. But all of them seem too poky for my pocket.

Now it comes to me. The other item that still lies quietly in the sock compartment of my suitcase. My hand finds it, and I add it to my outfit.

Four minutes early, a trio of knocks fall on my door. My heart leaps.

I open it to the sight of the most handsome boyfriend on the planet, *my* man, *my* first real love and hopefully my last. When my eyes manage to move from his fabulous face to his body, I'm stunned. "Fitzpatrick! A tuxedo?" He smiles serenely and bows as graciously as a prince to his princess. "Come in, come in, and let me take a better look."

"Morrow," he says, his voice full and throaty. He shakes his head and holds a palm to his chest. "I am . . ." He blows a toothpaste-scented breath through his lips. "I'm TKO'd by your beauty and may never recover." He takes my hand and raises it, then turns me in a pirouette. "That dress. It's *gorgeous* on you. Like it was . . . made especially for you."

I hold him at arm's length, then dip my chin and peep up under my lashes at him. As he stares, I bend my knees and drop him a small curtsy. "Thank you, my love. And *you* . . . you look like every woman's *dream come to life*." The tuxedo is coffee brown with velvet lapels. At his throat is a black velvet bow tie flecked with bits of gold. From his breast pocket a matching pocket square flares.

"Thank *you*, my love. Kwame, actually. He seemed like an elegant kind of guy. He hooked me up with a rental place. I wanted to surprise you."

I lead him to the mirror and take his arm. "I'm *awestruck*. Look at us. We're amazing." I recall the times I'd regarded us in the window behind the bar. We've reached pinnacle pair status.

He gathers me in his arms. "You waited to put on your lipstick, didn't you? How did you know I'd want to kiss you?"

I peep up at him again. "I had a hunch."

He chuckles soft and low, and I feel the rumble in his chest. "What shoes are you wearing?"

I close my eyes and grin. "My suede boots."

"Aw, my favorite. That's my girl." He raises his hands to hold the back of my neck.

"Careful not to muss my hair," I whisper before he pulls my lips to his. We kiss deeply, Rob tilting my head back and forth as though he can't get close enough.

Outside in the corridor, I hear the elevator bell. I break the kiss and step back, almost breathless. "Whoo. The bell tolls."

"Would you like to go to a Christmas ball with me?" he asks, and crooks his arm for me to take.

"Just let me put on my lipstick."

"Can I watch?"

"No way." I walk into the bathroom and pick up my zippered case. "If you do, we'll be more than fashionably late. Oh! See the little wrapped package on the chest by the TV? Will you grab it? It's for Kwame."

"Sure. That was sweet of you. Hey, your room looks exactly like mine," he says, as if he's just become aware of his surroundings. "Except . . . a lot . . . um, *messier*."

I laugh. "Are you surprised?" I call to him as I locate my tube of red.

"I am. I figured you'd be Little Miss Hospital Corners."

"Not in my bedroom. But in the rest of the house." I apply an even coat of lipstick and blot my lips. "Remember? I'm full of surprises," I say, walking back into the bedroom.

He smiles softly. "Never change, Morrow."

CHAPTER TWENTY-NINE

Rob

In the elevator, I worry with my bow tie. "Stop fidgeting, Fitz-patrick. You look grand," Mamie tells me.

"I'm just thinking of what my brothers would say if they saw me in this monkey suit."

"They'd be jealous. The whole brigade of them."

"Smoke would like it," I say as the doors open, thinking of our conversation this morning.

"Let's get the chief's opinion," Mamie suggests. We stand before the painting. She whispers, "He says you look splendid and worthy of being my date for the ball." I smile and move to kiss her. "Not yet," she reminds me. I give my fingers a disappointed snap as we move into the lobby. It's five fifteen, and the barstools are almost filled. "Just let me drop this off for Kwame?" Mamie asks. "And order me an old-fashioned? And water. A *big* water."

I smile. "Your wish is my command."

Tucker presides over the bar wearing a white shirt and black tie, a black apron around his thick middle. Two other bartenders, who must have gotten the dress code memo, polish glasses and fill orders. I take a seat and exchange greetings with Tucker. "Dude," he says, surveying me, "you look *almost* good enough to be with Mamie tonight."

"Thanks."

"You know once the ball starts it's cash bar?"

"Yah, I heard that and got some today," I say, and pat my breast pocket. I place our drink order and look back for Mamie. She's moving my way.

On her barstool, she leans back and moves her shoulders to Dan Fogelberg's holiday classic, "Same Old Lang Syne." I watch her and sigh with pleasure. "I *love* this song," she says. I should formally ask her out for New Year's Eve.

Tucker brings our drinks. "Enjoy, you two."

"What are we toasting to?" I ask.

"How about to two?" she suggests. "As in the two of us? *Only* we two."

"To two," I say, dying to kiss her.

We sip our drinks. "Kwame loved the little happy I got him. The sunshine sticker."

"Great. You're so thoughtful. I like that about you," I say, and touch her nose.

"*Thank* you."

"Ooh, is that a list of the hors d'oeuvres for pre-function?" Mamie asks Tucker as he passes by.

"Yep, from the caterer," he says, handing it to her and then mimicking exhaustion. "A hundred people will be here for the ball. Grateful for the extra hands tonight. And my seniority. I'm off the next five days."

"Oh, Tucker," Mamie says, dropping the list to the bar. "We're leaving Monday. We'll miss you. You were such a nice part of our meet-cute."

I smile at her.

"Aw, now," Tucker says.

"No, you've been great, man," I say. "Thank you." Another bartender calls to him.

"Well, it's been my pleasure."

"Hey, Tucker," Mamie asks him as he moves away. "Whatever happened to Whitney?"

"She up and quit," he says. "Nobody seems to know why. Somebody said she left town."

Mamie looks at me and shrugs. I sip my drink, pondering this news flash, as Mamie returns to the caterer's list. "Okay, Fitzy, you have to listen to this, but don't drool on my sleeve."

I laugh. "Promise. Shoot."

She takes several sips of water. "Bacon-wrapped scallops; deviled eggs with blue cheese, bacon, and shallots; bison sliders; six cheeses; baked coconut shrimp; jalapeño pepper poppers; and pecan-stuffed mushrooms. And for dessert?"

I hold my face in my hands. "I don't think I can take it."

Mamie cracks up. "I know! But listen: petite chocolate cakes topped with spun-sugar stars, pecan tassies, mini cupcakes with edible flowers, and assorted macaroons." She kisses her fingertips. "Sounds scrumptious."

I lift my head and drain the last of my drink. "Well, here's to Christmas gluttony!"

"Oh, let's see it all through, Fitzy," she says, snuggling into my side. "I feel so wonderfully festive."

At 6:20, the light through the window turns clear and bluish, like skim milk. I'd like to capture it, but the memory on this night will have to do. At 6:30, the doors to the pre-function room open, and everyone turns at the sound of xylophone notes. It's Mr. Reagan, who's also in a brown tuxedo—at once validating my choice and lifting my shoulders. His voice rings out. "Good evening, ladies and gentlemen. I'm Vaughn Reagan, manager of the Grand Bohemian Lodge. Thank you for joining us this evening for our inaugural Christmas ball. Please," he says, standing aside, "enter and enjoy."

"How special was that," Mamie says. From the ballroom, we

can hear the leader of the jazz combo kicking things off with the jumping Christmas music of Glenn Miller and "Sleigh Ride." The first people are moving into pre-function and having their hands stamped by a woman from the catering team. *Like Wonka's golden tickets,* I think.

"I see Betty and Gary," Mamie says. "She looks beautiful tonight in that green silk gown. I want to meet them."

I smile. "We'll make sure and chat." Mamie excuses herself to the ladies' room while I settle up with Tucker.

The combo's playing "In the Christmas Mood" as I enter the nicest event I've ever attended. Mamie lightly holds my arm. I smile down at her. "Thank you," I whisper to her just before we have our hands stamped.

In the pre-function room, Mamie's eyes reflect the gleaming décor. "Look, Native American decorations," she says. Thin evergreens lit by colored lights are lined up behind the food tables. They drip with Nativity figures, dream catchers, angels, drums, horses, and clusters of pheasant feathers, like the ones pushed into the back of Mamie's hairstyle. "Look at the darling felted papooses," she says as we move through the hors d'oeuvres line with glass plates in hand. My eyes are on the food, but Mamie gushes over dried red chili pepper garlands, white flowers, candles, and carved figures nestled between the service pieces. I pile my plate with one of each menu item, then go back and add another bison slider. Mamie's more selective.

"Our next selection is The Four Freshmen's rendition of 'I'm Dreaming of a White Christmas,'" announces the combo leader from the platform at the back of the ballroom. Mamie finds us an empty standing two-top.

"Let's get another drink and let this settle a bit before we dance," she suggests. I nod, my mouth full.

Then at last, the two of us step onto the dance floor. I move us toward the far side of the floor, hoping for a kiss or two. Mamie places a small hand on my shoulder as I lift her other and hold it firmly in mine. We move together to "Joy to the World." Nearby, Annelise and Isla dance with their dates. We exchange brief greetings and smiles. I move Mamie and me closer to the edge of the floor, wanting her all to myself.

"Did I mention that I'm a terrible dancer?" I ask.

"Yah nuh!" she says, and then laughs. "I am too. I tend to try and lead. *And* step on feet." She looks down ruefully. "And with those canoes of yours, it's inevitable. But so what?"

I grin down at her. "So what? Hold me closer, tiny dancer."

"Oh, Fitzy, what a marvelous night," she says into my bow tie. Then she lifts her gaze to my face. "I feel as though all my dreams are coming true."

"Mine too."

Emboldened, I make an attempt at dipping her as the jazz combo plays "Christmas Tree Boogie." She pivots, laughing, and as she pulls her arm back into her chest, a much-too-big-for-her silver-and-turquoise bracelet appears around her hand. It must have fallen from her sleeve. Where it's undoubtedly been all evening. I let her go and step back. Waves of shock and fear wash through me. I stand gaping at her and run my hands through my hair. The band plays on.

"What?" Mamie says, holding the bracelet with her other hand. "Tate left this to me. I brought it so he could be part of—" Alarm colors her cheeks. "Fitzy, what are you thinking?"

"I don't know what to think." I turn and storm away from the floor. It's Isla who catches up with me first.

"I saw what happened," she says, stopping me with a firm grip on my bicep.

Annelise appears, whisking a huge-eyed Mamie from the room. I'm profoundly embarrassed. Isla motions for us to step behind a caterer's partition. "Mamie," she says, "give me the bracelet." Her words are like punches to my hors d'oeuvre–filled gut.

Mamie, whose face is the color of old buttermilk, slowly removes the bracelet and hands it over, her hands shaking violently. Isla takes the piece and runs her fingers over the turquoise, surveying it closely before turning the bracelet to examine the marking on the inside. She looks up at me. "This is not ours. The craftsman's mark is unique." She lets out a great breath, along with the rest of us, and turns back to Mamie. Isla reaches for her hand and places the bracelet on her palm. "Mamie, I am deeply sorry. I don't know . . . how we . . . can ever make this . . . misunderstanding up to you."

Without a word or a look back at me, the love of my life flees the Christmas ball.

"Where are you, Mamie?" I shout aloud in the parking lot. I turn, the lodge rearing up at me. After rushing through the lobby, the restaurant, the whiskey bar, and even the private dining room and break room downstairs, I stumble through the market stalls and then down to our bench, and finally check her car. It's too cold for her to be outside, so I rush back to the registration desk. "Kwame," I pant, "Mamie is missing. I've looked everywhere."

The man looks gobsmacked. He stutters a little. "Have you tried her room?"

Isla, Annelise, and their dates appear. "How can we help?" Annelise asks.

I avoid Isla's eyes and answer Kwame. "She didn't run toward the elevators."

"Maybe the stairs," he suggests. "Here, let me provide you with a room key."

"I'll go up with you," Annelise says.

"No, I'll go alone. But look everywhere. Alert security."

When Kwame hands me the key card, I sprint for the stairs and then open the door to Mamie's hall, the night I'd mentally counted the doors flitting through my mind. *Mamie.* I fumble with the card; on the second try, the green light admits me. I slowly open the door and call her name before searching the room and finding nothing but the clothes and notebooks scattered about. I turn, my throat thick with unshed tears, and pull the door closed. Taking the elevator down, I try and calm myself. *Think clearly, man!*

Downstairs, a security guard speaks into a walkie-talkie and nods at me. I head back outside and am drawn to the bridge where, just this afternoon, I'd run through the rain and helped her make it inside. *Mamie, Mamie.* At the center of the bridge, the water seems massive, surging over rocks to smash those below.

I grab my phone and call Smoky. "Smoke," I say when he answers, "Mamie has gone missing. I can't explain it all now, but it was a huge deal, a huge misunderstanding with the gallery curator. But it's all my fault for doubting her."

"Rob, you're not like the rest of us. You're our hope, my hope, my hero. Go find her, idiot, and stop thinking wrong."

I end the call, my tears shored up but with a small measure of hope.

Back inside, I sit drinking coffee in the library with Annelise and Tucker. The security guards give us updates until the evening draws to a close. The ball guests spill from the pre-function room. I think of them heading out to their cars, full of cheer and love and joy in anticipation of Christmas morning.

At eleven o'clock, Kwame appears in the doorway. "Rob, the security guards have alerted the police."

The acidic fluid of nausea fills my mouth, but I swallow it back and take my mints from my pocket. "I guess that's best," I say, bone-weary, and put a mint on my tongue. I stand. "I need some air," I tell the others.

I move through the emptying lobby and remember the lobby porch. I push through the door and stride to the brick railing looking down at the falls. The mist reaches out and catches my hair and face, claiming me. An irresistible force majeure turns me around to the one place I would never think to look for Mamie. The egg.

I step closer and see the tip of a small boot sticking out. "Mamie?"

"I'm here, Rob."

I rush to the egg and sit on its edge.

The warmth from inside the structure moves around me, but my teeth chatter around my words. "Mamie, are you all right?"

"I'm okay, Fitzy."

"Don't move. I'll be right back." I stride back inside and hold onto the library doorway with both hands. I tell my friends where I've found her, safe and sound, and to let the police know. I ask them to give us our privacy, to go home and enjoy their nights.

Without waiting for their replies, I turn back for the porch, sending Smoky a text. I pass Isla sitting alone in the lobby. She leaps up and looks at me, but I just shake my head. Back on the porch, I whip off my tuxedo jacket and then climb into the egg, where Mamie lies small and curled on her side. I cover her with the jacket and then lie spooning her, covering her body with mine. She sighs, and the egg fills with the smell of sour alcohol.

"Mamie, what . . . How much have you had to drink?"

"Oh . . . I grabbed a bottle of wine on my way out here." She hiccups. "No . . . body was looking. I took it from Tucker's little fridge." She disentangles her arm and points toward the rail. "See? It's just there."

The bottle is only half-empty, but on top of the cocktails . . . "Mamie, can you turn over, darling?"

"I sure can." She rises to lean on her elbow, and I help her turn to face me. "I *like* darling," she says. "Guess what or who-o-o." She giggles a little. "A pair of owls have been calling to each other. A pair like us. Do you forgive me, Fitzy?" she asks in a tiny, thin voice.

"Darling, there's nothing to forgive."

"Thank you, darling, back," she says dreamily. She drifts off for a while. I lie holding her and racking my brain, searching for a path back to where we were before this night ripped us apart.

She stirs, and I can barely make out her eyes as she opens them. "I feel better now," she says, and then asks for a mint. We talk until only the moon and stars are awake, and I feel an extra space opening in my chest. Around three o'clock, we've found our path, and incredibly, after all that went down last night, I feel we're back on the good foot.

Mamie says she'd like to go to bed. I extricate myself from the egg and then bend to pick her up. I carry her through the dim and silent lobby and up the elevator. I still have her room key, so I take her inside and put her to bed, softly kissing her sweet forehead.

CHAPTER THIRTY

Mamie

I wake up at ten o'clock, and though Rob left me fully dressed and under the covers, the bed is cold. My nose feels like it would be well-suited for a snowman. I get up to check the thermostat, and a chisel drives itself right between my eyes. The heat is set, but none is coming through the vents. I pad into the bathroom and flip the wall switch, but the light doesn't come on. In the semi-dark, I dig out my travel bottle of Aleve and drink all the water I can hold.

I refuse to allow myself to dwell on all that happened last night because today is Christmas Day, my birthday, and I get to spend it with the man I love. Rob assured me in the egg that only the people who care about us know about the bracelet debacle. And that most of the guests were gone before he alerted security. Though Isla and Annelise are both on vacation now, I know I'll have to face an apology from Isla and maybe Vaughn Reagan eventually, but I am not going to dwell on that either.

I strip out of last night's clothes and, hoping there's enough hot water, get into the shower, then stand in my robe, regarding the steamy and dark mirror. I draw a heart around where my face should be with a finger, and then smile and say, "Happy birthday, Mamie. You are twenty-seven years old." My phone shimmies on the bedside table. Rob must have taken it from my pocket and placed it there. Could it be my mother calling? But *Fitzpatrick* is displayed on the screen. I grin and open the call, then fall back onto the bed. "Good morning, handsome."

"Good morning, beautiful," he says. "Should I say happy birthday or Merry Christmas first?"

I grin. "I think you just said both."

He laughs. "Guess I did. Your power out too?"

"Yep."

"I'm showered and dressed and heading downstairs to see what's going on."

"I'll be down in twenty or thirty minutes," I say. "I'm dying to see you, darling."

"Oh, *me too*, baby. See you soon."

Downstairs, a group of guests are standing around the front desk. I find Rob, and we exchange a big hug and kiss. Though he and I are dressed for the day, some of the others, especially the children, are still in pajamas. Someone says, "They're about to make an announcement."

Vaughn and Marco step from behind the front desk to address the waiting guests. "The transformer was hit by a truck this morning," Marco begins, "knocking the power out on one side of the hotel, as well as the lobby, the restaurant, and everything below it."

Vaughn picks up. "You can do one of two things: check out now and be reimbursed for last night's stay, or stick it out and see if the power is restored in time for the staff to prepare tonight's Christmas feast. Those who wish to stay and whose rooms are on the cold side of the lodge are welcome to relax in the lobby by the fireplace. The staff will bring out extra blankets and provide food, hot chocolate, and coffee."

"This feels like an adventure of sorts," I say to Rob. "What do you think?"

He grins. "I'm willing to stick it out."

"Let's do it, Fitzpatrick!"

An hour later, we're sitting on a sofa across from Betty and Gary Jones, enjoying coffee and donuts with a blanket over our laps. Gary asks us how long we've been together, and we give them the short version of our new romance. "It's easy to see that you're in love," Betty says.

Rob puts his arm around me and pulls me closer. "We are, though it's been less than a week since we met." I detect a sheepish quality to his usually assertive and confident speech.

Gary crosses his legs and grimaces as though the movement causes him pain. Betty gives him an encouraging pat. "Let me tell you a story," he says. "Betty and I met in 1964. She came to visit cousins in Winston-Salem. She was nineteen. I knew her cousin Pete. One night, Pete calls me up and says, 'I'm taking Nancy to the movies tonight. My cousin Betty's in town. Want to come along? Be Betty's date?' I was curious, you know, and said, 'Sure, I'll go.'" He looks at Betty and grins. "When the girls came to the door, I took one look at Betty, *and I knew right down to my bones* that she was the girl for me. She was gorgeous and soft-spoken with red hair, a shade or two darker than yours, Mamie."

Charmed, I interrupt. "Did you feel the same, Betty?"

She gives Gary a long and loving look. "I did."

Rob and I exchange smiles, then his brow furrows. "Wait. You've been married sixty years . . . ?"

"Right," Gary says. "We had another date three days later and got married two weeks after that."

Rob leans forward and brushes crumbs from his hands. He stares from Gary to Betty and back again. "*How* did you know?"

"When things are providential," Betty says, "they come with a supernatural assurance."

I smile at Betty while Rob seems to chew on her remark. He opens his mouth. "Did you . . . disagree at all in those two weeks?"

"Sure, we did," Gary says, placing a hand on Betty's knee and giving it a pat. "We had issues to work through like anybody else."

Rob falls back against the sofa.

Betty looks at him and serenely says, "If your love is true, your differences work out over time."

Gary gives Rob a wink and takes another donut from the box on the table between us. "We have three children and thirteen grandchildren." He looks at Betty. "They are our legacy of love."

I shake my head, marveling. "So many congratulations to you both on sixty happy years."

"Thank you," they say in tandem, the way Rob and I do sometimes.

Rob's phone chimes, and he's out from under the blanket and on his feet. "Excuse me, please," he says, and strides over to a window.

"I think he has some Christmas surprises for me," I say with a confidential smile at the Joneses.

Six other families are gathered here today, three of them with young children. Two of the women are pregnant. How could any of us forget a Christmas Day like this? It's a cool memory to share with your grandchildren. Someone has hooked up a Bose speaker to their cell phone, and Brenda Lee sings "Rockin' Around the Christmas Tree." The cute kids are whooping and dancing around one of the smaller trees in their holiday pajamas. I feel a memory coming and close my eyes. I'm dancing with Grandtate to some special Native American song, my head thrown back with joy. A man who seems like a friend of Tate's accompanies us on a drum. But I can't see their faces. Then as suddenly as the vision came, it's gone. But it's replaced by a note of reassurance that lands softly on my shoulders. If a few memories have come back, others will as well.

And my mother. Recollections of her have been springing up like mushrooms after days of rain. I remember walking up the big steps of the church for Mass in a little navy coat, her gloved hand holding mine. And a fun time sitting on the floor of the living room on Tradd opening gifts. Mama, the name that comes with the memories, loved Christmas carols. She'd play them on our console stereo, and we'd sing along. Mama taught me how to harmonize.

Rob returns, twisting his mouth against a grin that wants to have its way with his mouth. Betty and Gary excuse themselves to go stretch their legs. Rob sits down and kisses me lovingly and long. His body fairly vibrates with what I assume is anticipation. It's contagious, though. I grin at him. I can only guess at what he's planned. Maybe an elaborate proposal? My heart bobs like a cork in my chest. I watch him watching the children sing "Holly Jolly Christmas."

"Are you thinking about Christmases with your family today?"

He nods several times. "Yah. My brothers were rowdy, but we had some great times playing with toys St. Nick brought. We each got three. And Pop behaved himself because Christmastime was Mom's favorite . . . followed by Easter."

"I love that." I snuggle into his side and lay my head on his shoulder. "Mm, you smell so good, Fitzy." I pause as he kisses my hair. "Try and remember the good things about your pop, sweetheart." I rise in my seat and turn to him. "And do you think . . . you could try and forgive him?"

He looks at me a long moment. "I'd like to try."

"I have three presents for you, but one you can't have until the afternoon," Rob says.

"Three like St. Nick?"

"Yah huh."

"I hope you didn't go crazy over my birthday."

"Yah nuh. At least not monetarily."

Good. "I have two for you," I say. "Should we find a corner somewhere and take our blanket with us? How 'bout we go get the presents and stuff them in our pillowcases? We could play Santa!"

"Deal. Meet you back in ten?"

We hurry upstairs and then get fortification: fresh coffees and egg bites the staff's just brought in. The library's empty. Cold, but empty. We settle into a love seat and tuck the blanket around us. Rob pulls a clumsily wrapped package from his bag and hands it to me with a "Ho Ho Ho." It feels like a framed photo, and I love that he's gifting me with a piece of his work. But as the wrapping falls away, I'm staring at a photo of *me,* I assume at age three, with a Native American man in long braids. My face goes slack and tears come. "It's the one that was supposed to be in the box, baby," Rob says softly.

I wipe my eyes with the edge of the blanket, but it's an exercise in futility. "How? Who?"

"I can tell you soon. Trust me for now."

I hold the photo to my chest and weep over the best Christmas gift I will probably ever receive. Rob slips away and returns with a roll of bathroom tissue. He smiles. "You may need it."

I stare at the photo some more and finally set it up against the vase of fresh flowers on the coffee table with a long *who-o-o.* "Okay, your turn."

He opens my gift of the painting of downtown Greenville that he admired most in the gallery. "Wow, this is too much, sweetheart. But I love it. Thank you."

We hug and then kiss for a while, joy pinging back and forth between us, and then it's his turn again.

"A photo? We were on the same wavelength, huh?" He opens a framed sketch of himself as a man, based on the photo

I took with my phone that day on the bridge to send to Abigay. It's signed in pretty, round letters: *TF.*

It's Rob's turn to gape at me. "Mom?" He swallows. "You got in touch *with my mother?*"

I pull up my knees and hug them to my chest. "I have my resources. Remember, I'm good at foraging. I'll tell you later." He gives me his I-can't-get-over-you look. "I already love your mom, BTW." He gives me a big smacking smooch.

"Okay, my turn again," he says.

I open a small book: Kate Greenaway's *Language of Flowers.* "How precious!" I run my hand over the smooth, hard cover. "I know about this book, but I don't have a copy. Thank you so much, darling. I know just where it will go."

"You're so welcome. Okay." He heaves a sigh. "You'll have your birthday present this afternoon."

I survey the photo again. "It's already too much."

"I could never give you enough," he says simply.

Marco knocks on the doorframe. "Hey, guys. Just checking to see if you need anything. And I bring news." He smiles. "A huge crew's been working on the transformer all morning, and the foreman says they may have the problem fixed within the hour."

"Hurray," I say. "Will that be enough time for the chefs to prepare the feast?"

"I think so, even if we all have to roll up our sleeves. We'll do all we can to make this up to you."

Rob gestures around us. "Hey, man, *we're great*, but thanks. And Merry Christmas."

CHAPTER THIRTY-ONE

Rob

After Mamie's stared at every pixel of the photo of her and Tate again and shed happy tears all over my neck, we sit quietly. Then I suggest a walk. We take smaller blankets to wrap ourselves in. Not caring what anyone else thinks, we make a few laps around the now-closed Christmas Market on the Green and then tread over to the bridge. A few people stroll around the park. The once-frenzied river is receding, but swift water still tumbles from the falls. "You game to hike down to our bench and sit for a minute?" I ask.

Mamie gives me a brow-raised grin. "You have a one-track mind, Fitzpatrick."

I laugh shortly. "I know. I *totally* do. But truly, there's something I need to talk with you about."

"Okay," she says lightly, but then goes stone silent until we've made our way down to the clearing where the bench waits.

I survey the tops of the evergreens. "I'm not sure where to start. This conversation may feel a bit premature to you, but I intend it as preemptive." Mamie flinches and draws her blanket tighter, but then gives me a mild look. "I want to talk with you about finances." I let my blanket fall so I can use my hands as I speak. "Of course, you're aware that my career is on the launch.

But I have some money in savings. It's . . . important to me as we . . . build this relationship that I know something of *your* situation. You prefer to live modestly, but you come from wealth. We should talk about the implications of—of, you know . . . entering into—"

"Rob," Mamie says, "I get it. To be blunt, I have a sizable trust fund my mother set up for me when my father left. I gained access to the account when I turned twenty-one. I consider it an emergency fund and life insurance, though I did tap into it once to buy a new car"—she gestures toward the parking lot with an orienting thumb—"when I was twenty-three. Under the terms of the trust, I'm required to have a prenuptial agreement when I marry." My stomach knots, but I listen intently. "Of course, we don't have to worry about that anytime soon." She looks for a sign in my eyes, but I'm guarding them until I hear the rest. She continues, "But I did go ahead and call my trustee at the bank on Thursday. Kenneth DuBose. He said the trust is *revocable*. The terms can be changed if either my mother or I elect to waive the prenup."

Revocable. I choose and measure my words carefully. "It's always smart to think ahead."

She looks straight ahead. "It is."

I slap my thighs, get to my feet, and pull my blanket around me again. "Thank you for sharing that with me. Hey, birthday girl, ready to head back and see if dinner's on?"

I reach for her hand, and she mine on the walk back. When we step back inside the lodge, the chandeliers flicker, and my breath hitches in relief. But as quickly as the light comes to life, it dies. Disappointed noises echo in the lobby. I check my phone for text or email updates and notice that it's four o'clock. A new tray of fruit is on the registration desk, and Mamie and I each choose a piece. We turn back to the fireplace just as the lights rebound strong and sure. We cheer along with the others.

Mamie and I take a seat. She twists the stem of her apple while I scarf down a banana and a pear. Marco, wearing a heavy coat, comes through the entrance door with Vaughn Reagan. Vaughn smiles and announces, "Dinner's on, folks! Prepare to feast."

I smile at Mamie, and she returns it in spades. "I planned to go up and get my computer for your birthday surprise, but now that we have heat, would you consider coming to my room for a little bit instead?"

She stands. "I do." She blushes. "I mean, I will."

"Good."

In the sole working elevator, I think of Mr. Reagan. "You have to hand it to Vaughn for coming in on Christmas Day to check on his guests."

"He's a class act and smart businessman. Like you," she says. I smile and kiss her.

In my room at 4:25, I power up my computer and set it on the desk in front of the side-by-side chairs I arranged for us. "This is the most unusually wrapped birthday gift I've ever received, but *intriguing*," she says, taking a seat. I pull up Zoom, my heart beating like a wildebeest's.

Promptly at 4:30, I enter the Zoom room. At 4:31, I admit Tom Bylilly. His friendly and sun-cragged face appears. "Tom, hello!"

"Hello, Rob!"

Mamie flashes me a look, a vertical line forming on her forehead. She trembles so that I can feel it through my chair. I put my arm around her and make sure the two of us can be seen on the screen. "Mamie Morrow, I'd like you to meet Tom Bylilly, who lives in New Mexico."

Mamie gives the man a reserved smile. "Hello, Tom," she slowly says.

"Happy birthday, Mamie." I watch her reactions in the little box of us at the top. She tilts her head, and recognition seems to register in her pretty features. "TB?" she murmurs, and looks at me for confirmation.

I smile gently. "TB."

Tom speaks. "Mamie, I was your grandfather's best friend for over forty years. A finer man I never knew."

I worry that Mamie may be in shock because her tears don't flow. The hairs on my arms stand up. *Is this too much for her?* I get up and pull the duvet from the bed and lay it over her.

Tom continues. "I have a lot to tell you about him."

"Okay," Mamie says. She is very still. I get up and pour her a glass of water, and she takes a few sips.

"First of all, I'm sorry I didn't sign my name when I sent your grandfather's letter. I should have provided contact information, but I never thought . . . With only my initials to work with, it took your young man here hours upon hours to locate me. But he did it. He found me through the Navajo Nation." I smile. "He sure loves you, Mamie, and so did your Grandtate. You came up with that clever handle for him."

Tears begin to streak Mamie's cheeks, but she smiles through them. I let go a breath.

"Tate was as proud of you as one of the strutting young roosters out here. Even after you left the Nation. Your grandfather had a hard life before the summer you came, as a lot of us did. But when you arrived? It was like the planet started spinning again for him. The two of you bonded faster than anything I've ever seen. You were his sweet little sidekick. He said you had the voice of an angel and that you were the second most beautiful girl he ever saw. 'Course, he meant your mother, and that was a generous statement because Colleen could be a hard woman."

Mamie looks at me and takes my hand. "We're going to work on her."

Tom smiles. "Well, good for you. Anyway, you played *hard* out here, Mamie, always running around, exploring and getting dirty.

You seemed to feel free." Tom pauses and picks up a glass of water. "Excuse me," he says, and sips from the glass before going on. "When you were sleepy, Tate would take a seat on his front porch, gather you up in his lap, and hold you tight. You'd fiddle with his braids—a little darker than your hair, but red." A little *o-oh* escapes Mamie. Tom talks about Tate's best qualities, his incomparable skill for catching salmon, his way with words, and his creativity. He chuckles again. "When he learned that you were studying art and writing, he bragged that you got it all from him."

Mamie's tears fall and make big spots on the duvet. "How . . . how did he . . . know about me?"

"He was as good at research as your sweetheart Rob here, but he respected your mother's wishes. And settled on worshipping you from afar. Don't be sad about that. He wasn't."

Mamie slowly nods. Our time is almost up.

"What questions do you have for *me*, Mamie?"

"Well. I don't know where to start. Could we be . . . like, pen pals?"

Tom hoots a laugh. "I would love that, and Tate would have too."

Mamie asks me if the session is being recorded, and I assure her that it is.

"Tom," she says thoughtfully then, "I've recovered a few memories from that time. But do you remember a children's dance . . . with a drumbeat?"

"Ah, the rabbit dance, a Lakota tradition. The little kids out here still perform it. You could probably find it performed on YouTube. And the drum you remember?" Tom sits straighter. "That was me."

"Oh, Tom," Mamie says, "I'm so grateful to you for talking with me." She looks at me and holds my hand tight. "I couldn't have had a better birthday gift."

"I'm grateful too." He chuckles again. "I think this is the

beginning of a beautiful friendship." Though the sentiment's trite, it sends an arrow to both our hearts.

We say our goodbyes to Tom, and I end the session. She looks at me and simply says, "Hold me?"

I do.

The super troopers, as Mamie calls those of us who stuck it out in the lobby today, gather for the feast. Our new friends Betty and Gary are seated at the next table. Several parties of locals arrive, and soon the restaurant is full and bustling with merriment. The Native American prefix courses are fantastic. Mamie enjoys them all so much, I feel a *tad* better about her missing out on so much of the ball last night.

When the warm cranberry and ground corn pudding with vanilla ice cream is served, I pull a tiny box from the breast pocket of my blazer. Isla's friend, a Native American jeweler, made a special trip to the lodge and helped me select a stone for a minimalist ring I knew Mamie would like. I rise from my chair, lay my black napkin on the table, and get down on one knee. Mamie covers her face for a moment, but then shakes her head and gives me her most beautiful smile yet.

"Mamie, my first love," I begin. People have turned to watch, and a respectful hush falls over the room. "I asked TB for your hand yesterday. Don't cry, sweetheart," I say. But I could blubber any minute myself. "He said yes. Since I met you, I have learned the importance of striking a balance between wisdom and lightheartedness. I love your playful energy and creativity." I duck my head for a moment and then look back at her. "I *adore* you, Mamie Morrow." I search her eyes. "I can't imagine the rest of my life without your laughter and your green eyes. Will you please marry me and be my *last* love?"

"I will, Rob Fitzpatrick, my first and last love."

The room erupts into soft applause.

Later that night, we place two phone calls: one to my parents, the other to Mamie's mother. We wish them Merry Christmas and tell them that we love them. Without mentioning our engagement, we tell them we want to see them soon.

It's a start.

EPILOGUE

Mamie

Rob and I arrive at Tradd Street for tea with my mother. She greets us at the door and seems in good form, I think because of the calls I've made to her, the second one to tell her Rob's and my news. She has set a pretty tea tray and a plate of Gladiola's benne wafers on the coffee table. She takes a seat in her chair and invites Rob and me to sit, gesturing to the sofa across from her where I had sat when she told me about Tate. Sitting next to Rob, I pour tea for the three of us, my hand trembling slightly.

"Mamie, you are glowing," my mother says primly.

"Thank you, Mother. I'm very happy." I smile at Rob.

She begins, "Alicia Rembert gave me her tedious little report about meeting you in Greenville. At the bridge table for all to hear." She smooths her hair. "But she failed to mention what a handsome gentleman you are, Rob. And how your eyes shine when you look at my daughter. Even though I haven't or may never have the great love of my life, that love is palpable between the two of you."

I blow out a silent slow breath. Rob looks at me and takes my hand. He smiles at me and then at her.

I realize that my mother's usual five-word sentences have become lengthy strands of pearls. Hope peeks its head into the door of my mind. "Mother, I have a belated Christmas gift for you."

"Oh. Thank you."

I pull her wrapped coffee table book from the pretty tote bag Abigay gave me for Christmas. Opening it, she regards the beautiful cover. "Roses. How I love them. Thank you," she says. "I believe I may take up gardening again this spring."

Rob helps himself to the plate of benne wafers.

I suppress a grin and address my mother. "Mother, we want to talk with you about our finances. Specifically, my trust fund."

Colleen sips her tea and sets it on her saucer with an unnoticeable to the casual observer but to me a telltale clank.

"Mr. DuBose told me the trust was revocable." She gives me a sidelong look. Undaunted, I take copies of the list I compiled for her from the tote bag, hand her a copy, then set my copy on my knees. She puts on her readers and then peers over them at us. I continue. "First, Rob and I are starting a new business. We work beautifully together, bringing out the best of each other's talents."

Rob speaks up. "Our future is undeveloped property, and it's got one heck of a view."

I laugh and then ask my mother if she's seen our article. "I *have*." She points out a copy displayed atop the English chest. Rob and I grin. "I found it compelling and fresh. Unlike anything I've read in *that* magazine before." She smiles and sits straighter. "The bridge club is all abuzz."

"Thank *you*," Rob and I say in tandem. I redirect the conversation to business.

"I've done my homework. Rob has contributed $10,000 to open our new business account at the bank and serve as start-up expenses. I'd like to withdraw another $15,000 from my fund to update our computers, purchase office equipment, and create our branding." In my periphery, I see Rob stuffing two benne wafers in his mouth. "Speaking of office needs, after we marry, we plan to rent a larger apartment so we can have a home office. The rent Rob and I are each paying now will go toward that." I take a deep breath. "With your blessing, Mama, I'd like to alter the terms of the trust and update the beneficiary terms. I want to name Rob as the first beneficiary and any children we may have as seconds. As a third beneficiary, I want to name the Partnership of Native Americans who support the Navajo Nation, in Tate Atwater's memory. Last, again with your blessing, I'd like to remove the prenuptial contract. It doesn't feel right for what Rob and I have." I turn and gaze into his eyes. "While we were at the lodge, we met a sweet couple who have been married *sixty years*. He's a Presbyterian minister. Rob has asked him to marry us in Greenville at the lodge where we fell in love. He and his wife Betty, who also *fell in love in a week*, can vouch for us because we talked with them at length. At our wedding, we will commit to each other for life. We want you to be there, Mama. Neither of us had the happiest houseful of love, and I'm sorry if that hurts you—"

She closes her eyes. "No, Mamie, I understand."

"But we want that for our children."

My mother is quiet for several minutes, finishing her cup of tea. "I want to give you two a Christmas present. When you are married, I'd like to buy you a house." She gives us a wry smile. "Not South of Broad. But somewhere that suits your needs."

I begin to cry and get up to hug her neck. Rob's eyes are misty too. I would suggest a group hug, but we've pushed Colleen enough today. With time, I hope she will become a warmer person.

"About these grandchildren?" she asks, her eyes aglow.

"One step at a time, Colleen," Rob says.

On April 27, an impossibly lovely day, the only showers are those from pink and white dogwood blooms. Gary Jones officiates at our marriage ceremony on the Green at the Grand Bohemian Lodge. He builds the ceremony around love, trust, and forgiveness. Abigay stands next to me as my maid of honor, Smoky next to Rob as his best man. I'm wearing a beautiful and simple white vintage gown that Abigay and I found on consignment. Rob, who's never looked more gorgeous, wears an elegant gray suit. Sweet Betty's there with Gary. Rob's mom and pop, all five brothers and their wives, and Seamus O'Malley fill three rows on the groom's side. On my side are my mother and Gladiola, Abigay's parents, Jake, Farida, and Tom Bylilly. I spent Christmas at the GBL to get in touch with my Native American heritage, and thanks to Tom, my grandfather's memory is my personal legacy.

Annelise and Isla, Kwame, Josh, Tucker, and Marco, eyewitnesses to our falling in love, fill the next row. The ladies and a few of the men sniff through the vows Rob and I wrote for each other. We sail into each other's eyes and promise to cherish each other every day of our lives. We seal our vows with a kiss that makes everyone clap.

In our new-to-us home in Charleston, Rob's painting of downtown Greenville hangs above our bed. The framed photo of Tate and me rests on my bedside table, Treasa's sketch of Rob on his. On a living room table is a framed copy of the first award-winning article we created together for *Á La Mode*. Rob's favorite line of the review? "The photographs reach out to grab you and pull you into the story."

Mamie

I miss Abigay in my everyday life, but Rob has become my best friend and Jake, hers. She and I will always be each other's BGFFs: best *girl*friends forever. Rob's taught me more about old souls who often tend to be loners with few friends, which was true for both of us. But we're working on that. We have dinner with Abs and Jake regularly, and new friends we've met in the neighborhood are often guests for cocktail gatherings and game nights. Our friendships enrich our marriage relationship. Another cool old soul gift is the proclivity to be good at something you've never tried before. I've learned to bake bread using Grandtate's wood bowl. Rob reminded me that my earliest memory includes making benne wafers, so I whip up a batch for him every week.

Our new business card is stuck to our refrigerator with a magnet. It reads, *Morrow and Fitz*, which we decided was a catchy name. We don't care about whose name is first or last.

We're just two.

A Note from the Author

Dear sweet readers,

Thank you so much for being a part of Mamie and Rob's swoony love story and Mamie's quest to get in touch with her grandfather's heritage. I hope the book inspired and resonated with you and that you will share it with your friends.

When it comes to an author's success, it's really *all about you*. Will you please consider posting a brief review of the novel on the review site of your choice? Book clubbers can find a list of discussion questions for *Christmas at Reedy Falls* on my website: elizabethsumnerwafler.com.

Follow me on Instagram: @elizabeth_sumner_wafler

I'd love to hear from you at elizabethwafler9505@gmail.com.

I wish you the merriest of Christmases!
Elizabeth
XO

Acknowledgments

Christmas at Reedy Falls began with a Christmastime visit to the gorgeous Grand Bohemian Lodge in my hometown of Greenville, South Carolina. The hotel's Native American art theme and décor create a warm and cozy environment rich in history and tradition. I began to imagine a swoony love story developing beneath the elaborate antler chandeliers and surrounded by garlands of evergreens, pheasant feathers, and fresh winter blooms. I'm forever thankful to Katie Myers for giving me a special "media tour" of the hotel; to Ashley McMullen for her warm hospitality, permission to use the hotel branding, and efforts at coordinating author events for me; and to the gracious gallery director, Kara Soper, for taking the time to educate me on Native American artifacts.

I believe my experience writing women's fiction in which the plot is driven by the emotional journey of the protagonist helped me add layering and nuance to what could have been a formulaic romance. For this I thank my lovely writerly friends, and the members of the Women's Fiction Writers Association for years of comradery, workshop and webinar opportunities, and writing retreat experiences.

Early readers are an author's safety net. For this novel, I was blessed to have an extraordinary team. The amazing Summer Song, Christina Consolino, Lynne Niva, and Bob King's words of affirmation and countless hours spent on insightful chapter critiques meant everything to me. Special thanks are due to Bob, who is a gifted local photographer. Without his camera and photography tutelage, Rob Fitzpatrick's work as a photographer would have been a mere shell.

I am blessed by all my friends at Woodruff Road Presbyterian Church. Many thanks to my readers and cheerleaders and the prayers lifted by the ladies of my small group, especially at crunch times.

Without the team at She Writes Press this novel would not be in your hands and hearts. Major-league thanks to publisher Brooke Warner, my project manager Shannon Green, my cover designer Mary Ann Smith, and my editor Katie Caruana.

I am most fortunate to have the perspicacious and eagle-eyed support of editor Julie Klein. She's helped see me through three novels now. Not only is she wise and kind, but savvy and a real peach in a pinch.

And the best for last. Porter Wafler, my love of forty years, you are the dearest and most considerate husband on the planet and the romantic inspiration for all my male protagonists. I love seeing so many of our inside jokes sprinkled throughout these pages. I won't reveal here what your unflagging and heroic support meant to me as I finished this manuscript. But *you* know. All the kisses in the world, darling!

About the Author

Photo credit: Porter Wafler

Elizabeth Wafler is the author of five novels. She is a member of the Women's Fiction Writers Association, where she served as director of craft education for two years. Elizabeth can be found reading, working at her blue desk, poking through a bookstore with a luscious latte in hand, at a farmer's market, taming her garden into submission, or enjoying a pretty cocktail on her screened porch. Elizabeth resides in Greenville, South Carolina, with her husband and their rescue pup, Georgette.

Looking for your next great read?

We can help!

Visit www.shewritespress.com/next-read
or scan the QR code below for a list
of our recommended titles.

She Writes Press is an award-winning
independent publishing company founded to
serve women writers everywhere.